Praise for EAT THE DOCUMENT

Nominated for the National Book Award

"Brilliant and haunting . . . this is a novel prepared to grapple with modern history."   —David Thomson, THE NEW YORK OBSERVER

"Like a set of Russian dolls nesting in each other, Spiotta's newest fiction finds the country in the family in a single human heart. Eat the Document—but read it first."   —Mark Costello, author of BIG IF

"A pitch-perfect novel."   —Greil Marcus, INTERVIEW

"Spiotta's insightful depiction of the character is imbued with deep tenderness, whether she is writing of the young, passionate idealist or the lonely, self-doubting middle-aged woman."
—Barbara Spindel, TIME OUT NEW YORK

"[Spiotta] has rendered the details of her characters' world with clarity. She has a special empathy for her female characters . . . [and] understands those who feel lost and left out of a society that seems too corporately driven." —Steven Rosen, THE DENVER POST

"What should compel the reader are the rich characters who keenly explore their sense of identities . . . *Eat the Document* honors the timelessness of youthful passion, but also serves as a homage to its recklessness that can come to define us."
—Adam Braver, THE PROVIDENCE JOURNAL

"Spiotta creates a convincing and thought-provoking portrait of a generation that is growing up behind a computer screen."
—Holly Silva, ST. LOUIS POST-DISPATCH

"A terrific novel, which reads like a diary or a thriller. To Spiotta, words are controlled substances, and they make the text shimmer and vibrate."

—Laurie Stone, *Chicago Tribune*

"Infused with subtle wit . . . singularly powerful and provocative . . . Spiotta has a wonderful ironic sensibility, juxtaposing '70s fervor with '90s expediency."

—Caroline Leavitt, *The Boston Globe*

"Spiotta's writing brims with energy and intelligence."

—Julia Scheeres, *The New York Times Book Review*

"Scintillating . . . Spiotta creates a mesmerizing portrait of radicalism's decline."

—John Freeman, *The Seattle Times*

"A powerful and disturbing book."

—Joanne Collings, *BookPage*

"*Eat the Document* . . . brilliantly contrasts nascent and mature postmodernity through the lens of culture/counterculture. . . . [Spiotta is the] literary heir of Don DeLillo."

—Sarah Cypher, *The Sunday Oregonian*

"Spiotta calculates every word, character, and story line to illuminate the many faces of rebellion. Her book explores protests, bombings, underground filmmaking, and computer hacking, finding the personal and political ramifications of each."

—Ross Simonini, *Seattle Weekly*

"*Eat the Document* reveals its darkness and weirdness slowly. The corrosive nature of secrecy is there, as is the eerie ease of self-invention. Spiotta ultimately expresses a deep ambivalence to American culture and its affection for starting over, its 'freedom from memory and history and accounting.'"

—Anna Godberson, *Esquire* online

"A keenly observant and caustically funny tale . . . Spiotta succinctly and dramatically sizes up today's chillingly cynical corporate kingdom."

—Donna Seaman, *Booklist*

"A forthright and fascinating look at American counterculture."
—Christine DeZelar-Tiedman, *Library Journal*

"Gripping and compelling."

—*Pages* magazine

"Spiotta's crisscrossing of times and narrators creates a remarkable tension. . . . In all of this, Spiotta manages to create a very natural story: It is believable, uneasy, mildly violent, lovesick, and beautifully written."

—Laura Leffler James, *Cincinnati CityBeat*

"*Eat the Document* raises complicated issues with economical prose and significant insight, while penetrating its characters' inner lives with empathy and understanding."

—Richard Gaughran, *Daily News-Record*

"Fiction as documentary, a coruscating, heartrending fable of struggle and loss."

—*Kirkus Reviews*

"Spiotta has written a very American novel about dissent, which becomes more valuable but also more dangerous and unwelcome in times of war, and the ethical lines one cannot cross without, as Caroline says, becoming the thing you wish to escape."

—John Hammond, *San Antonio Express-News*

"*Eat the Document* is a good yarn. Spiotta is an irresistible satirist and taut storyteller."

—Gina Mallet, *National Post* (Canada)

"I like the way Dana Spiotta tinges reality with a dazzling now-you-see-it, now-you-don't quality. She uses her prose like a strobe light to give you enough of a freeze-frame on what's happening to make you stop and wonder whether you might be implicated in this curious, perhaps dangerous dance."

—Ann Beattie, author of *Follies*

"Fantastic . . . It blew me away."

—Katha Pollitt, author of *Virginity or Death!*
And Other Social and Political Issues of Our Times

"Such smart and delicious satire, yet so true and good to its characters too. More, please."

—Stewart O'Nan, author of *The Good Wife*

"With only her second book Dana Spiotta has become, I think, a major American writer. The ironic connections she makes between the cultural divide of the early '70s and late '90s are chilling and delicious. This scary and often brilliant novel comes together beautifully in the end—there's an intense satisfaction of seeing everything link up so movingly and with such warmth, and yet Spiotta is the only female writer I know whose prose reminds me of the cool ambient poetry and steely precision of Don

DeLillo, and *Eat the Document* is as darkly exact and thrilling as the political novels of Joan Didion."

—Bret Easton Ellis, author of *Lunar Park*

"Stunning . . . a glittering book that possesses the staccato ferocity of Joan Didion and the historical resonance and razzle-dazzle language of Don DeLillo. . . . Ms. Spiotta has a keen ear and even keener eye for the absurdities and disjunctions of American life, and this novel showcases those gifts in spades. . . . A symphonic portrait of three decades of American life."

—Michiko Kakutani, *The New York Times*

Also by Dana Spiotta

Lightning Field

Eat the Document

A NOVEL

Dana Spiotta

SCRIBNER

New York   London   Toronto   Sydney

SCRIBNER
1230 Avenue of the Americas
New York, NY 10020

First Scribner trade paperback edition 2006

SCRIBNER and design are trademarks of
Macmillan Library Reference USA, Inc., used under license
by Simon & Schuster, the publisher of this work.

For information about special discounts for bulk purchases,
please contact Simon & Schuster Special Sales:
1-800-456-6798 or business@simonandschuster.com

Designed by Kyoko Watanabe
Text set in Elegant Garamond

Manufactured in the United States of America

1   3   5   7   9   10   8   6   4   2

Library of Congress Cataloging-in-Publication Data
Spiotta, Dana, [date]
Eat the document : a novel / Dana Spiotta.
p. cm.
I. Title.
PS3619.P566E18 2006
813'.6—dc22   2005054050

ISBN-13: 978-0-7432-7298-8
ISBN-10: 0-7432-7298-6
ISBN-13: 978-0-7432-7300-8 (Pbk)
ISBN-10: 0-7432-7300-1 (Pbk)

To Robert Spiotta and Emmline Frasca

PART ONE

1972

By Heart

IT IS EASY for a life to become unblessed.

Mary, in particular, understood this. Her mistakes—and they were legion—were not lost on her. She knew all about the undoing of a life: take away, first of all, your people. Your family. Your lover. That was the hardest part of it. Then put yourself somewhere unfamiliar, where (how did it go?) you are a complete unknown. Where you possess nothing. Okay, then—this was the strangest part—take away your history, every last bit of it.

What else?

She discovered, despite what people may imagine, having nothing to lose is a lot like having nothing. (But there was something to lose, even at this point, something huge to lose, and that was why this unknown, homeless state never resembled freedom.)

The unnerving, surprisingly creepy and unpleasantly psyche-delic part—you lose your name.

Mary finally sat on a bed in a motel room that very first night after she had taken a breathless train ride under darkening skies and through increasingly unfamiliar landscape. Despite her anxiety she still felt lulled by the tracks clicking at intervals beneath the train; an odd calm descended for whole minutes in a row until the train pulled into another station and she waited for someone to come over to her, finger-pointing, some unbending and unsmiling official. In between these moments of near calm and all the other moments, she practiced appearing normal. Only when she tried to move could you notice how shaky she was. That really undid her, her visible unsteadiness. She tried not to move.

Five state borders, and then she was handing over the cash for the room—anonymous, cell-like, quiet. She clutched her receipt in her hand, stared at it, September 15, 1972, and thought, This is the first day of it. Room Twelve, the first place of it.

Even then, behind a chain lock in the middle of nowhere, she was double-checking doors and closing curtains. Showers were impossible; she half-expected the door of the bathroom to push in as she stood there unaware and naked. Instead of sleeping she lay on the covers, facing the door, ready to move. Showers and bed, nakedness and sleep—she felt certain that was how it would happen, she could visualize it happening. She saw it in slow motion, she saw it silently, and then she saw it quickly, in double time, with crashes and splintered glass. Haven't you seen the photos of Fred Hampton's mattress? She certainly had seen the photos of Fred Hampton's mattress. They'd all seen them. She couldn't remember if the body was still in the bed in the photos, but she definitely remembered the bed itself: half stripped of sheets, the dinge stripe and seam of the mattress exposed and seeped with stains. All of it captured in the lurid black-and-white Weegee style that seemed to underline the blood-soak and the bedclothes in grabbed-at disarray. She imagined the bunching of sheets in the last seconds, perhaps to protect the unblessed person on the bed. Grabbed and bunched not against gunfire, of course, but against his terrible, final nakedness.

"Cheryl," she said aloud. No, never. Orange soda. "Natalie." You had to say them aloud, get your mouth to shape the sound and push breath through it. Every name sounded queer when she did this. "Sylvia." A movie-star name, too fake sounding. Too unusual. People might actually hear it. Notice it, ask about it. "Agnes." Too old. "Mary," she said very quietly. But that was her real name, or her *original* name. She just needed to say it.

She sat on the edge of the bed, atop a beige chenille bedspread with frays and loose threads, in her terry-cloth bathrobe, which she'd somehow thought to buy when she got her other supplies earlier in the afternoon. She had imagined a bath as bringing some relief, and the sink into the robe afterward seemed important. She did just that, soaked in the tub after wiping it clean. Eyes trained on the open door of the bathroom, and careful not to splash, she strained to determine the origins of every sound she heard. She shaved her legs and scrubbed her hands with a small nailbrush, also purchased that day. She flossed her teeth and brushed her tongue with her new toothbrush. She tended to the usual grooming details with unusual attention: she knew instinctively that these details were very closely tied to keeping her sanity, or her wits, anyway. Otherwise she could just freeze up, on the floor, in her dirty jeans, drooling and sobbing until they came and got her. Dirt was linked to inertia. Cleanliness, particularly personal cleanliness, was an assertion against madness. It was a declaration of control. You might be in the midst of chaos, terrified, but the ritual of your self-tending radiated from you and protected you. That was where Mary figured a lot of people got it wrong. Slovenliness might be rebellious, but it was never liberating. In fact, she felt certain that slovenly and sloppy attention to personal hygiene surrendered you to everything outside you, all the things not of you trying to get in.

The TV on low, she looked but barely watched, hugging her knees toward her. Unpolished clean nails, uniform and smooth. Legs shaven and scented with baby oil, which looked greasy but smelled powdery and familiar. She inhaled deeply, resting her face on her knees and drawing her legs closer. She was a tiny ball of a human, wasn't she? A speck of a being in the middle of a vast, multihighwayed and many-sided country, wasn't she? Full of generic, anonymous and safe places just like this one.

She thought of famous people's names, authors' names, teachers' names, the names she made up when she was eight for her future babies. Abby, Blythe, Valerie. Vita, Tuesday, Naomi. She put on an oversized T-shirt and clean cotton bikini briefs decorated with large pastel pansies, size 4. She thought of girl-friend names and cheerleader names. Names of flowers and women in novels. She ate peanut butter on white bread and drank orange juice directly from the carton. She was ravenous, very unusual for her. She took a large bite and a big swig, the sweet, pulpy taste mixing into the glutinous, sticky mouthful. She didn't finish swallowing before taking another huge bite. Maybe I'll be a fat person in my new life. She started to laugh, and the peanut butter–bread–orange juice clump stuck momentarily in her throat, cutting off her airway. She imagined, indifferently, choking and dying in this motel room. She swallowed and then laughed even harder, out loud. It sounded crazy, her short, sudden laugh against the quiet mono sound of the television. She could hear her breath squeeze in and out of her lungs and throat. She turned up the volume on the television and stared hard at it.

Jim Brown was talking to Dick Cavett. Brown wore a tight white jumpsuit with beige piping and a wide tan leather belt through the high-waisted belt loops. They both sipped something out of oversized mugs, also white, and placed them on a mush-room-shaped white metal table between them. Brown smiled

handsomely and kept declaring—with exquisite enunciation—
his respect and support for his friend, the president.

A piece of lined paper in a spiral notebook, a ballpoint pen.
Karen Black. Mary Jo Kopechne. Joni Mitchell. Martha Mitchell.
Joan Baez. Jane Asher. Joan isn't so bad. Linda McCartney. Joan
McCartney. Joan Lennon. Oh, good, sure. Bobby would appreciate that. She almost waited for him to contact her—but she knew
he would not, not for a while, anyway. At eleven o'clock she
turned the channel to watch the news, tried to see if he, or any of
them, had been identified or arrested. Jane Fonda, Phoebe
Caulfield, Valerie Solanas. She liked these names. Mustn't reference her real name in any way. Brigitte, Hannah, Tricia. Just
don't get cute. Lady Bird. Pat. Ha.

"You are no longer Mary from the suburbs. You are Freya from
the edge," Bobby had said. They sat cross-legged on a handwoven
rug Bobby had bought in Spain. She spent many nights getting
high kneeling on that rug; she could examine it endlessly. Moor-
ish Möbius patterns took you in dervish circles back to where you
started but done in incongruous, rainy European colors—muted
greens and yellows—next to imperial, regal and regimental looking banners and shieldlike things. The rug wasn't authentic, but
whoever made it had worked meticulously to evoke something
authentic, studied relics of conquerings, exiles and colonies. It
clashed and conflicted the way real things often did. It was the
most beautiful thing either of them possessed, and they often sat
on it, next to their bed, which was just a mattress on the floor with
no frame or even box springs. All the kids she knew slept on the
floor; it softened the distinction between their bed and the rest of
the world. She felt safer, nearer to the ground. What did it mean,
a culture where people sit cross-legged on the floor, on beautiful
rugs? Were there horizontal and vertical cultures? Was living
closer to the earth free and natural, or was it simply meager? Was
it good, or better, or just different for someone?

"And what will *you* call me?" she had asked, leaning her head against his back. He often wore sleeveless undershirts, very thin and slightly ribbed; when she pressed against him he smelled both tangy and sweet. Pot and incense and sweat.

She tried to conjure him, with her eyes closed, in her midnight bed. She thought Bobby looked exotic, handsome not so much in the total as in the details. The closer in she was, the more attractive he became. His skin had a faint yellow-green undertone that was the opposite of ruddy: skin so smooth under her touch that she could feel every tiny rough spot on her own fingers or lips; skin so clear and fine she could see his blood pulse at wrist and temple and neck. And although she wasn't ever crazy about the random curliness of his long black hair, which grew out rather than down, she adored the silky way the hair slipped through her fingers when she pulled her hand through it, and the tension in his shoulders when she pressed against them, and how in candlelight she would see her white skin—her slender hand, say—against the dark skin of his broad back, and it would catch her off guard always, the contrast between them. She felt then exquisite and even fragile, which she liked. She wasn't supposed to, but she did. Perhaps because they spent so much time together, and dressed alike and spoke alike—even laughed alike—it was great to in some palpable way be unalike.

"Will you call me Mary, at least when we are home, in bed?"

"Only Freya. And you have to call me Marco. In these sorts of activities you can't use your real name. Ever. If you want to change your life, first you change your name."

"A nom de guerre? Isn't that sort of ridiculous?"

"All cultures have naming ceremonies. You have a given name, but then you get a chosen name. It's part of a transformation to adulthood. They tell you who you are, and then you decide who you are. It's like getting confirmed, or getting married."

"But I didn't choose that name. You did."

"I'm helping you. The first thing we do is make up a new name. A fighting, fearless name."

"A Bolshevik name?" Mary said, frowning.

"It's a Nordic goddess name. A towering priestess name. A lightning bolt name. A name to live up to."

She closed her eyes and rested against him. "Okay."

"A name that exudes agitprop. These are always two-syllable names that end in a vowel. Freya, Maya, Silda. Marco, Proto, Demo. If you don't like that name, come up with another." They never did use those names except in the press communiqués and on the telephone. Now she was choosing another name, its opposite—a hidden, modest, meek name—but truly choosing.

The next morning (was it morning?), when she woke after hardly sleeping, she sat down in the one chair, a molded plastic affair in mustard yellow, next to the motel bed, in the dead time between showers and sleep, with nothing to do but indoctrinate herself into her new life. She could not leave until it was done. She wrote it all out on the piece of spiral notebook paper. Her age: twenty-two. Birthplace: Hawthorne, California. Name: Caroline. Hawthorne was just another suburban town in California, which you could bet was more like all the other suburban towns in California than it was different, and it would do just fine even if her favorite band was also from Hawthorne. And Caroline is a pretty girl's name that also happened to be the name of the girl in one of her favorite songs. (Okay, there was no point in being witty about any of this, encoding it or making it coherent in any way, except if it helped her remember. But as Bobby had warned her, if it is legible to you, then it gives you away. But everything, of course, means something. However hermetic and obscure, it can't fail to signify, can it? Unless, of course, she wanted it somehow, however quietly, to be legible and coherent. Unless, of course, she wanted someone, at some time, to figure it out.)

Caroline. Caroline Sherman. Okay?

That first night, Caroline didn't know where Bobby had gone. Or when she would see him again. She knew only to get across state lines as soon as possible. Only then could she pause, anonymous in the great expanse of states between the two coasts, and hole up in a motel room composing her new life. They had agreed on Oregon as her final destination because she wanted to be back on the West Coast. Bobby said he would contact her eventually. Go to Eugene, he said, and when and if things are cool I'll get in touch. I'll find you. Otherwise they had determined a fail-safe plan to meet at a designated spot at the end of next year. But surely they would see each other before then. He'd get in touch when and if things cooled down.

And *if,* he said.

She fell asleep those first few nights committing the "facts" of her new identity to memory. And for a while it would be impossible not to be confused and self-conscious during even the most mundane exchanges. Do you drink coffee? And she would have to think, Well, I always have, but now, well, maybe I don't. And she would reply, "No, I never touch the stuff." And the extra step of comparing the present with the past would keep her in a constant state of reaction. Until it stopped, later and slowly—but she didn't know about that yet, couldn't even imagine it. Yet one day she would have lived her new life so long that the conjuring of the old life would seem like a dream, an act of imagination. Eventually it would almost feel as though it had never happened. This was the way it was supposed to go down. A secret held so long that even you no longer believe it isn't really you. But at this point she had no idea that this could go on indefinitely. She had no idea she would find that her identity was more habit and will than anything more intrinsic.

She had all her supplies. She pulled them one by one out of a brown knapsack and placed them on the bedspread. Blond hair dye. L'Oréal Ash and Sass. Scissors. Cash. About four hundred dollars, all in twenties. This was her whole life, the sum of her past twenty-two years and the path into her future. A spiral notebook, blond hair, scissors, a handful of twenties, a pair of jeans, a black sweater, an oversized T-shirt, a bathrobe and a blue blouse. Three pairs of underwear, three pairs of socks, one pair of brown clogs. Silver earrings, antique, that Bobby gave her on their one-year anniversary. His grandmother's. A watch her parents gave her for high school graduation—a quartz Timex, a Lady Sport model with a khaki-colored canvas band. She should discard these, but she couldn't. She had already discarded her phone book. She did that the night before, ripping her name off the front and burying it as deeply as possible in the big garbage bins outside the train station, pushing different pages through each swinging lid as discreetly as she could manage in the state she was in. Right before that she stood in the ladies' room, feeling ill, looking one last time at the phone numbers and addresses of her parents and her few friends. She knew by heart all she needed anyway, still did. That was the first time that expression made sense, *by heart*. Memorization and memory that was not intellectual or by rote but by heart.

When Bobby and Mary first discussed the day they might have to go underground, it had actually sounded exciting. She could admit that. In case of emergency, you must do the following. The escape plan. Change name, hair color, clothes. Social Security number. Remember the first numbers must match where you say you are from. Don't count on any luck. Count on bad luck. He made her go over all of it. She didn't really understand then that if it happened (and yet they knew it would happen, didn't they?), if all went well, all according to the plan, it would happen in silence and isolation. Unnoticed and unobserved. She would end up alone in an anonymous room somewhere with a pocked chenille bedspread and a watercolor landscape print in the same hues of mustard and green that were everywhere in the room and with only the TV on the broken swivel stand to remind her of the world at large.

By the second night, she had her new identity worked out. She then needed to determine what should happen next—not just how to evade detection but how to survive, to sustain herself for however long it would last. (She didn't, at that point, define what "it" really was. She projected a few months into the future and then stopped.) Caroline, a.k.a. Freya, a.k.a. Mary, did not count on luck but took stock of her advantages. She could see only two: One, she was a woman. Two, she was plain.

She was not ugly, she was not pretty. But just that old-fashioned word, plain. If she left the room, or if you tried to recall her to others, or even yourself, the adjectives would be limited—not hard to come up with but hardly worth the bother. Thin, yes; neat, yes; hair much more light brown than red, which also made it hard to describe, not so much both-this-and-that as barely-this-and-barely-that; light, milky blue eyes and pinkish white body. Her skin tone gave off a peeled quality that left the line distinguishing lip from face indistinct, her pale eyebrows lost against the nearly same-colored forehead. Bobby once described her as looking like a heroine in a nineteenth-century novel. To her that meant sickly, bland looks that suggested small, prim virtues.

"No." Bobby laughed. "They would have said you have a noble physiognomy."

"Right."

"A pleasing countenance."

"What does that mean, exactly?"

"Uh, a good personality?" He laughed and tried to kiss her.

"How sweet." She pulled away, frowning at him. He held her arm. She shrugged him off.

"No, listen."

She didn't look at him but examined the floor, lips pursed.

"You are so lovely," he continued, his voice softer now. "True, it isn't a loud-volume effect; it is subtle but quite deadly, I assure you."

She turned a little toward him. He was staring at her so intently she looked back at the floor. She could feel herself flush.

"You have a sort of—I don't really know how to explain it— what you might call an undertow, if that makes any sense. The longer I'm with you, the more I want to be with you. It gets harder and harder to imagine leaving you behind. It's not about enchantment or seduction or anything as light as that. It is more like being held captive. It's powerful and uncomfortable and gets worse all the time." She couldn't hear what he was saying. She just knew that her lover thought she was plain.

But as Caroline she could put these two irrefutable facts together, plain and woman. It meant she could move somewhere new and go to the store or apply for a job and people wouldn't feel threatened or aroused. She knew she could go unnoticed. She could not recall her own face if she wasn't staring in a mirror. This smeary obscurity that had caused her pain her whole life became an asset now, her anonymity her saving attribute. Her looks had finally found their perfect context as a fugitive. Born to it by being chronically forgettable. (Which was also part of how she got in this position in the first place. Walking slowly, half smile on her face, clutching an innocuous purse, or a package, or a suitcase. Would anyone bother to stop such a person?)

Caroline did possess other assets as well. She could cook. She had worked in her father's restaurant her entire youth. She could walk into a kitchen with a nearly bare pantry and create chilis and pastas and stews. This made her eminently employable. Restaurants hired people off the books. No legitimate Social Security number required. No references. No one would suspect this bland, wan woman was anything but harmless and ordinary. Because, despite the circumstances that had brought her here, she knew herself finally to be harmless and ordinary.

By the third evening in the motel she didn't feel nearly as fear-struck. She even had an hour or two of giddy confidence. She was almost ready. Almost.

She imagined in future years there would be time to go over the series of events that led to the one event that inevitably led to the motel room. It felt like that, a whoosh of history, the somersault of dialectic rather than the firm step of will. The weight of centuries of history counterlevered against what, one person's action? Just in the planning they knew where it would lead. Contingencies are never really contingencies but blueprints. Probabilities became certainties. She knew she would comb over how she came to be involved with cells and plans and people who believed in the inevitable and absolute. Someday she would explain her intentions to someone, at least to herself. And the event, which she could not think about, not yet, the event that she could not even name, she referred to in her thoughts as *then,* or *the thing,* or *it*. But surely in years to come she would think about it, over and over again, especially the part where Mary became Freya became Caroline.

What else?

She brushed her teeth. She ate more peanut butter and bread. She wished for a joint but settled for a beer bought at the store across the street. She exited briefly the afternoon of the third day, wearing large sunglasses and a scarf. She trembled in the fluorescence of the convenience store and hurried to pick up some juice, some beer, the paper. The *Lincoln Journal Star*. Front page, lower left quarter, a picture of Bobby Desoto. Just pay and leave. She stumbled back across the highway to her mustard-colored motel room. She read as she walked.

She opened the paper to the inside report and felt the fear come crashing back, making her stumble. She started to cry—noisy, hiccuped sobs and gulps as she closed the door behind her, staring at the lines of type. She learned that the group had been identified, although only one had been caught, Tamsin. She was the youngest and weakest. They must have gotten the names from her, just as Bobby suspected they probably would. (Behind her back he used to refer to Tamsin as M.L.C.—Most Likely to Crack.) But Tamsin didn't really know the details of the various underground plans. The authorities were looking, but they had few leads. Nevertheless, contact anytime soon with Bobby was definitely out. She already knew that would probably be the case, but she cried anyway.

She drank three beers in a row watching TV shows about regular people. She sniffed as her nose ran. She went over everything again and again. Had she already made mistakes?

Her motel room was outside the train station just south of Lincoln, Nebraska, which was practically the dead center of the country. She wondered—she stared at *Ironside* and then turned the channel to *Owen Marshall,* and then to a commercial for denture glue—if a lot of fugitives headed for the dead center of the country, stopping there to make a plan of where to go next. Maybe this was fugitive central, a magnet.

PoliGrip. Eat like a man.
Polaroid. Land Camera. SX-70. Almost part of you.
D-Con. House and garden spray. Against bugs.

She wondered if her every thought would be predictable, the same things people always thought in these circumstances, and if she would give herself away without even realizing it. She doubted, actually, that anyone else would follow her Nebraska strategy. Logic would say try to get over the border, to Canada or Mexico. Most would move to the perimeter. That was what they would be looking for.

What else?

She, Caroline, didn't have siblings, and her parents died in a car wreck years ago. She felt superstitious about writing that down. As if it would curse her poor parents somehow, or undo her younger sister.

For the first couple of years, Caroline wouldn't be able to resist the occasional phone call to her mother. She knew this was dangerous. She knew this was a big, stupid risk. She knew the FBI, COINTELPRO, the police, all of them, expected this and had tapped the phones of all her relatives and friends. If there was anything Bobby had hammered into her, it was the consequences of involving other people. Anyone she told the truth to could be charged with harboring a fugitive. No contact of any kind could occur. She only hoped that somehow her family understood this. That she was protecting them. Caroline would talk herself out of it as many times as she could, and then she would call from a phone booth. She would wait until her father or mother picked up the phone. She would say nothing. She would listen to the sound of her mother's voice saying hello, and then her mother getting annoyed and repeating that word, *hello,* in an urgent way. Then Caroline would hang up and start crying. Or continue crying, as that had already started when her finger first rotated the dial on the phone. She would go as long as she could and then call again, and swear it was the last time, until a few months went by and she couldn't resist calling once more.

And?

Choose a California Social Security number, start with 568 or 546. The next two digits relate to your age. Always even numbered.

She removed the towel from her wet hair. She opened the tiny frosted window in the bathroom to let the hot, steamy air escape. She took the towel and wiped the mirror clear. In the seconds before it fogged again, she glimpsed her newly blond hair. It was a daffodil yellow blond, not the ash promised on the box. The side-parted, sophisticated and liberated woman on the L'Oréal box. From the Champagne Blonde series. Honestly. But it didn't matter. She wouldn't feel liberated by her blond hair whether it was egg-yolk yellow or a pale, early-summer corn-silk flaxen. She didn't feel any relief in discarding her old look, or in no longer having to be the woman she was. She only felt an unnamed dread that had more to do with loss than capture. What do you discover when you remove all the variables? That you are the sum of your experiences and vital statistics? That you are you no matter what your name or whether people expect different things of you? She wanted to feel the joy of no one urging her to go to graduate school, or to get married, or even to give it all up for the movement. To get to be anyone is a rebirth, isn't it? But she couldn't be anyone, she got to be—had to be—anyone but who she was. In retreat and in hiding. She looked at herself, and she saw the same whispery, alone person she had been her whole life, more unlikely than ever to feel at home anywhere. And the dyed hair made her complexion more sallow. She looked not monochromatic but subchromatic. A pallid suggestion of a person.

The very last time she would call home was on her mother's birthday, March 9, 1975. Twenty-nine months, three weeks and two days after she first went underground. She called, and her mother answered the phone. She listened as her mother said Hello? and waited, not hanging up, because she couldn't, not just yet, and her mother said, "Mary, is that you? Mary?" with a plaintive, quiet voice. She instantly pushed the receiver button to disconnect, still pressing her ear to the handset. She could hear her breath, feel her heart dropping to her stomach, and her knees actually buckling at the sound of her mother saying her name. To her. She leaned against the phone booth and then felt a contraction and a heave as coffee-tinged bile rose up her throat and back down. She knew then she couldn't call again, ever. Never, ever, never.

....

She had written it all down, once, on the ripped-out piece of spiral notebook paper. Her name, her history, the members of her family. Where Caroline Sherman had spent every year of her twenty-two years. When she was done, she tore the paper into shreds over the wastebasket. Then she fished the shreds out of the basket and lit them one by one in the yellow glass ashtray. She had it all memorized. She had all the details already in her head if not exactly in her heart.

PART TWO

······························

Summer 1998

Jason's Journal

SHE, MY MOTHER, apparently walked by my open bed-room door as I was blaring "Our Prayer." I'd just gotten my hands on the Beach Boys' three-disc *Smile* bootleg—you know, the kind of bootleg where there are like ten versions of the same song in a row? All these versions are usually just alternate takes that vary only slightly from the other versions. Say, for instance, on this take Brian stops singing two bars from the end. Or the harmonies get muddled slightly. Or somebody says, "One, two, three, four," at the beginning in a soft, defeated, boyish voice. So these aren't versions per se, these are screwups.

There are plenty of other bootlegs featuring actual different versions of Beach Boys songs: they occasionally have an extra verse, or a different person singing lead. Or different harmonies, different arrangements. Sometimes completely different lyrics. What my extended-box-set-bootleg packaging of *Smile* offers though is almost exclusively alternate takes. Ten, fifteen, twenty takes that are nearly identical to each other. They have already worked out how it is going to go, exactly how it will sound, and the takes are all about executing it. Now, you might ask, why the hell does someone want to listen to all that? And in truth, when I realized what I had bought (ninety dollars, no less), at first I was disappointed. But, and this is a big but, there is something amazing about hearing the takes. It is as if you are in the recording studio when they made this album. You are there with all the failures, the intense perfectionism, the frustration of trying to realize in the world the sounds you hear in your head. Sometimes they abruptly stop after someone says "cut" because they lost it, it didn't break their hearts enough, they just couldn't feel it in the right places. Or someone starts laughing, or says, suddenly, "Could you hear me on that?" What happens is you jump to a new level in your obsession where even the most arcane details become fascinating. You follow a course of minutiae and repetition, and you find yourself utterly enthralled. Listening deeply to this kind of music is mesmerizing in itself; the same song ten times in a row is like a meditation or a prayer. So it is quite apt to listen to the song "Our Prayer" in this manner. I'm on listen number three of the full ten versions, at about version seven, and I am peaking—my desire to listen is being satisfied but hasn't been entirely fulfilled, fatigue hasn't crept in yet, I still yearn for more, and it is a premium experience at this point, the blast of wall-to-wall harmonies, five-part, singing no words but just beautiful, celestial ahhs, the voices soaring, pure instruments of sound. Really, the Beach Boys at their acid choir best.

She, my mother, stopped by my door, which, as I said, was open, in itself a very unusual thing. I must have just returned from the kitchen or the bathroom and not yet closed the door. Maybe I was so into the music and wanted so much to be back next to it that I didn't even notice the door. I think actually I had a sandwich and a soda in my hands and I was arranging them on my desk, and that's why I hadn't closed the door yet. I noticed her leaning slightly against the doorjamb. I thought perhaps she mistook the open door as some sort of invitation. But then I noticed this tiny smile creeping across her lips, and how she wasn't really looking at me, and then I realized she was listening to the music, that was why she was standing there.

Okay, it was about eight o'clock, and by this time in the evening—I've noticed this, really all the time and without really intending to notice—by this time she was a little drunk. I knew this because I occasionally go to the living room to watch TV. Or I go to the dining room to eat dinner with her. She does this thing where she pours like a third of a glass of white wine and then she pours club soda into the glass to top it off. A wine spritzer, I guess. A corny suburban housewife kind of drink. She thinks it's a light aperitif, I imagine. You might call it that, an aperitif, if you wanted to make it sound reasonable and almost medicinal. Thing is, she soon finishes and then does the third of a glass and spritzer routine again. Thing is, she does this all evening long. It's not like I'm counting or even really paying attention, but it is hard to miss when she does this all evening long, every evening. I'm not even saying there is anything wrong with it. She never seems drunk—she doesn't get all slurry or drop things. She just seems increasingly placid and a bit dulled by bedtime. She is already the sort of person who seems constantly to be halfway elsewhere. So this habit only makes her more and more absent or indifferent to the vagaries or boredom of being in this house. I'm not judging here but merely describing what it is she does. I am just observing her. I think maybe the whole third of a glass plus seltzer thing indicates she isn't quite admitting to herself how much she drinks, but surely at some point she goes to refill and she realizes she's down to the last third of a glass in the bottle (and we are sometimes talking a magnum here, a big economy jug) that started the evening full, and she must realize, then, that she is drinking quite a lot. But by then she must also be placid enough, plied enough, by the countless spritzers where perhaps this empty magnum doesn't weigh on her too much at all. She is by then, well, whoever she is, in her private, silent thoughts, and I don't really mind as long as she doesn't interfere with me, which she usually doesn't.

So she was feeling no doubt buzzed by eight o'clock, and this song caught her as she walked down the hall. She was lost in it, faintly smiling. She looked really young standing there listening, and sort of uncovered, which was unusual for my mother. She is generally so creepily guarded and cryptic in odd, sunny ways. Like she isn't really entirely sure she is in the right house or the right life. Like she's a guest here. I guess she lacks the kind of certainty one expects in a parent. She seems to lack the necessary confidence. The song ended, there were a few seconds of silence and then "Our Prayer," take number eight, kicked in. During the break she smiled at me—a flirty, sheepish smile, disarmingly unmomlike.

"Great song," she said. Then it began again, and I lowered it reluctantly.

"A teenage symphony to God," I said, quoting the liner notes that quoted Brian Wilson.

"Yes, that's right," she said, nodding. "They always sound most like that when there aren't any words. When they use their voices as instruments. Just pure, perfect form."

So she said this kind of smart thing about the Beach Boys and then wandered off to refill her glass or something. That's the first time I remember thinking, How can that be?

Antiology

NASH HAD SEEN it happen before—many times, in fact. He stared at the kid's racing-striped, voluminous nylon messenger bag. Nash recognized the carrier of the bag. Davey D., maybe, if he remembered correctly. D. had that long, snaggly-ass surfer hair, bleached and knotted. He had a habit of pulling at the knots, tearing his fingers through them, then discarding the clumped strands on the floor. And when he took off his knit skullcap, the blond and knotted hair sprouted up and out like a palm frond over his forehead. Nash stood next to the cash register and watched Davey D. shove a skateboarder magazine into his bag. Who gave a crap except it was one of those Japanese imported skateboarder magazines that came wrapped in plastic and sold for fifteen bucks, with a CD sealed inside. Davey D. just eased it into the bag, slid it from magazine stand to flap compartment. No hesitation. No look around.

Nash didn't do anything. He watched D. but berated himself: why have a fifteen-dollar skateboarder magazine for sale at all?

Sealed so it can't even be flipped through before you shelled out your fifteen bucks. Could there exist a more appropriate or likely object for shoplifting? But this was Nash's problem, or one of them. He felt waves of ambivalence about shoplifting, and usually at crucial moments.

That didn't mean it didn't upset him. He stared at that shoulder bag, at Davey D. as he continued wandering the store. Nash felt increasingly angry over it, in fact. What upset him (probably) was his sense that Davey D. was certainly one of those rich-raggedy kids. They looked poor, they acted poor, they smelled poor—but somewhere behind them or out ahead of them, somewhere in the surround of them, lurked big, ungainly scads of unearned money. Big Connecticut or Rhode Island Grandpappy dough. The more snaggly the hair, the worse the hygiene, the older the money. Nash didn't know for sure, but he had developed what he felt was an accurate instinct about such things. After watching a lot of kids at close range, you could tell which ones had nets and which ones didn't.

Nevertheless, Nash did nothing about this particular theft, or any other. And the thefts had become rampant. Prairie Fire Books had been open only eighteen months. Eventually he hoped it would be run as a collective, by and for the people in the surrounding neighborhood, but for now it was funded by his benefactor, Henry Quinn, who gave Nash complete control of the place. Prairie Fire in no time became highly trafficked by the local youth and on many levels exceeded Nash and Henry's expectations. Of course it never made money; it never would. But Nash had a modest ambition for it not to lose too much money. And if it wasn't for all the theft, it probably wouldn't lose money at all, even with the low pricing and the tables where people were invited to read before, or instead of, buying.

Davey D. approached the cash register. He examined some flyers on the front rack—clubs, bands, zines and meetings. He wore a huge gray überflak jacket with oversized welt pockets, and there were deep and versatile zipper-and-Velcro-sealed pockets on his cargo pants, too. A veritable shoplifter's uniform. Nash made eye contact with Davey D. and even greeted him warmly. Davey D. said "Hey" in a friendly tone, then calmly cruised out the door. Nash thought of his half-formed theory that if he could make these kids see the store as part of their space—or even worse, that word *community*—they wouldn't indulge in petty thefts. But it was more complicated than that.

Prairie Fire stocked largely fringe texts. They sold books that advocated subverting the status quo, abolishing property and ownership, resisting American hegemony, and embracing rebellion and nonconformity of any stripe. Books of this sort, it seemed, begged to be stolen, and lots were. Nash knew it was like a roach infestation: for every one you actually saw, there were dozens you missed. And he refused to hide things behind the counter the way they do at some bookstores. Henry suggested he ought to do at least that with the most frequently stolen texts. But Nash believed that created too much mystique for the stolen objects. It made the unstolen books look shabby. Or else the hiding of the books behind the counter made it less likely kids would buy those books because they had to ask for them. They couldn't be silent, shuffling and begrudging about it; they had to be public and certain.

He did however start writing notes and pasting them throughout the stacks and shelves. Especially in the areas he couldn't see that easily.

We are not a corporate chain—
please don't steal from us!

or

If you steal from us we will cease to exist.

even as bad as

> *Prairie Fire is not the "man," so why are you stealing?*

and

> *Petty thievery is not subversive, it is just petty.*

Henry—and after all he was the owner of the place, the man whose dime was on the line, Nash respected that—saw the problem as one of enforcement. If Nash would just bust one of these kids, they would stop. Nash conceded that Henry might be right about that. Word was out that they didn't bust anyone.

"The notes just remind them that stealing is an option. Hey, I should buy this, and then they see this note asking them to cut out stealing, and they think, Oh yeah, people steal. I forgot about that, that's a good idea."

"Punk city," Nash said. "Have you noticed they all use that word again, *punk*. And *punk rock*. But it seems to mean generally rebellious rather than specifically 1977. As in 'You closed down traffic on I-5 during rush hour? Punk rock.' Although they tend to say it in a sneering tone, so perhaps it is sort of ironic. Or both, everything is both earnest and ironic at the same time with them. Which is either a total dodge or some attempt at a new way to be."

"Those signs just don't work," Henry said.

"But they would never use *city* as an intensifying suffix. Not yet, that is. But it will be back eventually, in some mangled retread. Count on it."

"But I leave it entirely up to you," Henry said.

They were having their nightly beer after the store closed. Or, more accurately, beers, as Henry would consume five to Nash's one. Henry, bottle in hand, wandered through the store laughing at Nash's signs.

"But I still think that as we gradually make them feel it is their space, as more of them work here, they will respect that."

"Or you could just bust one of them," Henry said.

"Where do you stop? How much energy do you give it? Then you end up in lockdown. Beepers and cameras, mirrors and cops. Seizures and searches."

"You're exaggerating."

"Charges. Pressed charges."

"Okay, do it your way. The whole point—"

"Affidavits. Attorneys."

"—of the place is not—"

"To cede yet another part of our lives to over-ordinance and constant surveillance."

Henry finished another beer in a long swig. He tossed the bottle in the recycling bin, where it clanked against the others. His face stretched into a painful-looking horizontal grimace that Nash understood to be Henry's smile. He always had razor stubble along his cheeks and dark circles under his eyes. And he chain-smoked unfiltered Camels, which enhanced a rather nasty asthmalike illness. Nash watched as Henry downed beer after beer, only hesitating at the last beer in the six-pack, which he would unfailingly offer to Nash, and Nash would decline politely, and Henry would shrug and grab it.

Neither Nash nor anyone else who really knew him would likely describe his life as particularly golden, not in the larger sense anyway, but in small ways Nash felt he would have to say it was lucky. Truly. Luck with people, friends—he was lucky with guys like Henry. Nash first met him at the bartending job Nash had taken to pay the bills. Prior to that he worked small-time construction jobs, but as a late-forty, he couldn't take it anymore. Or his body couldn't anyway.

Nash was a lousy bartender. He didn't know how to make many drinks, he wasn't fast, and he gave drinks away (every other drink was a buyback if you looked like you needed it). But this particular bartending job mostly required a stoic ability to deal with drunks for twelve hours straight and not get drunk yourself. The clientele were clichéd lonely, older working men with cumulative, functional-but-chronic drinking habits. And occasionally the younger nonworking locals that liked to slum in dive bars. They ordered drinks and then smiled and whispered to each other, gesturing. They constantly telegraphed that they were there for a laugh only, as if getting older was contagious. Nash tolerated all of it, he occupied himself with wiping and polishing—*tending the bar*—as he listened.

Henry was one of Nash's regulars. He was one of those wiry, slight guys who could drink endlessly and never hesitate when he finally stood, never seem surprised by the sudden hardness of the ground beneath his feet. He did have bad days, though, days when he had that jumpy, look-over-your-shoulder habit. But Nash immediately liked him. They were about the same age, which for some reason seemed important. At the end of the night, or toward the end of the night, Nash would pour himself a beer or a drink and come around the bar and sit on a stool, and Henry would tell Nash stories about growing up in this neighborhood, what had changed and what hadn't. He told good stories, and he didn't repeat himself, both rarities in the drunk crowd. Henry did sometimes sweat a lot, but he never, ever slurred his words. Nash heard rumors from the other regulars that Henry had been an Army Ranger and seen combat. Or maybe it was the Marines, or the Air Force. Others said he had been in prison. It was obvious Henry had been through *something,* but Henry never told Nash anything about that. What was clear was that Henry had lost hearing in one of his ears. Nash noticed that he frequently said What? in an irritated voice if Nash had the radio or TV on. Whenever Henry came in, Nash turned the background noise way down or off. He didn't make a fuss about doing it, and Henry certainly never asked for it, but that was how their rapport began.

Eventually Henry invited Nash to get high with him. It was closing time, and after locking up they walked around the corner to Nash's apartment.

He lived on the top floor of a small house. The old woman who owned the place lived downstairs and never raised the rent once in eight years. Nash felt that was being lucky in small ways. Henry followed him up the back stairs to the entrance door on the second-story porch. He was winded by the climb and waved Nash off as he caught his breath. From the back door and windows the distant downtown of the city gleamed and twinkled. During the day Nash could easily see the Sound and even the jagged, painterly Cascade Mountains beyond like a two-dimensional backdrop, so pretty they looked artificial to him and not pretty at all. He didn't really believe in them. He would catch a glimpse of them on clear days and then shake his head and mutter, "Yeah, sure. Ha."

"Do you own this place?" Henry asked when he stopped gasping from the stair climb. "I get these breathing irregularities at unpredictable times. More to do with anxiety than lungs." Breath. "I guess."

"No. I just rent it." Nash turned on the light. He rarely had guests, and only now did it occur to him that his apartment had a college feel to it, peculiar in a man his age: a secondhand couch with a blanket slipcover, a recycled industrial wire spindle turned on its side for a coffee table, a stereo (an actual vintage hi-fi turntable) with stacks of LPs at its side. Books strewn everywhere. Books in shelves made of crates and actual carpenter-made shelves, and more books doubled in front. Books shoved sideways on top of the books on the shelves. The room had no decoration except an oversized Persian-style area rug. And against one wall, lined up on several built-in shelves, was a collection of broken things: a series of vintage plastic objects, not so much a plate or a radio but a piece of something, a curve, a handle, a corner. They were that old imitation ivory with faded, prefab, fake imperfections—more beautiful older and faded, even cracked. Nash knew everything about them: they were urea resins, or acrylic, or phenolic molding masses. Co- or homopolymers. They were called made-up words with futuristic, hybrid, exotic formations: melamine, Bakelite, celluloid. They were resiny yellows with strands of darker color to evoke tortoise, or they were unnatural blow-molded reds and greens, meant to evoke nothing in nature. They had curves that went nowhere, and Nash found them all in junk shops and dumps, garbage bins and giveaway boxes at yard sales. He was not a collector, but he felt drawn to these plastic remnants. He liked looking at them, touching them, smelling them. (All of them still emitted odd, vintage toxins that you could detect, faintly, if you pushed the piece right against a nostril and inhaled. The odor reminded Nash of their slow evaporation into the air, of how they would disappear after a thousand years of low vapor emittance, and of their true plasticity, unstable and variable.) But of course to the guest visiting the chances were that these industrial relics—these detrital treasures—looked like, well, garbage.

Henry stepped into the room, barely glanced at the plastic pieces, the stereo or the books, and sat on the couch. He took out a pipe and a lighter and began to smoke.

"It has been ages for me. I never smoke anymore."

"How come?" Henry said.

Nash put his hand on his chin and frowned, glancing at the floor and then back to Henry. "I don't know. It was an expensive habit. I have a no-frills existence, a modest life," he said. He took the pipe from Henry and inhaled while he held the flame to the bowl. Nash didn't smoke anymore because at some point it began to have an unpredictable effect on him; sometimes it made him uncomfortable in deep, existential ways, making even the feel of his breath suspect, as if he were inhabiting a strange, wrong body.

So Nash didn't mind that smoking after all this time wasn't making him feel high in the slightest. But the gesture of smoking, particularly with Henry, was relaxing. "How modest a life? How no frills?" Henry said, sucking in air, holding it and then gulping in more. Nash couldn't help noticing how bad Henry looked away from the low bar light, the ragged edges beneath the surface, the deep creases on his face and the yellowness of his skin. Nash shrugged.

"Pretty fucking modest. Humble, plain. In every way imaginable."

"Health insurance?"

Nash shook his head.

"Stocks? Mutual funds?"

"No. God no."

"Real estate?"

"I said really modest."

"A savings account? A bank account?" Henry asked, hard-grinning at someone unseen and shaking his head.

"I use money orders and cash. There is not much left over. What there is, I stash." Nash took the smoking pipe from Henry's outstretched hand, leaving a faint smoke trail of herbal sweetness. He put his lips to it and inhaled. He began to feel the diffusion of the pot easing his muscles. Good, that was what he had hoped for—a nice physical high.

Henry watched him for a minute and then started laughing and rasping. It seemed unlikely that he would be able to stop for a while.

"You stash your dough? Like under your mattress?" he said between guffaws.

"I'm not going to tell you, asshole. I'm not stupid." Nash started laughing too.

"Ex-wife?" Breath. "Kids?"

"No. No! Look, I buy thrift store clothes. All right? I never eat out—I cook everything myself. Is that all? Oh yeah, I don't have a telephone, man. Did you hear me? I get mail, so why do I need a telephone?"

Henry stopped laughing finally and just smiled. "That's amazing. You are off the grid. Right here in the city."

"Sort of, I guess. But I have electricity and refrigeration. I'm quite content with that."

"Off the fucking grid."

"No cabin in Montana."

"No goddamned phone."

"But you know, I wouldn't mind being one of those guys in Arizona or New Mexico who have spent twenty years building some massive landwork in the desert. Some earth-altering sculptural dream of the future and God, until you die one day in a tractor moving the never-ending piles of dirt, unfinished but still—up until your last breath you are implacable, relentless and alone. Alone except perhaps for the young acolyte wife, desert tan, a woman with braids and devotion, her never-ceasing and only ambition being to help you—a man thirty years her senior— realize your dream. Your lifelong project, monument, statement. Your unyielding testament to, uh . . . well, unyielding."

"Sounds great," Henry said. He offered the pipe again. Nash shook his head and leaned back on the couch. There was a second of silence, and then Henry barked out a huge laugh.

Nash nodded. "It sure does, doesn't it?" They laughed until silence gradually set in. Nash then got up from the couch and sat cross-legged on the rug.

"Are you married?" Nash asked.

Henry sighed. "I'm divorced. I got a kid, too. I have two houses and I own a few buildings."

"No shit? Really?"

"How do you think I can afford to be at the bar all the time? I'm a man of leisure."

"You don't seem like someone who doesn't work."

"Good."

They sat for what felt like a long time. Nash studied his rug. Then his ceiling light fixture.

"That's beautiful. Braids in the desert. A tractor," Henry finally said.

"Yeah."

"You know what you are? You're a fucking priest, man."

"No, I'm not. I just slightly exist. Lots of people in the world live like that, they're just more ashamed and less deliberate about it."

"Maybe, maybe not."

Henry agreed to fund Prairie Fire. Mostly, Nash guessed, because Henry wanted to do something for him. They took over the basement space of one of his buildings; Nash left his bartending job. Once the store opened, Henry became more interested in it. He would spend hours looking at the books, not exactly reading them but pulling them from the shelves, studying the back covers, looking at the tables of contents, fanning the pages with his fingers. He even sat in on some of the meetings, although he never said anything.

One of Nash's ideas to help the place make extra money and keep traffic up had been to stay open late for various local meetings. He modeled his idea on European "infoshops." They put in two long wood tables with benches in a recessed area at the back of the store. He hired a middle-teen high schooler, Roland, to sell coffeehouse beverages from a station in the corner. It was through these drinks that the meetings brought in some money. But most important, the meetings made Prairie Fire into a fairly interesting place: a sanctuary of subversion for misfits and scragglers. And even occasionally those kids referred to by the other kids as the *marginalites*. (Nash guessed they were either the elite among the marginals or considered only lightly marginal. Probably both.) They read books or magazines, met people or just watched, wrote, ate, and even organized various protest events.

Nash enjoyed sitting among them at the long table, working but also drinking a soda, listening and occasionally talking. It all fit into a subject dear to his heart, and which he called by various names: His Antiology, or study of all things anti. His Counter-Catalog. Compendium of Dissidence. Ana-encyclopedia. The Resist List. His Contradictionary. He liked to think he observed them with a nearly clinical objectivity: the scrappy outsider kids who either stood in the park and discussed various actions and take-it-to-the-street strategies or sat all day in the coffee shop inventing manifestos and declaring their opposition—often to a seemingly arbitrary object, as much, perhaps, for opposition's own sake and energy as for a desire for social change. Nash thought that was okay, in fact he loved that specifically adolescent perversity: the brief window when the monolith of the culture had not yet made a convincing claim on their souls and they were able to muster some resistance to it all.

Nash heard them explain how they would get this media or that media to notice. In these kids' mouths the media was not a force they feared or admired but simply a tool they understood. They were more connected and savvy, and also more smug, than any activists he recalled. Except they would never use that word, *activist*. They were protesters but not that either. They could call themselves resisters, but that sounded so reactive, almost puritanical. Instead they called themselves *testers,* and they organized not demonstrations or protests but *tests*. He kind of liked that, testers. What was being tested—the kids or the target? Okay, not bad.

But plenty of other things about the testers did not impress Nash. When he felt particularly uncharitable, he found them entitled in this very dumb and tedious way. Oddly enough, for all their sarcasm and easy, shallow irony, there was still not enough self-reference for him, not enough wit. There was self-obsession, yes, self-consciousness, sure (after all, they always lived as though their lives were all on the verge of broadcast), but no concern with self-implication. Just that ungenerous righteousness, as if merely being young was somehow to your credit.

Nash would nearly give up on them, bored, tired, but then he would notice something to make him interested again. Like the kid he saw the other day as he walked through a test held in Pioneer Square. He was a short, chubby middle-twenty in all-white cotton like an ice-cream man. At some Reclaim the Parking Lot event, or a Liberate the Cement something. There among the usual kids stood this lone fellow in a white coat and white shirt and even a white tie. Spotless. He held a hand-lettered sign over his head, his face expressionless and deadpan. The sign said

World War VI will be fought in my uterus

He held the sign aloft and never altered his stance of intense gravitas. Brilliant. Nash loved kids like that, kids that surprised you and made you feel old and out of it.

He tried to be patient. He would take a deep breath and listen to them. And he discovered that he liked some of them okay, they were funny and smart. They were idealistic and angry. And, let's not forget, they were stealing. One other way Nash dealt with the epidemic thievery was to hire the very people he suspected of stealing. Particularly if he found them likable and not spoiled. For example:

Roland, the coffee guy. Nash first noticed him hunched over the edge of the table, drawing in a sketch pad, never looking directly at anyone. Roland drew retro Utopian-looking skyscrapers straight out of Tomorrowland or *Metropolis* with Buckminster Fuller domes in meticulous, boyish detail. He drew mega-tech vehicles and environmental disasters. He wore the same long black duffel coat every single day, no matter how warm it was. Nash figured you gotta love a middle-teen like that. He watched Roland rip off some of the graphic novels—beautiful, expensive books. Nash gave him a job and a store discount. Roland liked working there, he seemed to view the place as his home. Nash was certain Roland was still stealing.

Or Sissy. She was impossible to not notice, with her shiny blue-black hair, sharp, high cheekbones, and wide-set, overly made-up eyes. Nash admired how she was so very pretty but did everything in her power to dissuade you of it. Not just the overwrought makeup, which at a certain thickness moved from augmentation to ironic meditation, but a general ultra-ornamentation. Multiple piercings and tattoos, of course, but she also wore weird, pinned-up clothes—rags that she got at thrift stores in a variety of sizes, often in synthetic fabrics, that she safety-pinned around legs and waist and shoulders. She layered mummy style. Half the time it actually worked; the jumble came across as a planned, intended thing. The other half of the time she looked like a disaster, a freak, a bag woman.

She also had the vapor-thin body of so many of the girls around. They all seemed to be either sensitive-girl doughy or about to disappear. Sissy had a painful, deeply wrenched thinness that radiated hunger but, oddly, not fragility. In fact what came through was a steely, obdurate intractability. He couldn't quite read that yet—what that whip-thin look meant to these kids. Was it cultural capitulation or rebellion against being a body in general? Against needing to consume at all? Sissy had stolen at least one book, the *Vicious Nation's Biographical Dictionary of Incorrigible and Inscrutable Women*. It was almost a junk book of shallow, easy-to-read entries, but somehow it exceeded its own intentions by including some cool and obscure figures like Voltairine De Cleyre, mistress of nineteenth-century direct action, or forgotten-

but-verging-on-newly-cool second-wavers like Shulamith Fire-
stone. It was a hefty forty-five-dollar boutique-press monster of a
book. As if he wouldn't notice that gone missing. She looked at it
every single time she came in, and then it disappeared. But Sissy
also bought things. Little broken-down used books of poems.
Kids' science encyclopedias from the '60s. Amazing little artifacts
that Nash collected for someone just like her. Every time he sold
one of his strange used books, he felt vindicated and happy. He
hired Sissy to run the evening schedule of group meetings. He
told her he needed her help because she knew everybody. Which
was true. She also continued to steal.

His hiring strategy may not have headed off thievery, but
Nash learned not to take it personally that they stole stuff. As he
talked with them, said hello, waited on them, even answered
questions, he knew it wasn't personal because they thought so little about him. He observed and even studied them and all their
foibles, but he knew the interest was not reciprocated. They never
betrayed the slightest curiosity about him or even addressed him
by his name.

However, there was one way Nash was pretty certain they did
refer to him, although he never actually heard it said. *Loser*. This
was an inexplicably resilient word, the epithet that would be
hurled at someone and then no more needed to be said. Like the
word *suck*, *loser* had, despite its long overuse, retained its capital
among adolescents. No intensifiers made them work better;
these were terminal, face-slap, teleologically absolute terms. And
both words nihilistically conveyed no real information, just a bot-
tomless disdain. Nash imagined he was often described by these
kids as a *loser* and also someone who *sucks*. As in *that loser sucks*.
In this respect, as in many others, Miranda was a different case,
right from the beginning. Miranda actually initiated conversations with him.

"You shouldn't drink Coke. You guys shouldn't even be sell-ing Coke," she said to him one afternoon, just when he was convinced he truly had at last become invisible. He already knew her name, Miranda Diaz. She was the newer kid. The one he hadn't noticed stealing. Her face looked ridiculously young to him, smooth and unmade-up, but he figured her for an end-teen. She sat next to him as he took his break. He had just finished hours of used-book pricing and wanted a minute to relax before the evening's events were under way. He took a swig of his Coca-Cola and nodded at her.

"Yeah, as it happens we don't sell much, uh, Coca-Cola," he said. "And, okay, I guess I shouldn't drink it, but I do."

She looked surprised for a second, then smiled and shrugged.

"I like this place. It's great," she said, again smiling. She didn't look as young to him now. Maybe it was the way her expression lingered in her face even after she stopped smiling. It was playful, wasn't it?

"Are you the owner?" she asked.

"Nope."

She looked at him as though she wanted him to elaborate, and when he said nothing more, she laughed again.

Miranda started to hang around the store at the beginning of the summer. Sissy brought her, or they knew each other. He guessed Miranda was another well-fed suburban girl; usually they look like that when they first move to the city, a little too soft and a little too anxious. Her arms perpetually folded across her chest, legs crossed and then crossed again with her toe hooked under her ankle. Her round face and heavy-lidded dark eyes were offset by a constantly working, overexpressive brow. A little bit of a scowler, this girl, until she suddenly broke into that easy all-points, grown-up woman smile. He decided he liked her. She always said hello to him and cleaned up after herself. She studied the flyers and even started to come to a few of the tester meetings.

Only months earlier Nash had inaugurated the night meetings with a few groups he helped organize, and already it seemed everyone was an organizer. Instead of starting a band, these kids started collectives and fronts and miniarmies. The store even had a wait list for some of the slots. He let Sissy handle all that.

Nash should have felt Prairie Fire as meeting space was a great success, but he found too many of these groups indistinguishable. They wanted to demonstrate in front of a senator's office with placards. Or they wanted to march papier-mâché effigies of the president to city hall. Some groups tended to be unimaginative and self-serious in Nash's estimation. This inspired Nash, against his better judgment, to continue devising some groups of his own.

Right after he finished his first real conversation with Miranda, he held a meeting of the Church of the Latter Day Drop Society, which was his neo-yippie, post-situationist group, with an open-ended policy to let anyone who happened to be in the shop participate. A whopping eight kids straggled in. He noticed Miranda stuck around as he put his boxes of books away and cleared the table for the meeting. After her one moment of chastising Nash for his soft drink choice, she didn't speak but seemed to be pensively listening.

She sat in the farthest seat in the back, in the corner, blowing on her chai tea, legs crossed. Her laceless sneakers had thick white rubber soles, on which she had written slogans and drawn graffiti-style pictures with a black marker. It struck him as sweet, the youthful gesture of writing on your shoes. A strange form of self-expression similar to writing on your school binder: half-motivated by declaring your difference to the world (an important thing) and half-motivated by a desperate enslavement to what other people thought of you (the terrifying thrall to presentation that intensified everything crappy about being an adolescent). She charmed and distracted him with her shoes, and he actually tried to decipher the slogans, which was impossible.

She began coming in most days for her tea. Nash also noticed her on the street one afternoon walking arm in arm with Sissy. They smiled at him and waved, and then did that thing that young women do—fall about in giggles as soon as you wave back, as if you disappeared after the moment passed and they were now alone, critiquing it. She turned up again the following week at another of his groups, the Kill the Street Puppets Project, an antipuppet guerrilla theater group. That got a big crowd, as many people seemed to have a secret aversion to papier-mâché and chicken wire. She sat again in the corner, her limbs double-crossed, her face stern and serious, and earnestly took notes. It wasn't until her third week of attending his group meetings that she finally spoke up. This was during the Brand and Logo Devaluation Front meeting.

She wanted to hijack labels on Nike shirts.

"We could alter them to indicate that they were made in China under appalling conditions. Make it look exactly like a Nike label, but instead of saying one hundred percent cotton, it says made from sixty percent Chinese prison labor, forty percent child labor."

"Yeah, and I think product tampering is like a major felony," said a guy in a slightly unraveled, fuzzy alpaca vintage sweater worn with an oversized trench coat. He had on a hand-knit cap and never sat or removed his hands from his coat pockets, as if to say, "I'm not really here," or "I am almost not here, I'm just going to stay long enough to try to make everyone not want to do anything."

Miranda furrowed her brow and gnawed at the edge of her fingernail. She had the raw, swollen nail beds of a chronic biter. It was always these self-devouring types who ended up here, hating Nike. (Nike, like Starbucks, originated in the Northwest and then exploded in horrendous global ubiquity. The local kid culture obsessively focused on these formerly local corporations. They had a sense of entitlement when it came to making them targets, even as they still loved and desired the products on some level, too. That love seemed to increase their desire to undo the corporations that made them. It used to be you had to make munitions to piss people off. Now it was enough to be large, global and successful. That made it a more radical, systematic critique, Nash thought. And more futile, naturally.) Nash figured there were worse ways for these kids to expend their anger and energy. Way worse ways. So he listened to them rant and plot against Nike, and it was good.

Nash's head throbbed; he couldn't sleep after the previous night's late meeting. Despite his fatigue, he caught himself looking around throughout the day for Miranda. He sat at the common table drinking coffee and sorting used books when he saw it happen again. And again it was Davey D. Again it was one of those extreme magazines sealed in plastic. It couldn't have been more than three weeks since the previous incident. Nash sat with clipboard and pen, surrounded by stacks of old books. He sneezed the whole time he priced the used books. These were books donated to them or acquired at estate sales or at flea markets. Many of them were mildewed, all of them were dusty. Sometimes it seemed to him the more unusual or valuable the book was, the more likely it would have acquired the stench of decay. He usually quarantined the bad ones. They infected the good ones. But he didn't throw them out. The main reason the mildew grew there in the first place was because the books were neglected—unread, uncracked even, for years. Admittedly many of these books were from small, do-it-yourself-type presses: cheap, disposable productions with high-acid paper that began decaying right from the get-go. There really wasn't a remedy for the mildew—he would end up putting those books in the free bin in front of the store.

Davey D.'s first theft was not particularly a blow, but its repetition, and the fact that it was right in front of him again, made it unusually upsetting. He didn't even want to carry these types of magazines, but some of the kids loved that crap—the semi-retarded, tiny subversion of extreme, physically expert but mentally unchallenging subcultures. He called it brat refusal, that skate-rat rebelliousness, but it was still alternative in some way, it still had the energy of resistance. And he was not convinced that these compromises were a bad thing, not convinced that the thinnest veneer of rebellion wasn't still preferable to none at all.

Nash's feelings, then, were complicated when he witnessed this repeated, petty theft: D.D.'s person as crypto rich, the object as base, and the shamelessness of the grab right in front of him. Nash also knew he would just suck it up and absorb the loss. Henry would tolerate it, he would make it up some other way. Because Nash would rather jeopardize the existence of the whole enterprise than bust this kid. Not because he didn't like confrontation but because he absolutely refused to be a cop of any kind. It really would be the last thing he would ever do. He was certain that the tiniest choices altered the world as significantly as larger choices. It was through accumulation that people gradually became unrecognizable to themselves. He would sacrifice a lot not to become an enforcer.

He watched as Davey D. walked out the door with no hesitation, just as before.

Nash returned to his stack of books. His skin itched. Itching always coincided with his being watched—he could feel scrutiny like a rash. He realized that this whole theft drama had been witnessed by one of the other kids.

Josh Marshall stood by the table and nodded in his direction. Nash recognized him. He stood out because he didn't have the customary appointments of the Prairie Fire crowd. He wore clean, well-pressed clothes. Short, neatly combed hair. He bought interesting books. Nash couldn't recall which ones exactly, but he remembered thinking he was an unusual kid.

Nash waited for him to say something, but he didn't. Instead he examined the top book on the stack. It was a cheap small-press paperback of Alexander Berkman's prison memoirs, essays and collected letters with no introduction, tiny Garamond type and thin, newsprintlike paper. And it was rancid with mildew. Josh picked it up and looked at the back pages.

"Revolutionist first, human afterwards," Josh said. He used his thumb to slowly fan the pages of the book.

"I think he revised that position by like page ten," Nash said.

"I hate books without indexes," Josh said.

"It's an old edition. I have a newer edition on the shelves that has an index. And explanatory footnotes. And an introduction—"

"I just check out the indexes to see what the reference points are and sometimes the bibliographies. I like to see what they are stringing together, where they came from. I don't need some academic hack's introduction to contextualize it for me."

Nash nodded.

"Sometimes I only read the index."

"That's very modern, isn't it?" Nash said. Now he remembered what a narc vibe this kid gave off. "Some books of philosophy and social theory from independent small presses didn't have indexes until someone, perhaps an academic hack, added them later."

"I don't necessarily want to read the essays as organized. I like to skip around and hunt out specific subjects of interest. I like things chaptered and sectioned. I like headings and subdivisions."

"Yeah."

"How much?"

"Fifty cents."

Josh smiled at that and took a calfskin billfold out of the inside chest pocket of his raincoat. He pulled a dollar out and put it down on the table in front of Nash.

"You shouldn't charge less than a dollar. It devalues things," he said, not looking at Nash and sniffing the surface of the book. "People won't respect things if they think you are giving them away."

"That is totally wrongheaded. You don't know what you are talking about," Nash said. Josh looked at him, his mouth now slightly open. He still held the book. "I mean," Nash said, softening his tone a bit, "I refuse to accept that."

Josh leaned down to the table so his face was close to Nash.

"Why didn't you stop him?" he said in a low tone. "I'm sure you saw what he did." Nash scrutinized the next book in his pile.

"That kid lifted a magazine. Why didn't you stop him?"

Nash marked a price on the inside cover of the book and then recorded it on his clipboard list.

"By the way, that's a very mildewed book, you know," he said, pointing with his pencil at the book Josh still held.

"You saw him. Stealing. I know you did."

Nash pushed the dollar back at him. "Thing is, I can't sell you a mildewed book. It wouldn't be right. You can have it."

Josh didn't move.

"Just take the book. It's yours."

Nepenthex

HENRY QUINN wore his mechanic coveralls. At 1:45 a.m. he moved quickly across a parking lot on Third Avenue. The streets were quiet but not at all dark. This didn't concern him. After several nights in this street at this time, he knew that very few people passed by. Very few cars passed by. The only time he had ever seen a police car in the area was at 2:30, and then only in pursuit of someone at some other place.

It was a cool early summer night, but Henry was already sweating in his coveralls. He pulled a black watch cap off his head and put it in his side pocket. He kept his head shaved, and when he looked up at the side wall of the building, deep furrows formed in the skin where the back of his head pushed into his neck. A pain shot down into his shoulder. He couldn't remember when his neck and back didn't hurt. He wanted a drink and to lie on his bed with the odd-shaped neck pillow and the heating pad. He walked onto the side street perpendicular to the avenue. The street banked steeply to a series of alleys leading to Elliott Bay, and he could smell the ancient midnight damp from the Sound behind the buildings at the bottom of the hill. Most of the street light came from the illuminated billboard attached to the brick side of the building that faced the side street. The vinyl face of the billboard had enormous sans serif letters that spelled *Endurit* and *Abiden*. The legend underneath read:

> *Cutting-edge psychopharmacology in the new*
> *Nepenthex Pairing System:*
> *what gets you through the longest nights*
> *and the hardest days*

He couldn't help hearing the liquid-toned voices of the television ads for the two drugs, the man's voice saying "longest nights," the woman's voice, barely overlapping the man's, saying "hardest days." Underneath the letters there was a picture of two curved and interlocking pills in a pink, luminous chiaroscuro that glowed in virtual three dimensions in the spotlights. Under that, in smaller letters, it said:

> *Ask your doctor if the Nepenthex System of*
> *Endurit and Abiden is right for you*

Henry stared for a moment, unable to stop himself from either reading the board or hearing the mellifluous voice of the woman from the TV ad. He stood and waited, sweating. At precisely 2:00, the lights on the board timed out. Henry tried to take another deep breath, but already it was difficult, and he walked away from the board to a fire escape that led to the roof. He tied a rope to one of the metal bars holding the board to the building. The board didn't have a ladder attached like most billboards. He hooked himself to the rope with a carabiner and attached it to a thick nylon belt around his legs and waist. He pulled at it and then walked to the edge of the building. He dangled the rope down the front of the board. Up close he could see it was thick vinyl sheeting. He took out a large retractable-blade knife. He lay on his stomach and slammed the knife into the corner, pushing it until it punctured the surface. He struggled to pull rightward, cutting the vinyl across the top. White, powdery dust that smelled of new plastic puffed out from the cut vinyl and filled the air by his head. He felt his lungs close as he inhaled. Fumbling with the zipper on his coveralls, Henry fished out his inhaler just as he was about to pass out. He sucked on the inhaler, lying on the roof and staring at the night sky. He felt the cold, wet spray of the Sound blowing faintly on him. He could see the blue-black of the water from up here. He wanted to go back to his house and take a pill and fall asleep. But he reached again into his coveralls and pulled out a bandanna and covered his mouth and nostrils. He very slowly resumed his cutting of the vinyl board.

He had considered every possibility—and certainly the idea that he shouldn't remove the vinyl from the wall but add to it instead. Some smart riposte to the ad. He'd seen others do it. The Gap Kids board by the freeway. The picture was of some beautiful Asian toddler in a pink corduroy hat. It just said "Gap Kids." But someone, or some group, pasted under it, in exactly the same font,

made for kids, by kids

He admitted it was clever. Smart-aleck clever. But to Henry that kind of addition made it all just a joke, a way of showing off that you had the technology to match the font. And the wit to torque their intentions. That you could hijack their ad through your own savvy mastery of ad language and technology. Leave that to these ad-addicted kids. Didn't it just pile onto the general noise and garbage? Besides, was that even true about the child labor? Well, probably it was.

After he finished cutting the top, Henry used the rope to slowly rappel down the front of the billboard, cutting the vinyl as he lowered himself.

The vinyl sheeting came down over him as he cut. At the very last cut he pulled himself off to the side and watched the whole sheet bend forward until the picture faced the building and the wall was clear. Henry was exhausted, his arms were shaking. There was no way he was climbing back up. He looked down at the vinyl sheet hanging below him. Its bottom edge was maybe five feet from the street. He loosened the hook from the rope and climbed down the vinyl. At the bottom he jumped the last five feet. He landed fine, actually, no pain at all. He stepped back from the building and looked at the gray brick.

At last, he didn't have to look at it. Henry pulled off his face scarf and breathed in the night air. He started to shiver. He pulled his fingers out of the finger holes of his gloves and balled them together for warmth. He stared at the brick face one more time. It was only after he started to walk to his car that he realized his face was wet. Salty drops streamed down the creases by the corners of his eyes and into his mouth and dangled from his chin. His vision blurred. Henry sighed. Christ.

Safe as Milk

MIRANDA'S LIFE changed over the course of the summer. After years of static inertia throughout high school, everything at last came alive, fluctuated, became constantly inconstant. Miranda often tried to trace the whys and hows and ways of it: the way she met first Nash; then how she met Josh; how it could all be traced back to the Black House, to her friend Sissy; and also, or maybe particularly, to the long days of the Northwestern summer, when not only did the sun shine every day but it would stay light until nearly ten o'clock at night—ten o'clock—and it would feel as though the city spun extra hours just for serendipity, or even destiny, depending on how she looked at it.

That summer held a particular glow because it was the first time she left her mother's house in the suburbs to live on her own in the city. It began when one of those things occurred that she thought only happened to other, more interesting people. She made a connection, walked into a score of a connection: a friend offered an available room in a house on Capitol Hill, the alternative, funky-even-for-this-funky-town neighborhood. And not just a room in any house but in the Black House. Miranda met her while she browsed in Shrink Wrap, a used-music store specializing in vinyl LPs.

Shrink Wrap was unbelievably located in a suburban colossus called the Bellevue Mall: a formerly upscale, '80s mall-boom monstrosity with sponge-painted pink-and-gray cement pillars, now exclusively occupied by second-string retail stores. All of Miranda's life she had watched the decline and tawdry aging of something designed to be extra new and perpetually now. Like the rapidly aging housing developments that surrounded it, the best Bellevue Mall ever looked was the day it was built. Time could add nothing to it. But here, somehow, in this now lower-rent environment sat Shrink Wrap, the sister store of a relentlessly obscure vinyl-and-CD store in the University District. Because of its remote location in the suburbs, Shrink Wrap developed a reputation for unpicked-through merchandise and became a magnet for hard-core obsessives and music geeks. In addition to their vast stockpile of vinyl, they also sold old cassette tapes, which were becoming trendy among adolescent boys again despite their inferior technology. Gradually that became the theme, the hook, of the place: outdated technology for young kids who already saw the vanguard in the past, the recent past, and not just in content but in format. Miranda liked that; she found it vaguely subversive, and besides it was the only place of interest in the whole suburb.

Her big break happened, or began, as she flipped through the LP bins one afternoon. LPs lent themselves to browsing. Unlike a CD's, their substantial covers could be examined. Unknown music could catch your eye and force you to take a closer look. She picked up an old Captain Beefheart record, *Safe as Milk*. She thought she might buy it because she liked the title. They should name the record store Safe as Milk. They could name the whole suburb Safe as Milk. She always did that, thought of new names for things. If you discover the appropriate name, not only does the named thing change but your relationship to the named thing changes. It becomes within your grasp. While she held this LP, she thought, This is a Long-Playing record, which people play on high-fidelity stereo systems. She could see the outline of the record itself through the shiny cardboard sleeve. As she regarded it—it had weight—a girl with emphatically girlish Heidi braids approached her.

She had short, blunt bangs, cut well above her highly plucked brows, and two jet-black braids wound tight starting behind each ear, each with bright green yarn braided in and tied with knotted bows at the ends. And not the skinny yarn that you would use for knitting but that thick, fat yarn Miranda had only ever seen in kindergarten, yarn so fat kids with fat fingers were able to tie it. The girl's braids evoked in Miranda a rush of disconcerting nostalgia: she thought of glitter in clumps, ashy blue construction paper and abstract dreamscapes of tissue paper, confetti and pasta shells. Miranda held her own long hair in one hand, pulling it straight, staring at the girl, who was now speed-talking (sniffling, jaw grinding, practically spark shooting). Miranda's breath quickened, and she felt a general ache that made her want something from or with this girl.

She wanted to show Miranda a clip on her laptop computer. She had ripped the entire Captain Beefheart box set, obtained somehow at no expense, including a digital video encoded on one of the CDs. She opened the computer on the front counter, and they watched a tiny Captain Beefheart shimmy and jam his way through a song on a French beach in 1967, with his Magic Band, zany freaks with a tight monster-blues sound, but blues with a fractured acid filter. The girl introduced herself as Sissy Cakes. She quickly told Miranda how she had just broken up with her much older girlfriend, and she had been on a three-day binge of partying and all-nighters ever since, so don't worry if she seemed to be hypered out. Miranda had heard of her, or read about her somewhere. Sissy described how she belonged to a performance/test group that had attempted and failed to shut down the Bumbershoot arts festival at the Space Needle each of the past three years. "They totally ghetto any local, noncorporate artists." She also wrote a music column for a local free paper. She explained how she made no money, but it was okay because she lived very cheaply in an old Victorian house off Fifteenth Avenue in Capitol Hill. And then she said it, there was a room opening up—maybe Miranda wanted it.

Sissy's house was known around town as the Black House. This was for two reasons: it was, in fact, painted black, and it also housed various black blockers, or want-to-be black blockers, kids from depressed rural backwaters and nearby college towns who came up for shows or political tests and demonstrations, and they were free to crash wherever space was available. The Black House was a squat but a benign quasi-squat. It was condemned but still standing. The people who lived there paid rent to the guy who owned it, but just enough not to get in trouble for trespassing. One day he would tear it down, but meanwhile he collected money on the sly and didn't do anything to keep it up. It had running water and electricity but no heat. The large L-shaped wraparound porch was still in pretty good shape, despite the kids forever perched on its rails and balusters. The house had a secret feel—it was set back from the road and hidden from view by large red maples growing in a row across the front yard. This kept the sun off the walkway to the house but also created an odd canopy of drizzle-edged dryness in all but the most dramatic downpours.

The asymmetrical entryway led to two connected parlors on the right and a stairway with a wobbly, oft-ridden-and-climbed banister to the left. One parlor was used as a bedroom; the other, with pretty triptych bay windows, was used as the common room. Which meant it was always covered with sleeping bags of crashers and visiting friends. There was one lone couch: a formal-looking Empire-style thrift store find. The upholstery was ripped and the wood scratched by the three cats that lived in the house. And although there was a makeshift coverall on it composed of an Army blanket further covered by a batik red-and-white throw (which could well have been someone's abandoned sarong left after a party and made part of the decor by happenstance), Sissy quickly warned Miranda that she would get fleas from reclining on it. "That is if you are the type of person fleas like."

Miranda moved there in mid-May, bringing only two suitcases of clothes and a cheap boom box. Her room was on the second floor, toward the back. It actually had a little anteroom attached to it, and someone had hung black beads in the threshold between the two rooms. With candles lit and her futon on the floor, it was practically paradise. Her main room even had its own dormer window, with black shutters that were permanently nailed open. It looked out over a side alley and beyond that Fifteenth Avenue. She could see a streetlight through tree branches outside the window, hear people talking as they walked by at all hours of the night, and she couldn't quite believe she lived in such an exciting place. Her first night she could barely sleep thinking about the whole city around her and actually residing right in the middle of it all.

The morning after her first night she discovered it wasn't necessary to sit on the couch to get fleas. She scratched frantically at her ankles. She woke early, stumbled out of her room half asleep and went to the kitchen to make coffee. She found three sniffling teenagers huddled by the stove. The electric oven door was pulled open and the heat on full blast, as well as all the burners on the stovetop, the coils glowing in the dark. The kids leaned over, warming themselves. The early morning air could barely be called chilly, but they rubbed hands along skinny arms, sniffling in self-pity and surprise at how they actually had to huddle for warmth—they were like real poor people, they really were. Later she would learn that the kids who did a lot of methamphetamine, or various other speed-type drugs, were often freezing, skinny and sniffling. She just stepped over them and hoped they didn't set the house on fire.

With the exception of the heat, which was an issue a few months a year, or in the early mornings or late nights of early summer, when enough partying and all-nighters might give someone the chills, and despite the various infestations of fleas, mice, roaches and cats, there were few other major deprivations at the Black House as Miranda saw it. The bathrooms on both floors worked, she had her anteroom and dormer window, and it was still, under it all, a good old house. But more than that, Miranda was certain it was a special place that might help shake the suburbs off her forever.

As they sat on the porch sharing a hand-rolled cigarette of tobacco and hash, Sissy told Miranda the impeccable pedigree of the Black House. How everyone knew the house, and how it was actually notorious in youth circles. It had existed for years as condemned but lived in, first in the late '80s and early '90s as a crash pad for rock kids (a strange conglomeration of Olympia and Eugene hipsters, fat girls with attitudes, post-grunge scenesters, and finally latecomer vultures). Now it was overrun with straight-edge anarchists, militant earth liberators, vanguardist pop culture pranksters, and hybrid testers and toppers from the very same hinterlands and suburbs. But no matter who lived there, the whole house smelled perpetually and deeply of tobacco, cat piss and Nag Champa incense.

There were no rules, but a few things were clearly not forgiven, depending on who dominated or paid the rent at any given moment. Most recently things were under the sway of a particularly humorless cadre of radical animal liberationists. Consequently, the food one found around was vegan and soy and free from animal traces. There was a big sign in the fridge indicating that out of respect for the vegans, the top two shelves were to be kept entirely meat free. The currently ascendant cadre also tried to make the Black House into a more formal experiment in group living. In addition to rules, they organized house meetings to divide chores and make group purchases of bulk food items. Sissy laughed it off. The house seemed fated to resist order, what with more and more baby anarchists camping in the parlors and hallways. Miranda followed Sissy's advice and put a padlock on her door. She soon discovered whatever food she put in the refrigerator was ipso facto communal and took her toothbrush and towel back into her room each night and each morning. The Black House was both the cushiest squat and the worst legit apartment she could ever hope to find. Paradise, though—pure post-suburban paradise for a girl like Miranda.

Living at the Black House indirectly led her to meeting Nash. It took several weeks for Miranda to get the nerve to actually enter the common room. She was looking for a phone, which she didn't find. People who wanted to make phone calls used their own cell phones. Sissy told her she could make local phone calls and even check her e-mail at Prairie Fire Books, where Sissy sometimes worked. The bookstore was just a block down Fifteenth Avenue, right next to what Sissy called Lesbian Hardware (because that was what it was, although the actual name was Mother Mercantile). Many times that summer, particularly after they smoked together, Sissy and Miranda would be on their way to Prairie Fire but get sidetracked and end up either blinking in fluorescence at the QFC supermarket or wandering through Lesbian Hardware.

Mother Mercantile was the fanciest hardware store Miranda had ever seen. It was run by middle-aged women with short, salt-and-pepper haircuts. Sissy referred to them as corporate dykes. (Sissy loved to shoplift there, mostly things she didn't want or need, like a piece of eco-conscious recycled Astroturf, or a very expensive garden spade with an ergonomic "Placoflex" handle made of durable polypropylene covered in a forgiving thermoplastic elastomer. Once she stole a can of Enamel Baby nontoxic acrylic latex paint; soon after, Miranda saw two people at the Black House inhaling deeply as they slathered the paint on the front of the refrigerator. Despite its being toxin-free, eye-watering fumes permeated the whole house.)

The store sold not only handsome tools and garden equipment but lots of sturdy clothing in third world fabrics cut in large, smocky styles. They sold little palm-sized books of spiritual inspiration, which lined the aisle leading to the cash register along with various kites, banners and wind socks in pastel solids or rainbow stripes. During one visit Sissy grabbed one of the wind socks and shook it at Miranda.

"What?" Miranda said. Sissy waved the festively colored fabric tube back and forth in front of Miranda's face. "Don't do that."

"Wind sock people. They are taking over this neighborhood. They take over all the neighborhoods after we've made them cool," Sissy said.

"I didn't make this neighborhood cool. I just moved here."

"That's not the point," she said, shoving the wind sock disdainfully into her large shoulder bag. Later she would wave it at someone, or toss it in the garbage. It was true, though. Miranda noticed that the owners of more than half the cute bungalow houses in this neighborhood refurbished them and then seemed to mark or declare themselves with a colorful wind sock. In the suburbs where Miranda grew up, people either hung cute "crafty" wood cutouts of ducks and dogs on their front doors or a year-round wreath of dried pastel flowers and brambly twigs. Here in the city they hung wind socks or sometimes wind chimes instead.

The subterranean front door of Prairie Fire, covered in flyers and blocked by kids smoking cigarettes, looked shabby and degenerate next to Mother Mercantile's marbleized portico. Prairie Fire was as much an anomaly in the neighborhood as the Black House. You knew eventually that the wind sock/hardware store element would not tolerate the Black House element, or its bookstore hangout either. But for now it all coexisted, in that exciting way city spaces sometimes contain things in opposition and transition. You could catch actual physical manifestations of larger cultural changes. For the moment tolerance was still the word, and the wind sock contingent considered Prairie Fire a good third place—a social space—for the neighborhood youth.

By the time Miranda starting going to Prairie Fire, Nash's open-door policy on group meetings combined with the growing social divisions in the neighborhood to create a volatile mix, irresistible to people like Miranda and Sissy. Miranda could feel things gathering their own energy. She could see things happening. And she thought herself quite lucky to have landed, only weeks after leaving her mother's house, so much amid it all.

Miranda sat beside Nash and again had admonished him about drinking Coke, which became sort of a running joke. Since she began regularly attending his Prairie Fire meetings, Nash increasingly engaged her in long, seemingly discontinuous conversations. No matter the subject, he responded to whatever she said with certainty and as if what he said wasn't off-kilter and incongruent with what had been said previously. She did think it funny—if someone were to tape them, it would seem as if big chunks of essential conversation had been erased. She attempted to be equally absurd in her return statements. He could read it as flirting, but that would be a mistake. At least Miranda didn't think she was flirting.

"I hate animal supremacists," Miranda said, biting at the nail on her thumb.

"I think they are actually called animal rights activists," Nash said.

She smiled at him and continued. "I do. Their blond dreadlocks and hemp clothes. Reggae-listening, green-panther, righteous rich kids."

"Are they green panthers, or are they more rightly called panther panthers?" Nash said.

Miranda spoke in a stagy whisper.

"Just look at them," she said. She tapped a finger on Nash's arm and indicated several kids loitering around the magazine stand. The usual marauders. Miranda gestured toward a petite henna-haired girl. She wore a camouflage khaki jacket that had a large circle painted on it with *fur* written inside and a red bar crossing it out. Her pants leg featured a Beef Nation = Killing Fields patch; she also displayed an American Animal Diaspora insignia, not sewn but pinned loosely to her hat brim. Everything she wore had that same contrived, raggedy look. "Especially those militants." She lowered her voice and shifted her eyes back and forth dramatically. "I live with some of them. Calling themselves Animal Marshals and Liberationists. All that pseudomilitary speak, and the uniforms. I don't trust them." She looked at Nash, bit her nail and then continued. "They are offended by fur coats. Yeah, fur coats are offensive, but it is because of the cost, not the animals. Someone spends twenty thousand dollars on a coat while there are people without food or shelter. Can't people ever feel any shame? What kind of society tolerates the idea of people sleeping in the street while other people walk right by in twenty-thousand-dollar coats? That's what's offensive." Miranda looked at Nash, her eyebrows pressing together, and she took a deep breath.

Nash shook his head. "I had no idea you hated animals," he said.

She had already made her point, but that didn't stop her because, well, sometimes she couldn't stop. That was one of her problems. She would start out trying to be provocative but end up completely earnest about what she was saying. She would start out intending to be cynical and aloof and end up with an embarrassing catch in her voice.

"I just hate people who have the wrong analysis, you know? Who miss the economics. Who just see it as one issue. Who have just enough compassion for the cute animals. Who care about the rest of the people in the world only when it starts to affect *their* world." She waited for a response, stared at Nash with her large brown eyes, her mouth a stern frown until she bit her lip, a waiting thing she did that she knew betrayed how anxious she felt and how urgent.

"That's good for you, Miranda. You must protect yourself with the 'breastplate of righteousness and the ammunition of determination' or something, more or less, like that."

His condescension upset her, but she also knew he was quoting something she should know but didn't, so she just swallowed it. She liked him anyway—he was smart and funny, yes, but something else, too. It was nice, wasn't it (or at least different) that he didn't feel he had to prove anything? Most of the time Nash seemed content to be anonymous and almost egoless. But despite that, if someone did look closely, it was hard not to notice things. The excitement he betrayed during the meetings—she could see it, or thought she could. He had a weathered face, unremarkable except when he broke into this lopsided, purely local smile. He would undermine his own expressions by only half-committing his face to them. His frowns were belied by amused eyes; his grins pushed the edge of smirk by a narrowing boredom in his brow. It could be noted, this tendency. And read as unsettling, or intriguing. Miranda, anyway, noticed.

Miranda also began to notice things in the meetings Nash led (or "facilitated," because naturally there were no leaders). They were held on Tuesday and Thursday nights under Nash's highly mannered and hermetic nomenclature: SAP (Strategic Aggravation Players and/or Satyagraha by Antinomic Praxis); or the Neo Tea-Dumpers Front; or Re: the "Re" Words—Resist, Reclaim, and Rebel; or the "K" Nation (single-tactic group that merely inserted the letter *k* or removed the letter *k*—dislokations were what they called them—to cause psychic discomfort and disturbances. As in *blac bloc* instead of *black block,* or *Amerika* instead of *America*. They sent out ransom-note-style missives to unnerve their targets: *Welkome, konsumers! You have been under attac. Better watch your bac,* et cetera). It didn't take long for her to realize that Nash's groups never met more than once under the same name. She noticed that the same kids were at each meeting. These were the most wounded looking of the kids who frequented Prairie Fire. The fattest ones, or the ones with the worst skin, or the ones with the most solipsistic hygiene habits.

Was it the same group with different names, or different groups with the same members? Each meeting always started with a demand that all cops and media identify themselves and be excused from the meeting. It seemed at first genuine, then a little self-aggrandizing, and finally, she realized, after the third week, to be a parody of left-wing paranoia, to ridicule the people who imagined they were constantly surveiled or infiltrated. But she couldn't be sure—it was all those things at once. They were planning to participate in some test or another with hundreds of other groups. Whatever antiglobal or anticorporate event that would occur. They discussed dozens of actions and prankster-type tests: pirating public-space surveillance cameras, infiltrating and disturbing business associations, staging website virtual sit-ins, performing seemingly ad hoc "plays" in malls and other retail environments. They planned to dress in suits and pass out dollar bills in Pioneer Square to the shoppers. They discussed defacing billboards and prancing nearly naked fat women in front of Barneys to ask people as they entered or left if there was anything available in their size. Always they were anticorporate. Mostly they were funny and absurd. And they wanted, it seemed to her, to point out the contradictions that had become so normalized in people's eyes.

There were other meetings, not run by Nash, but Miranda wasn't as interested in those. They were tedious and repetitive and conventional. Miranda kept coming to Nash's groups and became quite excited by the actions they discussed. She truly believed that if people felt the weight of what they did, understood the consequences, it might change their lives. Or they might change their lives. And this would—albeit in small, incremental ways—eventually change the world. It was simple and obvious to her, the truth of such a strategy.

She guessed that Nash had pursued these kinds of activities his whole life. He must know some secret way of being in opposition to the culture at large that didn't frustrate him. Miranda had felt a passionate and hopeful optimism about people for as long as she could remember, but already she grew frustrated when she realized that others still refused to see the way the world should be. It was like they'd forgotten how to be good. They'd made it complicated.

For all of June and into July, Miranda attended every meeting, and after every meeting she made it a point to stick around and help Nash pick up the recyclable paper cups, and then they would talk, more and more each time, stretching the cleanup into the evening. Nash would open the back door to get air into the hot, stuffy space, which finally began to cool down after the crowds left. She often stood in the doorway and looked at the night sky, reluctant to leave even after they finished the cleanup.

One night, after everyone had gone, Miranda lingered in the doorway, scrutinizing a flyer with the current week's schedule.

"What is with this group, SAFE? When is their meeting? I mean they are listed, but I've never seen them actually meet."

Nash shrugged.

"What does SAFE stand for?"

"I'm not sure."

"This isn't one of your groups?"

Nash shook his head. "I told you. I just facilitate now and then. Make a few suggestions. I believe they are the Scavengers Against Flat Effrontery. Or is it fatuous effrontery? It says on the flyer they meet after the 'K' Nation. But then again, I've never actually seen anyone from that group."

"So they don't meet here?"

Nash pointed to a footnote on the schedule. There was an asterisk next to the SAFE meeting time. The legend at the bottom said, "Meetings as needed and when necessary."

Miranda tossed the flyer on the table with all the other meeting papers and pamphlets.

"What about colors, Miranda?" he asked as if they were already in a new conversation. She smiled at him blankly.

"What about all the green and black?"

She shrugged. "It's all right."

"I think it's really from comic books," Nash said. "I know how you feel about militant environmentalists, but they are the badasses these days, you have to admit it. Did you see that green-and-black flag the ecoanarchist guys have? That looks good. You have those appropriated paramilitary colors and materials. That is powerful. Besides, guerrillas have always copped from the military. These kids mix superheroes with defunct army clothes, acronyms and slang. And those woodcut printed posters, too— sort of Soviet Constructivist looking. I think it's a legit symbolic strategy. Native Americans used to incorporate American flag designs in their clothes to steal the power of the white man by appropriating his symbols."

"Yeah? Did the Native Americans win that one?" Miranda said. Nash laughed. Miranda felt very pleased when she could make Nash smile, or even better, laugh.

"The point isn't to win. They'll never win, of course. They just make persuasive and powerful the beauty of their opposition."

"Yeah, I guess," she said. "But wouldn't it also be great to win? I think you should try to win. Otherwise it is just a gesture. That's not really good enough."

Nash didn't respond. He just crossed his arms and looked at her. She noticed he did that a lot.

Miranda turned away and went back to cleaning up. When she finished, she leaned out the back door and lit up a hand-rolled cigarette laced with hashish. Sissy had given her a couple, and she found them very calming. Nash came over and leaned on the doorjamb. He was slightly built, but sometimes when he moved Miranda noticed he had an underlying wiry strength, a subtle sort of power. She took a hit and offered the joint to him.

Nash ignored it and pointed at the empty meeting table. "I loved that one kid with the black earth painting on his jacket. He looks like a terrorist, not a doughy little geek like most of my guys."

"You just care about the aesthetics. What about the issues?" she said.

"And there is the pinning of badges instead of sewing. All those block-print silk-screened badges—they go to a lot of trouble to make those, and then to get that, well, recycled look. And the fingerless gloves, the torn stockings. The way they all match each other without even trying. That hobo solidarity."

"Clothes are shallow."

"No. What you wear reminds you of who you want to be. If you want to be fierce, or scary, or stealth. Those are the issues. They are part of the tactics. They communicate."

"But you don't wear fierce clothes. You dress like—" She

stopped, looked him over. Dark blue sweater, stretched and pilled, with beltless, baggy jeans.

"Like a third-rate lab assistant. Like an off-duty security guard. Like a guy whose boss is younger than he is," Nash said.

"Yeah, well."

"Exactly."

"What?"

"Look, I'm beside the point. I have been noticing these sorts of things for a long time, and I have high standards. I try to avoid being shrill and boring. Only someone your age gets away with, you know, being so instinctual."

"You think I'm overly earnest."

"No, I really don't. I don't think I could ever find someone too earnest."

"Shrill, you find me shrill," she said. He smiled. She took another long drag.

"But why should you care what I think?" Nash watched her through the cigarette smoke. "Miranda." And he just said her name, isolated and with enough pause before it to not seem part of the previous sentence. She didn't say anything. She felt a seriousness she couldn't quite locate as either his or hers. But there it was, now, between them. Nash raked his fingers through what remained of his curly gray and black hair.

How can anyone claim himself as beside the point?

He looked away first, and she realized she really, really liked Nash.

Vespertine

HENRY SAT ON the couch in his living room. The TV was off, the lights were off. He sat in the half dark, and he could not stop it. It came over him.

He has on a uniform. He is flying with two others. The sky is beautiful, an early morning green-blue. The water below is almost the same color. Only the jungle is different. It is a succulent green, the faint yellow-green of snake bellies and new leaves.

Henry sat on the couch, in his living room. He was awake—his eyes were open. He was sweating and clenching his hands, digging his fingernails into his palms.

It is a camouflage green C-123 Provider. He is not in the cockpit. He can see himself, the spray operator, by the bomber doors, operating and checking huge canisters marked with orange, white and blue paint. The canisters ride four across, snapped in, and he can see through the hatch in the bottom of the plane the spray of white aerosol trailing behind them. They are flying very low. They are buzzing rice paddies and villages. They are aiming for total saturation of the foliage. But it is all fucking foliage, isn't it? It's a jungle. Some of it splashes back on him when he adjusts the tanks. He can hear anti-aircraft fire from beneath him. They are so low-flying, bullets seem to back-spray from the ground. One of the drums gets punctured by a bullet, and defoliant sloshes on his arm and chest. The plane pitches back and up, gaining altitude at a sickening speed. He moves away from the hatch toward the interior of the plane.

It smells not of decay but of disappearing, of disintegration. An invisible eating away. But that's not how it works, it doesn't eat away like acid. It gets into the metabolism of things and overstimulates them until they die. It hyper-accelerates growth until the organism is undone. *Herbicide,* he thinks, is a better word than *defoliant,* but neither conveys the endless insinuation of the stuff, the occupation. He breathes the dank spray—it's heavy, oily, metallic. It almost doesn't smell, but it clings to you, gets between you and your sweat then sinks into your skin.

Later he will wash his face and hands. He will blow his nose. It's in his hair, his throat, his eyes. His throat is constantly sore; he rubs his eyes and they sting but they don't tear. It's not tears but the stuff itself welling up right under his eyelids. All night he can feel the inventory of its invasions: a stickiness now, between the legs, under his arms, after he showers. As the night gets hotter he realizes the stuff is coming out his pores, it is part of his body now. It inhabits him, in his lungs, in his cells, in his future, in his wife's uterus ten thousand miles away. It has a half-life, it has a genetic legacy. It will appear in the yet-to-be-born. It has sleeper cells hidden for fifteen years only for you to suddenly taste it, out of nowhere, in your mouth, a slick of oil in your spit.

He sees the plane from outside, like a movie. He is floating over the flat expanse of the whole Ca Mau Peninsula. For a moment he sees everything at once. But he starts to fall, he follows the spray down as if he were floating on it and sees it fall on forests of mangrove and jackfruit trees, rice paddies and rainwater cisterns. He sees people looking up, confused, standing under the trees. He sees them eating and drinking the stuff as it lands on everything in blanket coverage. It is extreme, jerky close-ups now. He hates this, but he gets so close he can see faces, mouths. He hears breathing. He smells their moist skin.

It can get really bad when this happens.

He shakes it off. In truth, he can force himself back sometimes. He feels his throat constricting, and that falling sensation, like when you wake too quickly from a dream and you jump in your bed.

He blinks and again sees the interior of the plane. He leans against the wall outside the cockpit, catching his breath.

He was lying down on his couch, covering his head, but it didn't leave him.

As he looks up, he hears the sounds of gunshots in quick, automated succession, ricocheting. The pilot turns from the controls and looks at him, his face young, smiling, and then as Henry watches he grows swollen red sores on his cheeks and mouth. It is that stuff again, trying to get out. Henry looks away. He sees the sign, handwritten, over the cockpit area, in white, over a drawing of Smokey the Bear in his hat. It reads

Only you can prevent forests

When it finally stopped, Henry's body was covered in a cold sweat. Hives and welts appeared on his face and arms.

....

Partial list of Henry's symptoms:

acne, or chloracne (adult, itinerant)
hypervigilance
insomnia (constant, chronic)
depression (underlying, with occasional acute crisis)
suicidal ideation (see above, crisis)
hallucinations / intrusive thoughts / night terrors
sense of helplessness: intractable, long-term, overwhelming
shame
despair

Jason's Journal

DID YOU EVER wonder what your body would look like by age forty if you never exercised, not even once? Gage, my next-door neighbor, answered any curiosity I had on that score. He has recently moved back in with his parents. Really. Apparently that is all the rage among the loser set these days. Gage, in all his dissipated glory, is someone I would call a pal. I first noticed him huffing his stuff onto his parents' lawn on a sunny summer afternoon. He had retreated to the home front for as yet undiscovered reasons. But the important thing here is that he arrived with crates and crates of long-playing vinyl records. Naturally, these caught my eye.

My friends—what few friends I have—are the types of guys who will argue about whether the rare RCA single version of "Eight Miles High" is superior to the track issued on *Fifth Dimension,* the Byrds' album release. It isn't, but it is cool to ask the question because it proves you know there are two versions and you are conversant with both. It is even cooler to maintain that the album—a common, reissued object—does have the superior version, and not the rare, hard-to-find single. (This is true, despite the fact, perhaps inconsequential, that the LP version *is* actually the superior version.) It is perverse, and very sophisticated, in these circles, to maintain the common, popular object is the better object. Only a neophyte or a real expert would argue such a thing. So are you getting the picture on my pals, here? I knew instantly that Gage was one of us. Or I should say, given his seniority agewise, we were one of him. We who live for bonus tracks, alternate versions, reissues, demos, bootlegs. Cover versions. Obscure European or Japanese reissues in 180-gram vinyl. Or original issue, original packaging. Authenticity. We like the inside story, the secrets. We constantly feel the best, coolest stuff is being withheld from us. In other words: there is never enough information. There is always more stuff to be had. A new master unearthed, a track unnoticed at the end of a long silence on a master tape. In a safety deposit box, in a basement. Someone didn't notice it!

Gage had thousands of albums in plastic protective sleeves. He had boxes of compact discs and stacks of 45 rpm records. I watched him unload them onto the lawn. He was wearing black jeans and a black T-shirt, which didn't conceal his paunch, despite what they say about the slimming effects of all black. But black, particularly all black, as we all know, is very rock-and-roll, very rebellious. Deeply subversive. So look out, right? I remember watching him as he sat and drank a beer, resting between the minivan he was unloading and his room in his parents' house. Apparently winded after like two trips upstairs. I watched him from our yard, and I saw my future, very possibly. At fifteen I already have an alarming jump start on a future paunch. Although mine is more pudge than paunch at this point, I could still see where I was headed.

As much as that thought filled me with disgust, I so badly

needed to look through his collection that I walked over and introduced myself. We had seen each other before when he visited over the last five years, but we didn't officially know each other.

At the very front of his stack of vinyl I could see one of the all-time great "lost" albums—*Oar* by Skip Spence, the schizophrenic guitarist from Moby Grape. He made *Oar* (an album, by the way, of Orphic longing and aching beauty) at twenty-two and then, naturally, like any rock-and-roll genius worth his title, spent the next thirty years in and out of institutions, never to be heard from again. I could tell instantly this was no reissue but an original pressing. I resisted the urge to comment on it, to hold it in my hands, to fondle it beneath its plastic protective sheath. Was it a gatefold? What did it have on the inner sleeve? Did it have a cryptic message carved in the run-out groove? All that would come in time. I didn't want Gage to get too much credit from me too soon. I played it cool, though I practically had a boner thinking about all the possibilities hidden behind that Skip Spence album. It is wonderful to care deeply about something so tangible and possible. It is wonderful to find such joy in something within your grasp, some specific, described, contained universe. Anyway.

He began to explain his temporary move back to suburbia, the saga of the failed offspring back at Mom and Stepdad's. He mock-shuddered as he said the word *suburbia;* we both sneered together at the idea of suburbia, but who are we kidding? We exist because of suburbia. Suburbia is a freak's dreamworld, a world of extra rooms upstairs and long, lazy afternoons with no interference. A place where you can listen to your LPs for hours on end. You can live in your room, your own rent-free corner of the universe, and create a world of pleasure and interest entirely centered on yourself and your interior aesthetic and logic. Suburbia is where you can pursue your individuality, no matter how rancid or recondite: the big generic-development mansions and three-car garages can harbor endless eccentricities. In your room and out of earshot. Sometimes an entire furnished basement—sorry, lower level—devoted to TVs and stereos and Ping-Pong tables; video games and computers and digital video discs. You can burn CDs and download music, catalog and repeat, buy and trade, all sitting on your ass in the rec room. The recreation room—in suburbia there are whole rooms dedicated to leisure and play and recreation. There is space and time here, and comfort and ease. Just look at me. Just look at Gage.

After our introduction, our brief paragraphs of biographical detail, we segued effortlessly into our obsessions. We have spent the last few weeks together in an orgy of listening. I was relieved to discover that Gage was no don't-touch-the-record collector. He was passionately into listening and playing things for you to listen to. We sat in his room—which has a black light, I kid you not, and the appropriate psychedelic posters to go with it—and we had listening jags, hours of intensity. Jumping promiscuously from "You have that?" to "Wait until you hear this!" But very shortly the novelty began to wear off. We quickly grew less patient with each other's interests. He was deeply into this '70s thing, particularly a lot of deep listenings of Roxy Music's mid- to late '70s albums. I was cool with that, but I had been through it all two summers ago. Naturally he tried to fly the rather perverse opinion that Roxy's late '70s discoish period was really the best stuff, rather than the avant-pop and math-fizz of their earlier experimental stuff. Something along the lines of the "glorious dance music of 1979" (a hyperbolic assertion, which is just so typical of Gage and his ilk, and so utterly false).

"Dude, listen, check out the percussion on this track. Totally conjured on a Jupiter 8. That is all of '80s dance music in a nutshell," Gage said to me.

"Yeah, *dude*. That's quite a legacy to claim."

"That is it. Nothing like those late '70s thick-as-a-brick ana-log synths, synthesizers that had no shame!"

It was the trend—unspoken but somehow felt everywhere at once—among some music freaks to be into synthesizers, but only the spaceship-landing, proudly precise and artificial vibrato of early- to middle-period predigital synths. Roland Jupiter 8s. Minimoogs. Yeah, sure.

"I don't know, the production is really flat. Like airless."

That was my bullshit response, to call the production "airless," because it just means this music is not flying my flag right now, and I've got several choice albums on deck, all without synthesiz-ers save perhaps a theremin and with production that could sup-ply enough oxygen to feed an army of asthmatic smokers for life. And of course Gage was being totally fascistic about what we had to hear next. But the thing is the guy was in the thrall, so deep into his obsession, his Roxy freak, that he meant it. He was drowning in the circular mess of relativity, the mindfuck of repeated listen-ing, the loss of perspective that comes with looking at something too closely. I know. I've been there. Don't even get me started on the Beach Boys. As I am writing this, it's there. As I was sitting at Gage's trying to listen to his records, I was fondling an original-issue 45 of "God Only Knows." I was humming, no, vibrating, *Pet Sounds*'s songs, in order. And I couldn't wait to satisfy my jones for it. So I knew exactly where Gage was at, but Gage didn't have much perspective for a guy his age, did he? He didn't have a clue how deep in he was, how tragically without perspective. I know the day will come when I won't feel this way about the Beach Boys. I know, at least intellectually, that day will come. Then per-haps I will be all gooey for the genius of early Little Feat or late Allman Brothers or something. And when I realize this I feel a lit-tle sad. I could be reading a great book, couldn't I? Or going for a bike ride or meeting a girl at the pool or hacking into someone's bank account. (Or even bathing more often, for God's sake.)

As I sat at Gage's feet—black light hurting my eyes, listening against my will to the perverse whispers of Bryan Ferry—I wondered if my life was going to be one immersion after another, a great march of shallow, unpopular popular culture infatuations that don't really last and don't really mean anything. Sometimes I even think maybe my deepest obsessions are just random manifestations of my loneliness or isolation. Maybe I infuse ordinary experience with a kind of sacred aura to mitigate the spiritual vapidity of my life. But, then again, maybe not.

As soon as I got home from Gage's, I threw on the record I longed to hear. Listening, I reconsidered my earlier despair—no, it is beautiful to be enraptured. To be enthralled by something, anything. And it isn't random. It speaks to you for a reason. If you wanted to, you could look at it that way, and you might find you aren't wasting your life. You are discovering things about yourself and the world, even if it is just what it is you find beautiful, right now, this second.

I am a person, I think, who feels comfortable in my isolation. Even someone like Gage (who is someone with whom admittedly I have a lot in common, a person with whom you might think I would enjoy keeping company) doesn't alleviate my feelings of loneliness. The effort it required just to be around him and tolerate him made me even more lonely. I am at home only in *my own personal* loneliness. The thing of it is I don't necessarily feel connected to Brian Wilson or any of the Beach Boys. But I do, I guess, feel connected to all the other people, alone in a room somewhere, who listen to *Pet Sounds* on their headphones and who feel the way I feel. I just don't really want to talk to them or hang out with them. But maybe it is enough to know they exist. We identify ourselves by what moves us. I know that isn't entirely true. I know that's only part of it. But here's what else: Lately I find I wonder about my mother's loneliness. Is it like mine? Does she feel comfortable there? And if

I am comfortable with it, sort of, why do I still call it loneliness? Because—and I think somehow she would understand this—you can have and recognize a sadness in your alienation and in other people's alienation and still not long to be around anyone. I think that if you wonder about other people's loneliness, or contemplate it at all, you've got a real leg up on being comfortable in your own.

Anyway, the really relevant part, the whole point of why I am writing about this, came yesterday, maybe a month after Gage and I started spending afternoons together. Gage was at my house, and it started creeping toward dinnertime. Dinnertime normally consists of my mother and me watching TV, or reading magazines, or watching TV while reading magazines. Our living area is of a contemporary "open-plan" style so common in the 1970s split-level vernacular. In other words, our dining room, living room and TV room all seamlessly segue into each other. A house designed—with sliding glass doors, cathedral ceilings, open kitchen counters instead of a wall, all of it transparent and divisonless—for bright Californians, not cloudy gray Northwesterners. Other families, like ours, are more suited to low-ceilinged, small, rabbit-warren-type rooms. We need corners and shadows. We need distinct spaces. The simultaneity of these open, integrated living spaces seems obscene to us. We lurk about, uncomfortable, shamed by our own house.

However, the open plan did afford one advantage. Not only are you able to constantly monitor each other but you can constantly monitor the TV, which is in the most central room. So if we were sitting at the dining room table, all we had to do was look up and we would see the TV. We don't have to actually sit in the TV room: no such commitment required. We just have to leave it on, and it will be visible from any room. There are rules, don't misunderstand, there are standards. We watch the news. Occasionally a movie. We do not watch a situation comedy, or a television drama. Not while we are eating. I mean, I don't care, I just like having it on. I usually have one of my crime novels, generally a serial killer book, on hand as well. I read true crime stories, or literary crime stories. But I prefer the real dark ones, thriller-killer stuff, to the corny kind of running sleuth series, but hey, I'll read any kind really. I read them constantly. Seriously, I read like a book a day. I can listen to music, read, and be on the Internet all at the same time. And watch TV. I'm not bragging, I mean I'm aware that this is no sterling accomplishment. It's pretty standard, isn't it? If I went to the gym, which I don't, I would see people reading, and listening to music while also watching the video monitors of TV shows they can't hear. Their eyes might even flick from their page to more than one monitor while getting their heart rates up into target zones and hydrating themselves from water bottles. All at the same time. So I don't think it makes me a genius or a mutant fuck to do all of these things at once. My point is simply that I am accustomed to a lot of controlled simultaneous stimulation.

So usually we would be sitting there and I would be reading one of my books and eating my dinner, looking up between pages or paragraphs, or during a bite, at Jim Lehrer—which is practically medicinal TV—and Mom might comment, and I would then comment back while still not interrupting my activities.

By the time I've finished my dinner, my mother, if one were to notice, still would not have eaten very much at all. But she will have managed to refill her glass of wine several times. She then will get out her trusty turquoise-and-silver *Tapestry*-era lighter and her little metal elbow pot pipe. Yeah. She usually gets stoned right at the dinner table. That's no shock, though, is it? During which I take my book to the bathroom, where once again, for the life of me, I cannot just do one thing. I get bored, even if it is just for a three-minute crap. Then I go back to my room, check e-mails, my cell phone voice mail, and finish burning a CD of music I've downloaded or traded with some other music freak I found on one of the fan sites.

But that's all the usual thing. The day Gage was hanging late in my room was unusual for us. I was unveiling my most prized possessions, unleashing the holy grail of my Beach Boys collection. The jaw-dropping stuff. So far, Gage seemed only mildly impressed. We were looking through my comprehensive collection of demos from the Beach Boys' fake lo-fi, unproduced, spontaneous, "non"-studio album, *Party!* when she knocked on the door. I ignored the knocking, figuring she would give up. But she continued to knock.

"Yes?" I said through the door. I am always instantly exasperated with her. She said something muffled. I opened up without lowering the music, which was pretty obnoxious, I mean it even annoyed *me*. Does it make sense to do things that annoy yourself? But I like to get her frustrated. I like to make her speak up. She stood there and tried to look past me into my room.

"What?" I said.

"Do you want me to set a plate for your friend?" She eyed Gage, who was mostly obscured behind my generously cut, mammoth jersey. Gage sat on my bed surrounded by stacks of CDs, LPs and 45s. He waved at my mother. He looked at me and shrugged.

"Sure."

She smiled, her eyes darting from Gage to the stuff piled on the bedspread and then to me, her hands worrying the hem of her sweater throughout, all of which I ignored.

"Ten minutes," she said, but I had already begun to close the door on her, so she really had to shout it, "Ten minutes!"

Gage held up an LP. On the cover was a bearded man in a faded, salt-stained blue-green T-shirt. He stands on a grassy hill with the ocean behind him.

"Wow. Is this?"

"Yes."

"I'd love to hear this. Where did you find it?" It was a bootleg of an unreleased solo album by Dennis Wilson, the drummer for the Beach Boys. This album is significant for two reasons, which I will take a moment to explain since it directly bears on a situation that I will soon recount.

First, lost albums. These are the legendary albums that never saw commercial release, or only had a very small release many years ago. Sometimes the tapes are said to have been destroyed, but the chance that they will resurface is always there. For example the Keith Richards–Gram Parsons heroin sessions in the South of France, 1971. The legend is that the music was a mess and Gram dumped the tapes, but one hopes it will be unearthed someday, however sloppy-slurry the playing may sound. Then there are the label disputes, or someone has died. Or the jam sessions meant for private reference only. These eventually surface in legitimate form after years of being available extralegally as bootlegs. The most famous one is *The Basement Tapes,* the Dylan and the Band bootleg that everyone preferred to what Dylan actually put out (*Nashville Skyline,* which, of course, I like and actually prefer to *The Basement Tapes*). There are also great albums that only saw a brief initial release and are now out of print, or were recorded but never actually released for some tragic reason, usually death: solo demos by Pete Ham, the lead singer of Badfinger (classic hugely popular power pop), recorded weeks before his suicide. The solo album of the obscure member of that famously obscure band Big Star (classic unpopular power pop), Chris Bell. Or the previously mentioned album by Skip Spence, or his British counterparts, Syd Barrett and Nick Drake. Made and then disappeared. There are a million. And if they are truly great, they do often make it aboveground. Eventually in expensive box sets or digipaks with liner notes and extra bonus tracks. But until then they are the holy grails of music freaks—probably all related to the finite nature of a dead artist's output. Couldn't there be one more secret album out there, or one more song?

So this album Gage had in hand actually hit all of the above points: it had one disc of an album out of print coupled with its follow-up—a genuine never-released gem. Naturally it was a find. But what is even more important was that this was by Dennis Wilson.

Dennis Wilson is a man I hold very close to my heart. To most people he is still a tragic joke, a colorful loser, a complete disaster. How could I not love him? Dennis was famous for being not only the only Beach Boy who actually surfed but for being so incredibly derelict for the last ten years of his short life that he actually drowned in a boat slip in Marina del Rey in like six feet of water. He was also the "good-looking" Beach Boy. He was also the Beach Boy who hung around Charles Manson because of all the easy drugs and easy pussy. (As if being a rich, handsome rock star didn't give him enough easy drugs and easy pussy and he needed Charles Manson's, or maybe there was something particularly potent in unbathed, helter-skelter cult pussy.) But what is hardly known about Wilson is that he recorded these two excellent if maudlin solo albums in the bad years before he drowned. This bootleg had both records in one double gatefold album. The second one is truly a "lost" record, nearly done but never released, and actually wonderful. Wilson was just too out of it to bother putting it out. Admittedly there are a lot of plink-plink sob-type piano songs sung in this almost embarrassingly sad, rusty voice. These real dirgy, messed-up vocals, unashamedly full of self-pity and raw emotion. I found it operatic, a complete expression of a tortured, not-too-bright, not-too-gifted, weary guy. But here is the thing, say what you will about skill, technique, control, brilliance: this stuff is truly moving. To me anyway. I don't know why, but I listen to that album and I start bawling, I really do.

So, anyway, Gage sat on my bed, listening to this priceless

artifact. I had it cranked way up. He started to roll his eyes, smirking and laughing a bit.

"It's so swoon-on schmaltzy, isn't it?" he said, giggling and then kind of moaning. After a few seconds I realized he was trying to make a parodic facsimile of Dennis Wilson's vocal track. Then he stopped. "Just pathetic, this drunken guy crying about all his suffering, all his cliché regrets." I flicked the needle handle up, interrupting the song, and snatched the album cover out of his hand.

"Time to eat," I said. We stumbled toward the dining room–TV room–kitchen area. As I said, the usual things were not in effect. For Gage's sake we had the TV off. The table was set with a little more formality than normal. My mother even broke out a bottle of some wine that came in a 750-milliliter bottle instead of the 1.5-liter power jug of oenological glory that she usually poured. She filled our wineglasses. I realized then that Gage was fully an adult and actually not that much younger than my mother. For a millisecond I entertained the horrible thought that they were attracted to each other and they would end up together, but that thought was discarded when she proceeded to ask Gage a series of interrogative-type, as opposed to conversational-type, questions.

Gage couldn't really give any answers, or any normal ones. He was eating heartily, though, and talking through his food, so that in fairly regular, small intervals partially masticated bits would fly from his mouth. Amazing. It wasn't as if Gage was saying anything scintillating or really of any consequence at all— surely we could all bear to wait the three seconds it would take until he swallowed his food and chased the swallow with a large gulp of the gold-hued wine from the 750-milliliter bottle. Which, by the way, we finished in no time.

I didn't like the scotch-and-butter smell of the wine. Or the glistening raw yolk yellow of it, but I did like the buzz.

"Why did you leave Los Angeles?" I heard her say as we began bottle two.

"My recording career didn't really take off," Gage said.

"Did you make a living at it?"

The wine was making me more generous. You know what, it made me less bored. I actually listened to this conversation. I listened to it raptly. It compelled me.

"I did some gigging, but mostly I bartended and wrote some rock criticism, which I rarely got paid for."

"I'd like to read it," I said. I really meant it, too.

"Do you like music as much as your son?" Gage finished his food and pushed his plate back toward the center of the table. After he asked his question, I saw him eyeing the remaining food on my mother's plate. He wanted more, but instead he refilled his empty glass, killing the second bottle.

"I do like music, of course. I mean I used to, quite a bit. I don't listen to much anymore," she said. She got up and started clearing the dishes. She returned to the table with another bottle of the same wine. She smiled slightly and went back to the kitchen. We could hear her washing dishes. Gage opened the bottle.

"So what happened to your dad?" he said to me in a semi-whisper.

"Dead," I said, not whispering at all. He nodded like he expected the story.

"Eight years ago he was driving home one night. It was during a snowstorm—do you remember the year we had that freak blizzard? The roads weren't cleared, so conditions were pretty bad. He drove off the road and crashed in a field. He saw some lights, which I guess he thought were a nearby house, but the lights were on the other side of the field. He got about halfway there and passed out in the snow. He died of hypothermia."

"No shit."

"He was totally drunk. He was also a drug dealer. Neither of which I know, of course. All I know is that he was a contractor who died in a car wreck."

"Really."

"He even did time for drug dealing. As I said, I don't know any of this."

"Actually, I think I heard something about that."

"Of course. It just required the most nominal investigating to verify what happened."

"She seems pretty sad about it still."

"Just look at the newspaper report. Five minutes on Lexis-Nexis. But I never talk to her about it. It is clear she doesn't want to discuss it, so it's not like I have to pretend not to know. It never comes up. It's easy. It's amazing how easy it is to live with not talking about the Big Things. Particularly of the past."

"She must miss him, she seems—"

"She's always been like that."

"Like what?"

"Like when I was a kid, I always had this idea that one day she might go out for a bottle of milk and never come back. She would disappear forever."

Gage looked up. She had appeared again.

"What music were you listening to right before dinner?" she said.

"What did you think of it?" I asked. Gage shook his head.

"I liked it," she said. She pushed back her hair and readied her little pipe as she spoke. "That voice sounded so familiar. Who was it?"

"Dennis Wilson. He was the drummer for the Beach Boys," I said.

"Honestly, Jason, I think I know who Dennis Wilson is. I grew up during those days. You're the one who shouldn't know who Dennis Wilson is," she said, now annoyed. Gage laughed.

"I didn't realize you followed popular music," I said.

"How much do you have to follow to know the Beach Boys?" she said. "It's not like the Beach Boys are obscure. I mean Nancy Reagan liked the Beach Boys. I think that disqualifies them from 'cult' status." Gage really guffawed at that. I was unused to my mother being so sarcastic, but I can't say I didn't completely deserve it.

I began, calmly, patiently. "The Beach Boys' extreme commercial popularity is precisely one of the reasons they are cult figures. Cult objects are one of two things: genuinely undiscovered artists and objects that deserved recognition—often with music that is quite conventional, quite as poppy as what is on the charts, but just unheard—or they are famous mainstream artists with secret counterlives in which they created risky, edgy experimental work. Work that very possibly deconstructs their more commercial work. That's the thing—the perversity of it. The subversive, even courageous, quality. And the price must be paid: sometimes they almost ruin their careers. Usually they get destroyed by their label and the mainstream press. This sort of cult stuff is almost always unconventional, formally radical, hugely ambitious, drug-fueled follies that destroy the artists emotionally and physically. But I don't expect you to understand my appreciation for the Beach Boys."

My mother nodded, smiling. She paused for a moment as if she were about to speak, but I had not finished.

"Dennis Wilson is the double whammy, because even though he is well known as the only good-looking Beach Boy, as a musician he is an obscure member of this very famous band—"

"I met Dennis Wilson once," she said softly.

"—and his solo records are therefore truly cult—" She smiled at me. I stopped for a second. She sucked daintily on her pipe.

"What?"

"I said I met Dennis Wilson once," she said.

"Are you serious? When?" I said.

"I met him in a bar in Venice Beach. In 1979, I think. Or maybe 1980."

Okay. A bar in Venice Beach. Do I ask her what she was doing in a bar in Venice Beach? It was pre-me, my mother to be, how can I really imagine that? She is unformed, she is waiting-to-be in my mind. So she started to tell this tale about some scummy bar called the Blue Cantina.

"It was where the surfer guys hung out. And bikers. Hells Angels too."

I struggled to envision my mother among drunken Hells Angels. But I said nothing. You don't want to remind them of their audience at this point, at least not until you get the goods.

"Living in Southern California was pretty depressing in those days. You know, everything was less than it could have been. Just casualties everywhere, drugs and venereal diseases. All dissolute and sleazy—that's what it felt like in 1980. Anyway, I was by myself and I noticed this very tan guy in his late thirties. He was still handsome despite having uncombed hair, a ratty beard and a bloat around his eyes. He wore, I remember, a white linen shirt, which was unbuttoned and hung open. And white painter's pants. His body was still muscular, his belly was still trim. If you didn't look too closely, he would seem just fine." She put down her pipe and picked up her wineglass.

"He kept staring at me, and it was then that I noticed he was barefoot. He had wide, filthy, beat-up feet, and I remember thinking, Why would they let him in with no shoes and pretty much no shirt? He came over to where I was sitting. I knew this would happen because I did make eye contact with him, which is the equivalent of an open invitation in a bar like that."

I could've been spared, couldn't I, the knowledge that my mother knows the lingua franca of seedy biker bars?

"He said hi. I looked at him up close, and he seemed very

familiar. Somewhere behind the beard and the shaggy hair. His neck was kind of short, but he was quite striking. And so familiar.

"'I'm Dennis,' he said."

"No way," I said to Gage.

"I realized it was Dennis Wilson, the cute drumming-and-surfing Beach Boy. He sat down on the banquette across from me and put his hand on the table between us. I wasn't hiding very well my thrill, and how extremely impressed I was that I was talking to Dennis Wilson, however barefoot and disheveled. And drunk, which I also realized. In fact, he was sort of eyeing my drink.

"'Would you like another?' he said.

"'Sure,' I said, draining my glass. 'A grapefruit and vodka with salt on the rim.'

"'Would you mind covering it? I'm short right now.' I shrugged and bought us two drinks. He retrieved them from the bar but this time sat next to me, on my side of the banquette."

"No way," I said, whispering now. For a moment I entertained the fantasy that she was about to reveal that I was actually the love child of Dennis Wilson—no doubt one of many—thus explaining not only my sense of her caginess but also my fixation on all things pertaining to the brothers Wilson—Brian, Carl and Dennis. But of course I wasn't born until 1983, which means I was conceived in 1982, and this story we were hearing just somehow doesn't feel like the beginning of a three-year love affair, you know? No, it sounded like something other than that. She took another toke on her pipe. As did Gage.

"Anyway, I felt sort of bad for him. I had heard how both Dennis and Brian Wilson would go on benders for days at a time. They would tell people in bars, Hey, I'm a Beach Boy, buy me a drink. And sometimes they would even play piano for free drinks. But he didn't say anything about the Beach Boys."

"Are you sure it was him?" I said.

She sighed.

"Okay, okay, go on. Please."

"There was a jukebox. He went over and put a quarter in. He asked me if I wanted to dance. That old Procol Harum song, 'A Whiter Shade of Pale,' started playing."

"Wait, did he pick it or did you?"

"He did."

"He picked a Procol Harum song. What were the other songs on that jukebox?"

"I really don't know, Jason."

"Then what happened?"

"He said, 'I love this song.'"

"I said, 'What does this song mean?'"

"He said, 'It doesn't mean anything. It feels something.'"

"Right. Wow. Did he put the moves on you?"

My mother smiled at this question. "No, not really. I mean he was probably more interested in getting drunk than getting laid."

"Yeah, right."

"But it was somehow a sweet moment—the afternoon light, the innocent song and this sad guy swaying with me. The world was going from bad to worse, I had been in L.A. way too long, Ronald Reagan had just become president, but America was still a place where you could dance with a barefoot rock star in a nowhere bar in the middle of a weekday afternoon."

So there my mother was, telling me about her moment with Dennis Wilson. And my mother had no business being in L.A. in 1980 and saying she had been there too long. But what did I actually know? She graduated from college in 1972. And she had me in Washington State in 1983. So there are like eleven years I know nothing about. I recall her once saying she left California after she finished school. That she had a falling-out with her parents, and she didn't keep in contact with them. But I don't remember asking for any specifics. Here was a perfect opening to pin her down on some things, but I said nothing. She smiled her vague, receding smile, half apologetic, half fuzzy with substance, and the conversation was over.

Okay, so here's the thing. You don't question these sorts of details, why would you? But what kind of fight do you get in with your parents where you never talk to them again? And moreover, who is this woman, drinking in bars, alone, on weekday afternoons? I'm no genius about people, but something is definitely up.

Night Ops

ALL-NEW PVC-coated, pressure-sensitive, UV-resistant flexible-face vinyl. A building wrap, a bulletin. Not a billboard. This plastic hugged and clung to the brick face. And it was enormous, the whole wall of a building, with one hole for the lone window on that side. It upset Henry that they couldn't even bother with painting anymore. The quaint ghost signs still visible fifty years later on the old brick. No, this was a computer-generated image, sleek and instantly reproducible. But not, at least, immune to the effects of a Stanley knife, a pair of decent bolt cutters, or any bladed implement. In fact, it was a fairly low-tech endeavor to cut these vinyl wraps down. But physically it was demanding—the sheer size of the job, the time constraints on accomplishing it, the low light available to do the work required—all conspired to nearly undo Henry.

Three times Henry undid their ad: the beginning of May, the end of July, and on September 3, his birthday. And three times the same ad was restored. They were in a dialogue, a private battle of wills. Go ahead, Henry thought, I got nothing but time. But it wasn't true. Clearly they would outlast him. And what would he have accomplished? It wasn't an appropriation. A displacement. An edit. A postmodern modification or improvement. A détournement. None of that. It was just his get-gone will. And it was his undeniable, get-gone need.

PART THREE

....

1972–1973

Speck in the Cosmos

BY THE TIME the bus reached Portland, Oregon, Mary had been Caroline for two days. Caroline had pulled her newly blond hair into a low ponytail. She pulled two tendrils loose over each ear and curled them into short spirals on her finger, blasting each with hair spray. She wore large round plastic sunglasses. It was decidedly different—she and Bobby always wore similar wire-framed National Health–type glasses, her hair always center-parted and pushed flat behind each ear. A carefully executed carefree look. Mary occasionally had snuck concealer here and there, but overt makeup was plastic, frivolous and shallow. Now, as Caroline, she put on some coral lipstick and felt unrecognizably safe. And as Caroline she hitched a ride south to Eugene and got the first job she applied for, cooking in a cafe. She would have made more money waitressing, but she wanted to be on the line cooking, hidden from view. And no one wanted a Social Security card or a driver's license or even an address or a last name. They wanted to pay you under the table, in a white envelope of cash, just like the illegal Mexicans who prepped food and washed dishes and bused tables. And the apartment wasn't so hard either, someone looking to rent out the space over his garage, a notice tacked to the co-op's community board. All you needed was a security deposit, no lease, no credit checks required. And there was no reason not to trust her. She was hardworking and well groomed and inconspicuously average; and at night Caroline sat up in her bed and struggled to breathe, her throat tight and hard with fear.

She saw most-wanted posters in her head, her college picture. In her dreams she ran into people she knew, classmates and neighbors. She tried to say, No I'm not her, you must be mistaken, but then she would get confused and blurt out her name. Shout it, Freya, Mary. Caroline. She dreamt of jail cells and trials. Of Fred Hampton's mattress. She even dreamt of telling them about Bobby, betraying him and saving herself. And she would wake up disoriented and ashamed. It would confuse her for a moment; then relief would start to come as she remembered that she hadn't been caught, that it was only a bad dream, and then horror as she realized she was in hiding; that part was not a dream but her life now. She was Caroline from Hawthorne, California. Caroline Sherman. She had had a bad relationship. She had left Los Angeles to start over. This would suffice—people would find it quite reasonable for a woman to change her life over a bad love.

It had been fifteen days. Years would go by before she stopped counting days.

She cut vegetables in piles. She trimmed red peppers with wet hands until she became sore from it. She cut mushrooms, she piled them into prep containers for the line. My *mise en place,* she said, and the other line guys stared at her. "What, your Mr. Plas?" They laughed. She knew she was the *garde manger,* but they just called her the cold side. That's me all right, the cold side. She threw lettuce in the stainless steel bowl with sprouts and sunflower seeds and just the right amount of dressing. She tossed it in the bowl with only one hand, just short jerks of her lower arm as she held the rim.

She made an odd discovery—no one asked her *anything*. She had her carefully worked-out tale of love lost—just enough Bobby to ring true. She realized or guessed that one day she would get to the point where she wouldn't even know what was true and what she had made up. So she wouldn't be lying any longer, even though some of it wasn't true. Someday time would turn the lies into history. But she wasn't there yet, a long way from it. Fortunately there was a kind of restaurant code that ignored people's past. There was the dinner or lunch prep time, but talk was of baseball, or the song on the radio, or gas shortages, or the president, or how expensive rent was, or the guy in the news who killed his wife and two small children. No one said, "Caroline, why are you here?" "Where is your family?" "How old are you?" "What is your mother's maiden name?" "What is your Social Security number?"

At the end of the shift some of the waiters and some of the kitchen staff would go next door to the Wheat Pub for a glass of thick, locally brewed beer or a cocktail. Caroline said no, she felt tired, and even that elicited barely a nod from the others. She was doing okay, she guessed. Twenty-eight days in and no problems except the airless terror that seemed to visit every evening.

Time just went by. There was of course the news. She hardly paid attention. She watched as the released American POWs from Vietnam walked down the steps from the planes and then fell to their knees on the tarmac and kissed the ground. The president seemed to be creeping toward disaster. It had nothing to do with her, nothing to do with them, any of it. She felt everything at a distance. She didn't follow the Watergate scandal. But it was in the air she breathed. Breaking the law had become endemic. She saw the sweat on the president's upper lip. She didn't feel anything. No glee, no satisfaction. Instead she couldn't stop thinking about Mrs. Mitchell self-destructing right on TV. Her sad, puffy hair. How even under all that stress and her obviously hysterical, perhaps drunk state, she maintained this elaborate, highly puffed coif. And then Mrs. Dean, also coifed, less puffy but equally blond, pale lipstick, shiny, polished face. Both of them stuck with their sweat-drenched husbands.

Faintly, barely, she told herself maybe no one cared about what she had done. She was like John Dean, who described himself to the press as just a "speck in the cosmos." That was deeply reassuring, and it was also her worst fear. Time just went by.

Caroline walked nearly every evening to the food co-op. She bought bread and vegetables, a refillable plastic gallon jug of local beer. She found a glass of beer, or two, made the move from wake to sleep less fraught. She started a friendly rapport with one of the women at the co-op. She was a big blond girl, braless in a sleeve-less T-shirt and proudly sloppy. She first smiled at Caroline, then started to say, Hey, how's it going? An acquaintance like that is pleasant and then becomes tiring, as there isn't much to say except Good. Just getting more stuff. How are you? And then you kind of wish the person didn't work there anymore, so you could buy your things and not have the same conversation over and over. Caroline figured it would be like that. She was surprised when the woman introduced herself one day, about a month after the hellos began.

"I'm Berry," she said, extending her hand.

"Caroline."

Berry gave her a wide, straight, white smile. She was more earth baby than mother, fresh and attractive, even with her hair falling out of its clip and her unshaved underarms, which were hard to ignore because Berry enjoyed long over-the-head stretches often. Right as she rang up food, while she waited for your money, she would put an arm over and in back of her head and use the other arm to push on the bent elbow.

"I'm part of this women's CR group, and we're having a potluck dinner tonight. You know, empowerment, the usual raising of consciousness, blah, blah. But it's fun, cool people. Beer, food. Maybe you want to come?" Berry waited a moment, then began bagging Caroline's purchases. At the co-op you were supposed to bag your own groceries, but Berry maybe needed something to do while she waited for Caroline's response. Caroline watched her finish, and she thought, What harm could it do? A little company, she realized, was what she desperately wanted.

"Okay." She smiled at Berry. "I'll make a sweet potato casserole."

"Far out," Berry said and winked at her. Caroline walked home clutching the scribbled address in her hand. She wondered if Berry was a lesbian. Maybe Berry would fall in love with her and help her somehow. Somewhere she remembered Bobby warning her. It was so confusing—she shouldn't be social, but she couldn't be conspicuously antisocial. Make sure to stay away from the rads and the movement scene. This was okay, it didn't sound too radical, it sounded small town and sweet.

Caroline remembered the first time she went to a consciousness-raising group. When you walk into a political group meeting without any men, you get a kind of rush. You realize you can say what you want, you are free from trying to win the approval of the men, the attention of the men, or figuring and worrying over the power relations of the men. Women in these groups made a real attempt at deep, foundational questioning: everything in your identity is potentially not real but an artificial creation of the cultural status quo (always patriarchal and suspect). It had seemed brave and bracing to her at first. She appreciated the issues, but in truth she would resist anything that included questioning and excluding Bobby. She refused to find solidarity that superseded their intimacy. Being "with" Bobby precluded her from questioning everything—and the point of these groups was a little mind-expanding, fundamental questioning. With some serious psychological self-analysis thrown in. After a few meetings, she had dismissed these methods as a kind of narcissism. The other women thought her doubts suspect, if not downright counter-revolutionary. And perhaps they were right. Her reluctance was cowardly. But she had her justifications: other issues and things she cared about were more important than women's rights. She focused on opposing the war—and what did women's issues mean in the face of the war?

But now she was Caroline, a woman alone. The Eugene Women's Collective was totally different. She felt safe instantly. And this group of women seemed to have long recovered from initial reactionary anger and moved on to something more appealing. It was less a witchy coven of man-hating lesbians— a possibility that secretly freaked her out—than a social group with a political agenda. She imagined she had been missing subcultures of mother love, forgiving and nurturing. Nothing like the catty cliques of high school and college, where beauty reigned and all subjects related to men. These women acted easy and friendly. They ate and drank, and then began, nearly reluctantly, a discussion of various issues: women's rights, certainly, but also vegetarianism, ecology and local businesses. Two of the women ran the Black & Red Book Collective. One had an Angela Davis Afro and her smooth, militant demeanor to match. That was Maya. She was the only black woman at the meeting, so the others constantly deferred to her. The other woman, Mel, never touched Maya but nevertheless made it clear they were a couple. The discussion turned to local politics, the University of Oregon and the chauvinism of the student activist organizations.

"I prefer the loggers to these ego-tripping U of O radicals. At least the loggers don't pretend to care about women's rights," said Beth, a dark-haired, very thin woman.

"Yeah, these guys want free love and then they want you to do their laundry." And so it went, and Caroline just listened quietly.

"Enough about men. We are not going to spend the evening discussing men, even criticizing men." This from Mel. Caroline listened to Mel and then saw Mel carefully check her out. Caroline thought of how she looked to the others. She probably was the only one with shaved legs. And definitely the only one wearing lipstick, albeit a practically undetectable neutral peach tone. Caroline thought it went with the dyed blond hair. It wasn't her, but that was the point. But no one seemed to notice. She felt okay here, inspired even. These women reinvented themselves: political lesbians, or merely libbers. Ah, liberation! Caroline always had to take a minute and work out what words the abbreviations stood for, or what the initials and acronyms referred to. She always had trouble with that, the way all the groups and movements shortened things and slanged them, or designed names just so they made acronyms, which were what they actually wanted to be called—like WITCH, the Women's International Terrorist Conspiracy from Hell. Designed for insiders—exclusive and status conscious, when you thought about it. Besides, the prepositions always tripped her up when she tried to remember what the letters of the acronyms stood for. Her brain didn't naturally work that way. Bobby loved it, he created an acronym or initialism or nickname whenever possible. Bobby pointed out how that all comes from the military, how every subculture ultimately imitates the military, which is the mother lode of all exclusive subgroups. But Caroline thought it mustn't be just exclusivity. The military has the most slang and acronyms because it has most need of euphemism. What does that tell you?

She believed failure of language belied deeper failings in the counterculture. The names just became more and more divorced from their meanings. What was the point of using a name in that way? Shouldn't a name remind you of who you are, or are trying to be? Did they really want a name to be part of a secret, exclusive language—a club that intended to exclude, that deliberately obscured things for outsiders? Was the need to be exclusive sort of reactionary, oppressive and even patriarchal? Caroline knew she was onto something, she was learning how things get away from people. How gradually they, what? Become the very thing they long to escape.

What were these women up to? Trying to recast their lives without men. Trying to forget the entire culture, trying to question all the things they had presumed their whole lives. And why couldn't Caroline have done that? Why couldn't she have been a radical separatist, at the margins? How different it would have been if she had tried to save just herself instead of the whole world? But that was what she was now—a movement of one. The most radical separatist of all. You are moved to save the world, and then you are reduced to organizing everything just to save yourself.

Mel dominated the group: when she spoke, and although she spoke softly, the other conversations yielded and attention was paid. Mel's aviator-shaped wire-rimmed glasses caught some of her hair in front of her ears, under the frames, Steinem-style. Mel spoke of entrepreneurial self-sufficiency, not domesticity. She wanted to expand the co-op. She wanted to force banks to give low-interest loans to women-owned businesses. Mel didn't have anything to say about abortion, the pill or the hierarchies of orgasms. After it was over, Berry walked Caroline home.

"Freaky group, huh?"

Caroline smiled.

"Melinda doesn't respect me because I still fuck men," she said. Caroline nodded. So Mel was Melinda. She already hated the name Caroline. She made a promise that the next time she had to come up with a new name, she would choose one that had a man's name for a nickname.

"But she's trying to free herself of all the disempowering stuff that gets fed us from day one. I agree, look at the women you see in the movies and on TV. Ask yourself what we are being sold by the establishment." Caroline nodded but kind of lost interest. She was weary of those words. *Empowerment, establishment, military-industrial complex. Male chauvinism, imperialism. Syndicalism. Leftist. Marxist, Maoist.* The oppression of all that freighted rhetoric, the *ists* and *isms,* made her feel spiritual fatigue. She knew this connected to her current predicament in profound ways, if she cared to examine it, which she didn't, not yet.

There was an undeniable innocence to her first year underground. Before Caroline's big screwup (which, really, she should have seen coming), she existed in nunlike simplicity. Her constant fear ordered her life and gave her purpose. Everything pertained to her maintaining her liberty, nothing else applied. Every decision, every waking and sleeping moment was enclosed and ordered by her fugitive status. Sometimes, as she lay in her bed, she considered the possibility of turning herself in. But she knew what happened to other fugitives when they turned themselves in—unless they informed on their colleagues, they got long punitive sentences.

Time just went by. She began to think of time as something she had logged in since the event, as if that might earn her something. Later she would look at time like scenery outside the window of a train, just a way of noticing what had passed her by, or what she had passed by. Another birthday for her sister, or her mother. As time accumulated, she thought less and less of turning herself in—being a fugitive was becoming her identity, the journey turned into the thing itself, the reason for being. In and of itself, her underground life felt like an accomplishment. She was recast, and it grew harder and harder not to continue. Prisoner or fugitive? But couldn't she perhaps live forever at the margins, and have a good new life? By the summer of her first year underground, she even enjoyed occasional periods of comfort.

She continued to cook for the CR meetings. Vegetarian chili. Rhubarb pies with wheat crusts. Nut loafs and spinach lasagnas. Everyone loved her food. She even became friendly with Mel. Mel believed traditional women's work needed to be reclaimed for their own purposes. She tried to help Caroline.

"You should quit the cafe and work at the bookstore. We could offer some light food in the back, where the reading tables are. We could start with baked goods and coffee." Mel pushed her glasses up. She held herself stiffly. She didn't wear a bra, but her sweatshirts concealed her breasts anyway. And when Berry flounced around falling out of her shirt, it was obvious that Mel found it all a bit too voluptuous. This annoyed Caroline; she sensed it was something complex and unfair in Mel.

"I think Berry is lovely," Caroline said to Mel one day as they sat on the couch and ate chili. There was a lounge area upstairs from the bookstore, and they often had the CR meetings there. Caroline didn't know why she said it, except Berry was finger-combing her hair absently and she did look lovely. Berry always seemed to be touching herself, and it made her appear suggestive and sybaritic. But it wasn't for show, it wasn't a display. It was just her, and the way she felt free to enjoy the thousand tiny soft delights of her own body.

"She's a slob. She has this flower child gluttony about her. It's a waste of energy," Mel said without hesitating. "You get the sense that she wants the easy way out of everything."

"That's a pretty shallow extrapolation. Do tough people have to look tough?"

Mel fixed her eyes on Caroline. "If you look tough, you get treated a certain way and it helps you become what you want to be."

"You want to be tough?"

"Hard, in fact. Immune to the whims of the body. And what weaknesses I have are my own business." Mel turned away, and Caroline knew the conversation was over. Mel had such certainty. But she didn't rant, she didn't bluster. Caroline admired that. Mel somehow escaped being smug because she didn't say more than she had to. Rants always make it seem as though the person ranting is desperately trying to convince himself of something. Or maybe the ranter becomes so interested in the rhetoric of what he is saying that convincing is beside the point. It is just about language and pattern and repetition. And the rush of words and adrenaline as it all spills out, exhausting any opposition with an overload of words. Mel was not evangelical in this manner.

Strange Caroline felt this way now. Bobby, after all, made ranting such an art. Whole days could go by and she wouldn't think of him. Already.

Less and Less

CAROLINE AND Berry ate dinner at Caroline's small table and watched the president give a speech. Again, Caroline noticed the sweat on his upper lip. It was hard to listen to him. He spoke about himself in the third person and described the "rather rough assaults" the president must suffer. He stood at the lectern with a peculiar, forced smile on his face. It was very specific, this expression of resentment and humiliation. What was it? Caroline shook her head. It was vulnerability. The bastard. He was melting before their eyes, and it was a lousy thing to watch. Berry ignored the TV. Animated bubbles advertised Dow Bathroom Cleaner. "We work hard so you won't have to." Caroline turned it off.

Berry sipped wine from a pottery mug. She described, in detail, her last breakup. Her last sexual fling. Caroline listened and drank her wine and watched Berry wind a piece of blond hair around her finger.

"I don't know why I do it, sometimes." Berry pulled her finger from her hair, and the little curl sprang back toward her face.

"I feel like when I don't want to I'm being uptight or something. You know, we are supposed to be open-minded and loving, right? And not make sex into these power games between men and women but make it equal."

"But you still feel lousy about it in the morning."

"I have some hang-ups still."

"Maybe you just don't want to have sex every time. Isn't that allowed?" Caroline said.

"But I do want to, I just think it still means different things and we all pretend it doesn't."

Caroline poured what remained of the wine into her mug. Berry lit up a joint pinched in a roach clip and took a drag.

"Maybe I should just become a lesbian. Like Mel." Berry offered the smoke to Caroline. Caroline took a hit and exhaled slowly. She thought it risky, but then it was okay. Time between sentences elongated and expanded. She felt good, all in one place for a moment.

"Is that really how it works, you just decide?"

Berry started to giggle. Caroline found this funny too, and she laughed. It was strange to hear herself laugh.

"Can't you tell that Mel has the hots for me?" Berry said, still laughing.

"Yeah, I noticed. You've got her wrapped around your little finger." Caroline snorted into her hand, then coughed, laughing. "Everyone wants you, Berry."

"Of course they do." And Berry thrust her breasts out a bit and made mock bedroom eyes. Caroline opened another bottle of wine. Berry scrounged in Caroline's purse for some cigarettes. She pulled out one broken Parliament. "You should lose the purse," Berry said. "Let go of all the stuff you lug around every-where. Do you really need it?"

"No, I don't." She stared oddly at her purse. It seemed a foreign and ridiculous object. Then she was at a loss, fixated on the
leather shoulder bag. Caroline forced her attention back to Berry
and tried to think of something to say, something to keep the
mood going. But she shouldn't have worried, Berry would never
allow conversation to lag for too long. She just needed to take
another hit off the joint. Berry tilted backward in her chair until
it hit the wall behind her. She smiled as she looked at Caroline.

"Well? Aren't you going to tell me about the big heartache
you seem so sad about?"

Caroline shrugged.

"C'mon, what's the big mystery? Was he a married man? Was
he a woman?"

Caroline sipped her wine. "He was a Republican."

Berry giggled and coughed on the wine. "I have always had
a thing for David Eisenhower, myself," Berry said. "Or even
Nixon. I'm serious. I watch him on TV, going down, angry, trem-
bling, scotch on his breath, hunched in his awful suit. And I
think I'm attracted in some perverse way. His repression—"

"Okay, enough."

"Do you think I should bring that up at the next CR meeting? Oh, Mel, I'd like to discuss my sexual fantasies about the
president."

"I met him at a demonstration," Caroline said.

"Where?"

"Berkeley. He was active in, you know, the usual groups. It's
like you always see the same people at the demonstrations. Well,
he stood out. He was from L.A., but he became involved in the
campus activities around San Francisco. He was very plugged
into the scene, you know, everything I wasn't."

"I met Sandy at a demonstration. I picked him up the first
time I saw him," Berry said. She munched on a fat, cigar-shaped
pretzel stick in between tokes and playing with her hair and sips

of wine. Crumbs landed on her breasts, and she brushed them off without really breaking her chewing stride. "Do you want to know what I said to him?"

"Sure," Caroline said.

"I seriously said this, Caroline. I'm not kidding."

"What?"

"I said, 'Do you want to come home with me and get high and screw?'"

"That was clever," Caroline said.

"He didn't say a word, just followed me right out of there."

"You don't say."

"I was very pleased with myself. I just picked him and that was it. What is his name?" Berry spoke through her now soggy pretzel stick, still perched cigarlike in the corner of her lips.

"Who?"

"Your man. The heartbreaker."

"Bobby." Caroline was pretty high, and she also thought she just wanted to say his name, feel it come out of her mouth, hear it hang in the air for a second. But then Berry repeated the name, and when Caroline heard Berry utter it, she wished she could take it back. She felt the hollow in her stomach, then a queasy, drunk feeling. Berry smiled and waited for her to speak again. Fuck it, Caroline thought.

"He had a lot of creative ideas about the world. He was buoyant and possible in a way that most people aren't. And he fell in love with me, which was probably the thing I found most impressive." Berry crossed her legs on the chair and leaned forward. She looked pretty in the candlelight. They were listening to the latest Dylan "comeback" album, *Pat Garrett and Billy the Kid*. Berry played "Knockin' on Heaven's Door" three times in a row. They both agreed it was the only good song on the album. Caroline thought Berry looked like the women Dylan wrote about, bejeweled and disheveled and bewitching, ornate in body and soul, or at least it looked that way from where Caroline sat, stoned and a little drunk.

"I never had a lot of men interested in me," Caroline said.

"C'mon," Berry said. "That's not true."

"No, it is true. But I wasn't interested in a career in men. So it wasn't a problem. I was interested in, well, society. Improvement. Moral perfection. I could have been a nun. But he was playful and passionate. Always very bright, and unfailingly convincing. And he had incredible confidence in his opinions."

"Like what?"

"Like?" Caroline paused and collected herself. She shrugged. "Hmm. Like Dylan was great *because* he went electric. Or my Beach Boys records were shallow or even reactionary. Or that you should only smoke pot in a pipe. Or that the business world was more the enemy than the government. Or that you should be a vegetarian. He was certain of a lot of things. I was not certain, but I was learning to be. Anyway, I was certain of him, at some point."

"So what happened?"

Caroline watched Berry get up and cross the room. She sucked at the pretzel as she walked and tossed the record she was playing on a pile of other uncovered records. She pulled out a Roberta Flack album and put the record on the turntable. She began to sing along to the music, looking at Caroline.

"I can't talk about it yet. If that's okay." Caroline was too tired, too high to figure out how to lie or not lie at this point. "I can't talk about it."

There was a pause. Berry finally chomped down on her pretzel, chewed briefly and swallowed.

"The first time ever I saw your face," Berry sang to the record and started laughing. Caroline also laughed, suddenly relieved, then sang with her a bit, laughing harder. Berry choked on bits of pretzel dust in her throat.

"I'm sorry," she said, laughing even harder.

"No, it's funny."

"Love is very heavy," Berry said, not laughing any longer. Caroline began to understand she could just not say anything, and people would make up their own lies for her. She just had to remember to say less and less. Say and do less and less.

In August, Caroline started up a tiny cafe at the Black & Red. She had been at it only a few weeks when Bobby came up again. Mel sat in the back office talking on the phone. She nodded as Caroline entered. Caroline looked at the books and newsletters on Mel's desk. She must have had every counterculture rag in existence. The top paper was the issue of *Rat* with the infamous Radical Lesbian's declaration in it. Caroline figured Mel had positioned it for effect. The cover was smudged and hard to read. Why must revolutions always have crappy type and poor ink quality? Why aren't they beautiful? Mel finally said, "Okay, thanks," and hung up the phone.

"Bobby wants you to know he's okay," she said to Caroline. Caroline felt her chest completely empty out.

"What?"

Mel just looked at her.

Just breathe in, Caroline thought, and say nothing. But she heard what Mel said.

"How did you know?" Caroline finally said, her voice choked.

"I didn't know, I just suspected."

"Did you talk with Bobby?"

"No, I didn't. I think he was at a safe house in Los Angeles a while back, but I don't know where he is now."

Caroline felt enormous relief. He was safe somewhere. Then, more than relief, she felt suddenly hurt that he hadn't really tried to contact her. That there really was no message. Some part of her believed somehow, still, that she would be in contact with him. And there was only Mel, staring at her.

"Look, I don't want to talk about this with you. You are safe here for now. I'm the only one who's figured it out. But who knows how long that will last. You better be prepared to move soon. You're still hot, you know that, don't you? You have to keep moving, especially the first couple of years, and everywhere you go you endanger what's going on there."

Caroline looked down at the dirt on the wood floor. Why dirty floors, always?

"Caroline?"

"Yes?"

"You have no right hanging out with us—it is dangerous. Dangerous for you and for us, do you understand?"

"You're right. I'm sorry."

Mel moved the papers together on her desk as though she was finishing a grueling performance report, or an employee termination, or a blackball.

"There are places you can go. I know some safe places where there isn't scrutiny, or they don't mind the scrutiny, or where everyone is hiding out so one more doesn't matter."

"Our intentions—" Caroline said quickly.

"—look, I'm not a supporter of tactics that give them an excuse for more harassment of the left. But that doesn't matter. What's done is done."

"But—"

"I don't want to hear about it. It is already too much. It is all too much."

"Yes."

Sunday Morning Coming Down

CAROLINE WAS Freya and the feds pounded on the door. She was in the motel again, but for some reason there were weapons all over the room. She wore a miniskirt and knee boots, like Bernardine Dohrn, bullets strapped across her chest, commando-style. They were pounding at the door. "Open up!"

She awoke in her apartment in Eugene, no guns, no Bernardine Dohrn getup, just washed-out blond Caroline. But someone was pounding on her door. She jumped up, looked at the bedside clock. 3:30.

"Caroline, it's me, Berry. Please, please open the door." Berry was knocking and begging at the door; she sobbed and was getting louder.

"Berry?" Caroline said and unlocked the door, undid the chain, turned the dead bolt. Berry was leaning against the door. Her nose bled and her lip bled. She pressed her scarf against her mouth.

"Oh my God, what happened? What happened to you?"

"Oh, Caroline, it is so bad," she said and started sobbing again. Caroline pulled her into the apartment, and Berry ran past her to the bathroom. She heaved and retched into the toilet bowl. Caroline held her hair back as she vomited. Berry caught her breath and winced. She touched her split lip. "That hurts so much," she said and then retched again.

When the heaving finished, Berry sat weakly on the floor by the bowl of the toilet. Caroline wet a washcloth and wiped Berry's face very carefully.

"Let me see. What happened? Who did this to you?" Berry started crying again. Caroline wiped the blood off her nostrils and cheek. Berry winced and pushed her hand away.

"Does it hurt bad?" she asked.

"Not too much, but I'm pretty drunk right now. Look at me. I'm a total fucking mess. I am going to have black eyes tomorrow, too." Berry's lip was already swelling. Caroline went to the other room and grabbed an ice cube tray from her minifridge's tiny freezer. She dumped the ice in a dish towel.

"We have to ice it so it doesn't swell."

Berry still sat on the bathroom floor, her legs spread in front of her. She wore flimsy Indian leather sandals, with just a center tie and a strap around the big toe. Her feet were dirty. Her purple gauze peasant dress was pulled up over her knees, and there were drips of blood on the blousy drawstring neckline. She tried to pull her frizzy blond curls out of her face with one hand while the other held the ice pack to her lip and nose. She still cried but no longer sobbed.

"I'm so sorry," she said.

"Are you finished throwing up?"

"I think so."

"Do you want to lie down?"

Berry shook her head emphatically. "God no. If I close my eyes I will be very ill."

"Well, let's get off the bathroom floor and go to the couch. That will be a start." Berry nodded. Caroline helped her to sit and wrapped a Day-Glo orange caftan around her lap.

"Maybe some food? I baked bread today, and I have tahini to put on it."

Berry nodded. With the swollen lip she looked like a pouting little girl, nodding through her tears at the idea of food.

Berry slid from the seat of the couch to the floor. She sat cross-legged, leaning her back against the legs of the couch, gingerly and slowly eating Caroline's bread covered with jam and tahini. They sipped tea, and Berry stopped crying. She pressed the ice against her face between bites.

"Better?"

She nodded. "Thank you."

Caroline shook her head.

"I was having a drink at the Timberline."

"A logger bar? Why would you go there? Who were you with?"

"No one. I went on my own."

"Why?"

Berry shrugged, sniffing. She wiped her nose with the edge of the dish towel.

"I wanted to. You know, I wanted to go to a bar by myself, and I wanted to see men with muscular arms. I didn't want some groovy guy. I wanted to see real, straight men—the guys who look good in their jeans. And I know women don't go in that bar by themselves. So that's what I wanted. I didn't want to be scared of any place."

Caroline nodded.

"I wanted to see if I could pick up a guy, in a real bar. And not have a relationship, just use a guy like a sex object. I wanted to overcome my hang-ups about sex, you know? And I wanted some unhip guy so I could blow his mind with my liberated ways. Besides, some of these guys are sexy."

"I guess."

"Anyway, I thought there would be a sort of Kris Kristofferson type, you know, working class—"

"Unpretentious."

"Yeah, down to earth and at least a little grateful for my attention, not entitled to it or expecting it like these longhairs around here, you know?"

"I guess, but Kris Kristofferson is like a Rhodes Scholar. And he has long hair. And a beard," Caroline said.

"Okay, you're right. I'm dumb, I know. But I felt lonely and I needed some attention."

"Actually, I understand, I do."

"You don't, but anyway. I sat at the bar, and right away this group of guys starts talking about me to each other, whispering but not hiding it at all. Sort of pronounced whispering. This was happening quick. Everyone knows freak chicks will fuck anyone, right?"

"Or women who go into lumberjack bars by themselves, anyway."

"But what I hadn't expected was this whole group vibe, you know? And this whole hostility trip they were on, like, right away?"

Caroline nodded, frowning. She uncrossed one of Berry's legs and undid the sandal. She pulled it off and undid the other.

"But you do know men find women like you threatening?" Caroline said.

"Why? Men want sex. What could be better than a sexually liberated woman, you know?" Berry said.

"They don't really want free sex. They don't feel comfortable with women. They want fraught sex. They want to go to the bar and be with other men and be far away from women. They are in the bar to *not* look for women. But once you are there, once a woman is in the room, they all have to try and screw you, and they're mad, because they really want to drink a beer and not deal with women. If they wanted free love, they'd go to a hooker and pay for it."

Berry sighed and chewed the last bite of bread. She no longer seemed so weepy and drunk.

"So what happened?" Caroline said.

"One guy did approach me and said something real clever about my forgetting my bra. And the other guys he was with laughed and stared. So gross. This guy was way too aggressive. Besides, I wanted to pick, I wanted to approach. That was the whole point. My feet are filthy."

"They are. Do you want to take a bath?"

"No, not really. So I saw this cute guy in the back, by himself. Do you have any more of this bread?"

Caroline cut another piece and handed it to her on a napkin.

"Thank you. So this guy by himself was very young, maybe nineteen or twenty, and he was sipping a beer and smoking a cigarette as though they were still novelties to him. Like he wasn't quite sure he was pulling it off." Caroline sat on the floor next to Berry. She wore the loose embroidered cotton nightgown that Berry had given her. She started to rub Berry's feet, pushing her knuckles into the soles, kneading slowly. She liked taking care of someone. It made her feel less wounded and more solid. Berry always wound up sitting on the floor, and Caroline again noted that this had a definite effect: it made you feel earth-tied and natural and safe. You can't fall or get tipped over. Furniture towers around you, but you are self-contained and somehow liberated from the structure of chairs and couches. It sounded silly, but it was undeniable. If you were sitting on the floor, you would be one sort of person and not another. You couldn't picture Spiro Agnew on the floor, say, or Henry Kissinger. It was a litmus test, one of many—can you picture them cross-legged on the floor?

"I walked over to him and asked if I could sit down. He said,

'Of course,' and then got up to hold my chair. I swear. I said, 'Don't, I can sit by myself. I can do lots of things by myself.' Anyway, I asked him if, for instance, I could buy him a beer. He said he would buy me a beer. I said, 'No way, I buy or I don't stay.' So he let me buy him a drink. He looked at the other guys, who naturally were all staring at him. I ordered a shot of tequila. Then another."

"At least you were being cautious."

Berry frowned.

"I'm sorry. But what were you thinking? You don't even drink tequila, do you?"

"I don't drink tequila with you, Caroline, but I do, in fact, drink tequila. I do when I want to get my nerve up. I really wanted to see this through. But I admit, it gave me the heebies having them stare at me. And I think I was off a little, I didn't read it the way I should've. I didn't take very long to ask him to leave with me, to go to my room was how I put it. I didn't want to be coy or have repartee or use any bullshit euphemism. I just wanted to be real and straight about it. So he blushes. I'm not joking. He says, Sure, all casual-like, but he is totally red, even in the dark of the bar."

It was nearing dawn. The room started to fill with weak, gray Oregon morning light. It was unlovely, flat, toneless light; not at all golden, not tender. The damp sunsets were subtle and lovely; the sunrises diluted, murky, unremarkable.

"The others made comments as we left. Really nasty stuff, like 'Watch it, these libbies have dicks' and 'Use a pool cue on the dyke.' I was getting a little queasy at this point. It was not yet fun. I was thinking maybe this was a bad idea. But there we were on the street, away from the bar, and I reached for the guy, kissing him. He tasted like Budweiser and unfiltered cigarettes. He was instantly shoving his tongue in my mouth. And grabbing at my tits. Apparently not wearing a bra really gets them tit obsessed, even with the baggiest dress. I said, 'Hey, hey, let's take our time,' like couldn't he kiss my neck a little. He pressed himself against me and pushed his leg between my thighs. I was turned on but sort of grossed out too, you know? Both at once. I can't really explain it, but I hesitated, and he pressed my hand against his cock and said something corny like 'You know you want this.' I had this vision, suddenly, of a porno film I saw once, you know, where the guy is just balling the chick and she's practically bouncing around, and it is superaggressive and not, you know, at all Kris Kristofferson–like, and I thought, I am not into this. I didn't want to get screwed by this guy, and no matter who I think is screwing who, that's how he'll look at it. For once I actually figured out that getting pummeled by some smelly John Bircher who thought he was really gonna show me was not going to make me feel too hot. So I lost my taste for it, just like that. I told him, sorry, I wasn't into it, I had to split."

"Now I get the picture."

"So he grabbed me, and I said, 'Get away.' He saw the fear in my face, and he slugged me. He fucking punched me, one shot, knuckles to nose and mouth, bam. And he held his hand like it hurt him and I ran."

"I'm so sorry."

"Yeah, especially how am I going to explain it? Mel will take one look at me and she'll know. They will never understand, not like you. You know what I am about. You know that I am not a joke, I am a genuine person. That I think about things."

"Of course. And you don't just think about them. You act on them and put yourself right on the line."

"She'll say it's destructive and self-loathing."

"You take your own hits. It is none of her business."

"Screw this town. I should get out of here. I have to get away, I do. Oh God, I am starting to really hurt now." She felt her lip with her tongue. She pulled herself up and went to the bathroom mirror. "I can't believe it. I'm screwed. That dumb-ass. He thought I was making fun of him, but I don't think I was. This better not scar."

Caroline called Mel the next morning.

"I think you're right. I should leave town."

"Probably a good idea. Before there is any real reason to. A woman I know can help you. She lives in a women's commune near New Harmon, New York. Ten miles north. She doesn't have a phone, but I will send her a message that you are coming to see her."

"What's her name?"

"She goes by Mother Goose."

"Really?"

"It's these rural acid lesbians—everyone has a 'special' name, like Alice or Mother Goose or Medea."

"Gotcha." Caroline took a deep breath. "Mel?"

"Yeah."

"We never expected it to go down like that. We were being so careful, I swear."

"You've got to be joking."

Caroline pressed her head against the phone, crying.

"It doesn't matter anymore. It's done," Mel said.

"I know, I know."

"And Caroline?"

"Yes."

"Don't call me or contact me again, okay? You have already made me an accessory after the fact, and I don't want to be a part of your mess. I don't want to hear from you again, ever."

PART FOUR

Fall and Winter
1998

Jason's Journal

I AM THE center of the culture. I am genesis, herald, harbinger. The absolute germinal zero point—that's me. I am the sun around which all the American else orbits. In fact, I am America, I exist more than other Americans. America is the center of the world, and I am the center of America. I am fifteen, white, middle class and male. Middle-aged men and women scurry for my attention. What Internet sites I visit. What I buy. What my desires are. What movies I watch. What and who I want; when and how I want it. People get paid a lot of money to think of how to get to me and mine.

Everything is geared to me. When you see those herky-jerky close-ups in action movies, where the camera jumps and chops its way in rather hyperly to the close-up of the hero, that is not for anyone but me. That is a movie being made to look like a video game or, rather, a computer game. That's right—the superior technology aping the inferior technology, which was trying to be like a movie in the first place. The mannered, telltale visual grammar of the computer graphic becomes the cool thing itself. It identifies cool. The real question is, if you don't get it, why are you watching it? It is for me and mine. It is legible to me and mine. It is our grammar, our visual slang and our rhythm—the speed and the super-percussive blowout sound effects. The most advanced technology making reference to and imitating inferior technology. Don't worry if you don't get it—that's the point. You are excluded.

I should feel proud. By the mere fact of my youth, I am entitled to so much power. I feel the world spinning around me, the NASDAQ, the Dow, every index and indicator, the focus group, the cool hunters, the yearn forecasters—everything. So then why do I feel the way I do? Worse than ever I feel excluded. Worse than ever I feel singular, freakish, alone. I don't care for computer gaming. Or computer gamers. I am not a fat, clammy kid who spends all my waking hours online and then either takes a machine gun to school in some perverse extension of the gaming life or ends up slumped among pizza boxes and tissues full of jizz as my fatty heart finally gives out, my game hand palsied and my parents full of guilt and halfhearted excuses about the distance of three-car garages, two-career marriages and six-thousand-square-foot houses.

That's not me at all.

Yes, I spend time online, sure. Yes, I have the kind of pasty, fat body that will one day evolve into adult-onset diabetes if not total morbid obesity. Yes, I spend money on stuff. But there is nothing carefree about my life. Not anymore. Something has changed. I no longer have the privilege of total self-absorption. What I need right now more than anything is to figure out what her secret is. I have determined she is hiding something. I don't think I am being overly imaginative, although all the crime books I read do affect my level of paranoia. They convey an ordered, systematic-but-rotten universe. And nothing is ever as it seems.

I followed her last night. I have started questioning everything about her. She teaches cooking twice a week—or so she claims. I waited until she left the house. She drove her Nissan even though it is only ten blocks to the community center. I got on my bike, which is a rare occurrence, and followed her. When I got to the community center, her car was parked there. I went down the halls, peeking slyly through the small windows in the classroom doors, the shatterproof glass panes with fine wire deeply embedded in them making everything a grid or like the crosshairs of a rifle. I heard my mother's voice. I stopped and leaned against the wall. It was brick painted an industrial white. I stared at the speckled vinyl composite flooring. I couldn't see in the classroom, and the people inside the room couldn't see me.

(Incidentally, if you have never stalked someone close to you, I highly recommend it. Check out how it transforms them. How other they become, and how infinitely necessary and justified the stalking becomes when you realize how little you know about them, how mysterious every aspect of them seems with an at-a-distance-but-close examination.)

"It is important to rinse inside and outside the bird."

Have you ever closed your eyes and listened to the sound of your own mother's voice?

"You must pat the skin and the cavity of the bird dry with a paper towel. Otherwise the seasoning will not adhere as you wish it to."

She exists, you know, wholly in the world apart from me. She spoke slowly and with deliberate emphasis. She sounded authoritative but not a bit shrill. No ugly breaths or underweighted sentence ends. Not girlish or apologetic. Not sexy either, but soft and serious.

"I like to put slivers of garlic and truffles under the skin of the breast. Also pats of butter. It makes the breast moist and the skin crisp and flavorful."

But I wasn't there to admire her voice or hear what she was saying. I'm not quite sure why I was doing this. But then I realized I was trying to place her accent. Does she truly have a California inflection, or is there a hint of the East Coast or Midwest to her speech? As I listened, leaning against the cold white brick, I couldn't remember what any of these accents sound like.

I headed out to the parking lot. I sat behind some trees with a view of her Nissan Maxima. It is a metallic, high-saturation blue-green. I waited. What for, I don't know. Did I think she would meet someone after class? Is it merely a liaison I suspect her of? I waited. I noticed several other cars in the lot were the same blue-green, no-name color. Or else a deep red flecked with gold underlights. Or shiny black. It occurred to me—have you noticed that there are no longer any beige or brown cars? I know they existed once—I have seen them on old TV shows like *Hawaii Five-O* or *The Streets of San Francisco*. Brown, chocolate brown, or that taupe beige color, like a raincoat. It is strange how color schemes of various times are different. People used to like browns, military greens, creams and mustards.

You know, she doesn't have one baby picture of herself? I think that is odd. She's estranged from her parents, but I presume they exist somewhere. For some reason she just left all that behind.

Someone apparently decided that nobody wants brown cars anymore. Some fifteen-year-old, no doubt, in some information-gathering test situation declared brown old looking, uncool, or it made him not want to drive. And that was that.

Contraindicated

THE PILLS CAME in a small opaque plastic bottle. He pressed down hard on the cap as he turned it to open. Fastened to the bottle was a folded piece of paper with chemical chain diagrams, case studies and long lists of side effects. Charts with percentages of groups that experienced some of (but not limited to) the following: peripheral neuropathy; facial and testicular edema; impotence; stroke; hallucinations; myocardial infarction; sudden, unexplained death.

The pills were ovule, innocent shapes. Peaceful shapes. It was called Blythin. The improved supplement to his Nepenthex regimen. He swallowed two. Because. This was a new one, taken to augment the others he already took. You don't ever stop taking any of them, you just add new ones or alter dosages. But things had gotten so bad lately.

Henry couldn't sleep, and he decided to take a bath. He put on the lights everywhere in his house. If he were to look out his windows (he never did, particularly at night), he would see faces looking back (or probably he would), so he pulled all of his curtains closed. He didn't even like to think about the covered windows because he could imagine so easily what he feared seeing. He also, for similar reasons, avoided mirrors. It hadn't been quite this bad before. Things were getting worse. He couldn't take showers anymore because he couldn't hear well enough through the rush of water (hear what exactly?). But he could take a bath, in the middle of the night, with the door to the bathroom open, and most times make it to the morning undisturbed. Then he could take an exhausted drop into bed. He lay there and listened. His breathing.

Henry is in a plane again. This is a B-52. It is predawn darkness. He is in the tub, but he knows that he is flying over Quang Binh Province. He hears the loud-to-faint sound of bombs being dropped. He looks beneath him through the open hatch. The sky is lit up by showers of white phosphorus, arching in floral, organic, symmetrical shapes; the lines they describe are graceful. They are otherworldly, these electric trails and their already fading illumination. Light reflects off the water, glitter sparkles in the smoke. Then the bombs make contact, and beneath them and behind them he can see explosions.

Henry no longer feels the water on his limbs; he no longer sees the bathroom. He is on the ground, beneath the plane, not suddenly but as if he had followed the bomb down, he sees the ground come closer and closer in silent jump cuts. Henry hits the ground running, and he sees an explosion and then feels the breath sucked right out of his lungs, out of everything around him. The heavens are ignited, and the air has collapsed. Then he feels the burning on his skin. Something sticky on his skin, eating it. He runs and it burns worse, burrowing into the flesh. It has a gasoline stench. He knows what it is. It is jelling to his back and arms. He rubs at it, and it doesn't come off, it just burns his hands. He jumps into a swampy tide pool, covers himself in water. But it still sticks, and he can really smell it now, gasoline, burning plastic, and burning flesh. NP2, or Super Napalm. He doesn't feel anything but numb, but he watches the stuff burn through the layers of skin to the bone. He yelps and clamps his hand on it. It seems to stop, somewhat, but as soon as he lifts his hand it resumes burning down into him.

Henry lurched in his bath and then leaned over the side of the tub and vomited. There was some white, chalky goo, which may have been the Blythin. He can't quite breathe. I am being followed by fire and brimstone, but fire that burns with no flame, just a chemical constancy. He still smelled a sharp whiff of gasoline. They frightened him, these smells from nowhere, their conjured passage from imagination into experience. How can you know things you don't know?

Agit Pop

MIRANDA EXPECTED August 5 (the date of major tests every year, ostensibly because it was the anniversary of some infamous Seattle Wobbly action in the 1920s) to be a focus for all the actions Nash's groups discussed. The day came and went, with lots of groups participating, but none of Nash's did anything. And nothing was said about it. Labor Day weekend was also full of various tests and actions. Again, nothing from Nash's groups and nothing said about it. By the next planning meeting, this one of the Sovereign Nation of Mystic Diggers and Levelers, it finally dawned on Miranda what Nash was really up to. His groups had no intention of executing any of it. None of them. Not the Barcode Remixers. (They made fake bar code stickers that would replace existing ones. Everything rang up at five or ten cents. This was strictly for the chain, nonunion supermarkets.) Not the New American Provos (inspired by the antiwork Dutch provos, they got jobs at Wal-Mart and then executed ad hoc sabotages). Not the Radical Juxtaposeurs (they rented mainstream films from Blockbuster and dubbed fake commercials onto the beginnings of the tapes to imply dislocated, ominous, disturbing things). The same weird misfits, week after week, with different names and new ideas, new actions, long discussions of smart-ass tactics and tests. But nothing ever acted on. Of course: para-activists, not actually acting but running beside. No one ever said it, you would never know unless you had gone to meetings and paid attention. But it sort of made sense: he always said the actions were for their benefit, not to educate or humiliate the public, even the most evil of corporate bureaucrats. The actions were about keeping their own resistance vital. Direct action to keep you from being absorbed and destroyed. To remind you of what was what. Nash, she realized, had no plans to save the world, or enlighten people or change anything. She was both appalled and impressed, and she couldn't wait until the day's meetings were finished and she could talk to him. She wanted to let him know she'd figured it out.

"Want one?" he said, after everyone left. He held up a twenty-ounce bottle of Coca-Cola, its plastic hourglass shape in imitation of or homage to the old eight-ounce glass bottles.

"Once," she said, "I had this conversation with my elementary school soccer coach."

"Where was this?" he asked.

"Bellevue. Just on the other side of the lake. We had a great game, and the coach took us out for pizza after. Even in our pretty, suburban, tree-lined town, there was a desperate-looking man outside the pizzeria asking for money."

"Bellevue, Woodinville, Avondale. Where do they get these names? I mean honestly, Bellevue, who are they fooling with that?" Nash started to get up. Miranda followed.

"We all walked by him, already knowing somehow to ignore him, like how old are you when you learn this? Do any of us even remember when we learned this? So we were stuffing our faces with that doughy pizza and talking about the game." As soon as they were outside Miranda pulled out one of Sissy's hash-laced Marlboros.

"I don't believe you," Nash said, pointing at the Marlboro package. She shrugged and inhaled.

"It's more subversive than capitulation or straight opposition to have deliberate, conscious contradictions," she said.

"Of course, how could I think otherwise?" he said.

Miranda wasn't flirting, but she did like the way older men (she assumed it was a function of age, even though she had no experience with any other older men in this context) found her weaknesses somehow endearing. And someone like Nash could appreciate her ability to run his game right back at him, to underline his most treasured vanities. He could appreciate the rare form of attention that it indicated; she listened carefully to everything he said to her. After all, what was the point of any of it unless someone paid attention?

"We headed back to the van and walked past the guy lying outside. No one looked at him, and it was even worse because we were all jolly and overfull," Miranda said.

"You, Miranda, run back and give him your allowance." Miranda stared at Nash for a long time. He crossed his arms and smiled at her.

"Look, I only smoke hash-lined cigarettes that I get for free or steal."

"And you realized then and there that you, and you alone, were different, special even. Yes, you, Joan, would save France from the English."

"And then I only smoke them around people like you, who are so bothered by what other people do." And she smiled back, but she felt stung and didn't want to talk to him anymore. She didn't tell him about how she sat in the van the whole ride from the pizzeria staring out the window, ignoring her teammates. She stared at the big houses set back from the road and remembered when her father drove her family by the public housing projects in the city, and how the people loitering outside glanced at her through her car window, and she looked away.

Miranda sat silently in the back of the bus and listened to the singsong voices of the other girls. The lilt of their young, carefree voices. Finally, she couldn't help it, and she blurted out, "How can you be happy when there are people with no homes and no food? How?" There was a momentary silence. Then one of the other girls started giggling. And then another girl laughed.

"You have to be an idiot," Miranda said with a righteous hiss at the girl.

"Well, I must be a complete idiot, because I am hap-hap-happy!" Giggle. Heh, heh. Miranda felt her face get red and hot tears start.

When they got back to school, Mr. Jameson, the soccer coach, asked her to wait a minute. She nodded and wiped her nose. He went past the seat she was in and sat across the aisle from her. He turned to her with a serious frown from which he pressed a tight smile.

"Miranda, you have to understand—" he said. She fixed her gaze on him. She really wanted to understand.

"There are people who are born into this world Indian chiefs and people who are born Indian braves. That's just the way it is. And that is the way it will always be. Your not enjoying your life won't help change that. It will just make you unhappy."

That was his answer; he actually said that to her, and she knew right away that it was a lie. Everyone knows what's true: you make the world a better place than you found it or you make it worse. Anyone who tells you that isn't so is just making an excuse for his own inaction. At twelve she vowed to herself never to feel comfortable in the face of things obviously unfair and not right.

Miranda walked away from the bookstore toward the Black

House wishing she had stayed and continued talking to Nash. She wished she hadn't been so sensitive and hadn't said good night and left. She wanted to talk about the soccer coach and what he had said. And what she really wanted to tell Nash. She'd figured it out, she finally got the joke: The Cult of Lasting Material Invasion, as it was called in this week's flyer, didn't ever do any of its actions. Or, another way of putting it, its actions were the discussion and planning of actions. This was a conceptual direct-action group, and no one ever spoke of it—you figured it out or you didn't.

She wanted to tell him that she'd figured out his para-activist stance and it wasn't good enough. Not nearly. That it was just another kind of lie. And that's not all she wanted to tell him. See, it wasn't just the hash Marlboros. She sometimes ate hamburgers from McDonald's. She was indeed the one to take big, luxurious wads of toilet paper and inches of Kleenex at a time. It got even worse. When no one was looking, she sometimes threw stuff in the garbage. Newspapers and glass bottles. Easily recyclable stuff. Right in the garbage. Shoved it down so it was buried. Even her mother didn't throw that stuff in the garbage. Because she couldn't help it, she just did it and felt guilty about it. That was part of why she talked to Nash in the first place. Because she saw him there, at the meetings, drinking a Coca-Cola.

And finally she wanted to tell him that the world offered horrendous terms, a terrible, huge price was paid in actual suffering, and if you didn't try to change that or mitigate that, your life was indefensible, wasn't it? And if he was being clever, or cynical, in the face of that, well, it was wrong. And if she was overly righteous and simpleminded about things, then so what? And maybe she wanted to say something else, but she didn't even know what that was yet.

Loaded

HENRY SAT through one of Nash's meetings and then lingered after all the kids left. Miranda wasn't in, and Nash realized he had spent the evening wondering why. He had been waiting to talk to her all day. It had always been this way with women and Nash. He rarely felt struck, but when he was he would discover the woman somehow insinuated into the deep reaches of his psyche in some complicated way. She became an essential component of his well-being. He was glad Henry was there to distract him.

Henry drank his beer lying out on top of the common table. Nash put on some very old Appalachian folk music (Harry Smith's *Anthology* that Sissy burned for Miranda and Miranda lent to Nash) and started to shut the place down for the night.

"How come you are never around anymore?" Nash said. Henry shrugged. He looked thinner than ever. He smelled of old beer and cigarettes.

"Do you think it's possible—" Henry started.

"What?" Nash said. Dock Boggs was singing about honey and sugar through some fast banjo.

"Nothing." Henry finished his beer and pulled another from the six-pack. "Hey, it's your birthday, isn't it? You're fifty now."

"Not till next week," Nash said.

"Happy birthday, man."

Nash waved it off.

"Here's to fifty," Henry said. "The beginning of the end. I feel every minute of my fifty-two years, I swear it, I wear them every day."

"It's funny, I don't feel fifty," Nash said.

Henry turned on his side, propped his head on his hand and studied the flyers on the table.

"I'm turning fifty, and it is just now dawning on me that I have limited time," Nash said. "No kidding. I always felt my life was circumscribed, but I believed it was because of me, because of the choices I made. Now I realize—and only now, I am ashamed to say—that my life is circumscribed by definition. We are all circumscribed by the finite terms, you know? There is a whole world of things I missed out on and will never experience. Whatever I have done, there is an endless amount I have not done. Do you know what that tells me?"

Henry shook his head.

"It tells me it is not meant to be this all-encompassing journey. It is not meant to be catholic or encyclopedic. By now I have carved some grooves in this life. A few. What I need to do is hunker down and make those grooves deep and indelible. Not the time to dig new ones, you know?"

Henry sat up. "I guess. But."

"The time now is for depth. Make that grab for profundity."

"But."

"Yeah?"

"What if they are the wrong grooves? What if you made mistakes? Shouldn't you try to make it right, no matter how late it is?"

"Well, of course."

"Hey, can I ask you something?" Henry said.

"What?"

"Do you know what kind of plastic explosive works best with a delayed fuse?"

Nash stopped midswig on his beer and looked sideways at Henry. "No, I don't know the answer to that. Why do you want to know?"

"Nothing. It's just information I'd like to have, you know, in case. I thought you might know because you seem to know a lot about plastic."

"Right. The explosive isn't really made of plastic. HMX and RDX are nitroamine explosives. They are combined with a plasticizer, like mineral oil. The binder and stabilizer is made of a plastic precursor, like styrene, but not the explosive substance itself. It is called plastic explosive because it is in malleable form."

"Okay."

"Because it has plasticity."

"Thank you."

"You're welcome."

Cellophane

"YOU REALLY shouldn't drink Coke. It's like totally under-writing American corporate hegemony to buy Coke," Miranda said.

Nash nodded and swallowed. "I prefer to call it a bottled soft drink. Or the Coca-Cola Company. I never call those companies Coke or Pepsi. Or McDonald's Mickey D's or the International House of Pancakes the IHOP. They're not my friends. Why should I call them by nicknames?"

"Bottled soft drink, huh?" Miranda said.

Nash nodded. "There's a generic movement—never use brand names. It's a kind of mental hygiene."

"No Kleenex. Facial tissue."

"Right, no Q-tips but cotton swabs. No Jell-O. Gelatin dessert. There's a group called Counter Corporate Contamination. They promote generic nonbrands. They fight the infiltration of brand into everyday language. No 'fun' corporate acronyms, no trademarks, and God, no nicknames."

"There isn't really a group for that, is there?" Miranda said.

"It's more difficult than you might imagine," he said.

"No exceptions?"

"Well, there are always some exceptions. Some names are so perfect, so apt, so electrifying with promise and eponymous in an almost magical way that to not use their names would be to deny some delight and truth to the world."

"Such as?"

"Cellophane." Nash folded his arms. "Cellophane. It's beautiful. Much better than plastic film wrap. And it was also appropriated as slang for a drug—a kind of LSD on dissolvable squares of film."

"And we know what a big fan you are of appropriations. But guess what? So was Coke."

"Yeah, but Coke is a motherfucker's drug. And cellophane is also obsolete. It has been defunct for years. Dupont's Cellophane was overtaken by Dow's Saran Wrap. Which by the way was made of polyvinyl chloride instead of cellulose, so it was a much more synthetic plastic than cellophane. With an inferior name. Cellophane is a failed and defunct brand, so I'm not promoting anything when I use it. Which, admittedly, is not very often. But mostly I give it a pass because it is beautiful."

Miranda was lovely. It was true. Nash woke on his fiftieth birthday, and this was the first thing he thought. She didn't quite realize it. She almost did but not to what extent and why.

The night before, Nash had watched her having a conversation with one of the late-teen testers at the store. She was smiling and talking, but the kid just looked over her shoulder, unsmiling, half-nodding. Nash remembered being a late teen. He wanted to shake the guy, grab him by his ripped jean jacket and shake him, tell him, Look, would you, look and notice please, let yourself see how beautiful this woman is, how perfect, what a masterpiece with her soft thighs and her bitten nails. If only he knew at nineteen what he knew now about how to love a girl like Miranda. To not be scared she might want things from you. To want her to want things of you.

He didn't want to protect her, or her to restore his youth. Nothing like that. He didn't exactly know what he wanted. Yes he did—he wanted to be close to her, closer than anyone else. She was awkward and impatient. Too sensitive. She wore the wrong, unflattering clothes, had yet to inhabit herself convincingly. She seemed to have no ambivalence, and endless energy—anything he mentioned she would read practically overnight. She was combative, judgmental, angry. She utterly dazzled him. What a complicated mess of a woman she was, and how desperate he found himself feeling about her.

So here, on his fiftieth birthday, he was giddy with his crush on her, lying in bed with a lazy erection and longing for her. This was a pleasure in itself, just to lie in bed and long for someone. He felt ridiculous, happy, foolish.

But she liked him, didn't she? That also amazed him. Last night she appeared at his door. She brought over a bottle of wine and even cooked him dinner, didn't she? She wanted to celebrate his birthday. Sweet, her total incompetence in the kitchen. She fought against her spoiled suburban self, even washed the dishes.

"Don't condescend to me," she said, but he wasn't, she just read his expression wrong. Later, flushed with wine, she began to flirt with him. He could feel her wanting him, and he let her lean toward him across the table, touch his hand. It was heaven when she closed her eyes and leaned in to kiss him. He wanted it so much. She pulled slowly back, opened her eyes and smiled. She leaned in again, and he pulled back. She opened her eyes.

"I'm sorry," she said.

"Don't, *don't* be sorry."

"I think I have a little crush on you," she said, all of a sudden willing to give all her trust in the truth. She smiled broadly.

He looked around the room and sighed. "I think you are terrific," Nash finally said.

"You think this is all very adorable, don't you?"

"Yes," he said.

"Yeah, I know you think that, truly. It's what I like about you." She watched him from across the table. "I should go before I make a total fool out of myself."

Nash handed her her sweater. She started to laugh when she stood up, apparently a little drunker than she had expected.

"Watch it," he said, taking her arm.

"I'm only a little drunk, you know. That's not why I kissed you."

"No?"

"No, I did not kiss you because I'm drunk. I got drunk so I could kiss you. That's different." She started to move toward the door. Nash grasped both of her hands and squeezed them.

"Be careful, Miranda," he said softly. He let go, and she left, and he imagined she thought he meant, Be careful, he would kiss her back if she stayed any longer. But what he meant was, Be careful with me. Please. *Please.*

The first time Miranda talked to Josh was under the auspices of Prairie Fire. Under the auspices of Nash, really, which she found ironic. After his birthday dinner, she had avoided Nash and the bookstore for a few days. She expected him to call her or seek her out. But he hadn't.

Seven days passed, and she couldn't bear it any longer.

She walked straight to the back of the store, right past Nash, and ordered a chai tea from Roland.

"Hi, Miranda," Nash said from the table where he sat.

"Hey," she said, cupping her tea and studying it. She walked to a secluded corner and sat. She picked out a book and began to read, furrowing her brow and concentrating. She read the sentences, and then read them again, but all she could think was, Why did I have to come in here, looking for him? After all, I kissed him. She parsed through that evening again, as she had been doing all week.

Not only did she kiss him but he didn't really kiss back, did he? He just handed her her sweater when she said she was leaving. How foolish she was. By the time Nash came over to where she sat holding her book, Miranda felt close to tears.

"Why haven't you been in?" he said.

"I've been busy."

"We are having a big plenary tonight—remember?"

"Of all of your groups? That should be interesting since they all have the same members." Nash laughed, and she glared at him, refusing to laugh.

"It isn't any of my groups, I promise. It's the Green and Black Action group. The GABA Group. I merely facilitate it. You should come."

"Maybe." She shrugged and turned a page in her book.

"Miranda."

She looked at her watch and got up. "I'll try."

The GABA Group plenary was not promoted, and people heard about it only through word of mouth. Despite that (or because of that) everyone in the Black House, including Sissy and Miranda, went.

Nash was interjecting during a discussion on direct action, not leading, of course, but moderating, guiding. Facilitating. Miranda thought, Ha, right. He had been talking for at least fifteen minutes.

"It is not so much that we do direct action to get a certain result, you know, like pass anti-global-warming legislation," he said. "We do an action for the action itself. Our act is the end, the point."

"But we do also want to direct the action at something, don't we?" Miranda says.

"Sure, we do. But I'm saying in our quest for whatever goals we have, we should make sure the tactics themselves are reflective of those goals. We dance in the street and stop traffic not because we want to be on TV to get our message out but because we like to dance in the street. It's the world we want to live in." Nash took a deep breath and smiled in spite of himself. "It is in itself organic and original and full of a delicious solidarity that is usually difficult to come by."

"Or we could just talk about actions and never do them. Not dance but think about dancing. That would be really subversive," she said flatly and looked at the ground beneath her sneakers.

Miranda hated when Nash used words like *organic* and *solidarity*. He sounded like an old hippie then, worse, like a caricature of a hippie. He of all people should know subversion started with the language you used. But Miranda couldn't help but feel bad for Nash, despite her hurt feelings. And she knew the other kids weren't really listening. The guy with the black-and-green flag on his jean jacket? He just couldn't wait to break the window of a Starbucks for whatever reason.

"I have some plans for an action we should do downtown. The new shopping-oriented downtown. We dress in business suits and are stationed in all different locations around Fourth Avenue. And just at 12:30 p.m., the most trafficked time of day, we all head toward the traffic island at the center of the street. We approach at precisely the same time, briefcases in hand. Incidentally, this is where all the surveillance cameras converge."

Nash crossed his legs. Miranda thought he should sound less calm and more angry. He should sound like there was something at stake. But that wasn't even it. He couldn't resist himself, could he?

"So we approach the traffic island at precisely the same time, maybe thirty or forty of us. The clothes have to be perfect. It is fine if we have dreadlocks sticking out or whatever, but it must be suits and ties and briefcases. Women can wear the skirt and jacket, the power bow. The point is to look uniform and of an easily identifiable type. We originally wanted car-mounted sound systems to play *Swan Lake* or something. But I think we would be arrested in no time for public loudspeakers without a permit."

"So what?" The green-and-black flag guy. "Let them arrest us."

"Well, if we get arrested we can't do the action. The object is not to merely be arrested. At least, that is not my object," Nash said. "We do a kind of Busby Berkeley synchronized dance, a serious, deadpan, perfectly synchronized show, with briefcases aloft. We stop people going into the stores and in their frenzy of shopping, not because we physically block them but because we entertain them for a moment, we amuse them, intrigue them. There among the glittering billboards corporations pay thousands for, we engage everyone's attention out of sheer whimsy." A girl spoke out from the back of the crowd. "So what the hell is the point? Are we going to even have information for people about the sweatshops that produce the Gap shirts they are buying? Or the way their fast-food restaurants are destroying the ecosystem?" The tone of her voice—the tenor of the earnest whine—contained a sort of tremolo that hung perpetually between an accusation and a dissolve of weary, resigned tears. Miranda found it tremendously unpleasant. "What is the point?" she repeated.

"The point is for us, the players, and perhaps them, the audience, to feel for one second as if we didn't have AOL Time Warner or Viacom tattooed on our asses," Nash said. Miranda chewed at her fingernail. He was right.

"And disruption is liberating, especially if it is a formal, organized disruption," Miranda said. Nash smiled at her. "Mere chaos causes anxiety. Preaching didactically causes boredom. But a formal disruption—"

"Then it approaches beauty of a kind," Nash said. "Then you begin to really be dangerous."

After the meeting, she went outside to smoke one of her edge-erasing hash tokes. Nash sat by himself drinking a soda. She walked right past him to where Sissy stood talking to another girl. She left with Sissy, arm in arm, until the next scheduled group began.

The so-called hactivists were up next—the Net geek guys that advocated hacker-type direct action on the Web. She wanted to hear about this, but she especially wanted to see them, the ones who could break laws and destroy things all from the comfort of their homes. Miranda didn't trust these guys—and naturally, they were all guys. She imagined them to be the same pale, socially isolated creeps who chronically masturbated to Internet porn—not even photos of real women but those cartoon-video-game chicks, the gun-wielding pinups with their glutes bursting out of torn, tight short shorts, all made by some other sweaty, pale guy in a room somewhere. She wanted to check out the kinds of guys who were turned on by these virtual, man-drawn women.

A group of young men crowded the back of the store. They didn't look all that different from the usual crowd, save a few skinny guys in T-shirts that said OPEN SOURCE or COPY LEFT— GNU/LINUX or simply FUCK MICROSOFT. Nash sat toward the front with a thinly veiled expression of condescension. All at once Miranda felt bad for him again. She wanted to take Nash by the hand and show him how to use Listservs or something. And then, out of nowhere, she thought it. She thought about Nash, in her room at the Black House, in her space. She thought of kissing him and how he would hesitate at first and then kiss her back. She imagined undressing herself and pulling him down on the bed. She imagined his adoring expression. It excited her to be eighteen to someone like Nash. So much more fun than being eighteen to someone who was also eighteen. She really flushed thinking this, and Nash smiled at her because she was staring at him, and she quickly looked away. She turned to the front of the room, where some e-freak pornographer was about to begin.

It was Josh. Josh Marshall, from her old high school. He graduated two classes ahead of her, and certainly she didn't know him very well, but she used to see him every day. He was not a sweaty little social misfit. No, Josh Marshall was the straightest boy she could imagine. Tall and good looking in an unremarkable, clean way. He wore a uniform of button-down shirt, flat-front khakis or tidy jeans, and brown loafers. Shirts always tucked in.

"Mostly what I thought we could go over is how denial-of-service or flood attacks work and—my specialty—how to hijack sites. You might remember how the address for the IMF meetings was redirected to the green anarchist site. This lasted for about twenty hours. Their site was not altered, we just inserted a program that redirected anyone accessing their address to another site."

He glanced at her and smiled in recognition. He had never smiled at her in high school. Miranda tried to piece it all together. Certainly Josh was a smart guy. But he was so sunny and so destined for full-steamed establishment success. As he spoke she began to understand. His normalcy was so extreme as to be perverse. No one was that clean-cut, that inadvertent, that unobtrusive. That shy.

"The best kind of hijack is to create an alternate site that looks and behaves just like the real site. I call these parasites. But the links are altered, the information is rearranged so that the truth can be disseminated, but also so misinformation can be posted about where they are meeting and other logistics, as well as some irreverent information just to ridicule them and underline their hypocrisy."

"How long do you get away with it?" Nash asked.

"If you do it gradually, and don't shoot your wad all at once, you can string them along for weeks. Monsanto took two weeks to notice. People look at their sites but don't really 'read' the rest of it. And if you imitate their language, and their design, you can often tamper extensively and extendedly."

"But ultimately detected."

"Oh sure. Especially if you are giving out false information about meetings and such. It is admittedly a limited gesture, but you can really humiliate these corporate site designers. And these organizations."

Who would have guessed, Josh? That was how it should be done, she thought. Look and seem straight and law-abiding but actually do things to subvert the status quo. Do something genuinely subversive.

When the meeting ended, Josh walked over to her and asked what she'd been up to since graduation. She invited him down the street to check out the Black House. She didn't think twice about it—Josh was the kind of guy she generally didn't get any attention from. She liked listening to him. And she really liked leaving with him.

After everyone left, Nash sat for a while. He didn't feel like cleaning up the flyers and coffee cups by himself. Even Henry wasn't around to distract him. Instead Nash lay down on one of the benches and listened to *Mingus Ah Um*.

It was okay, really, because Josh was her age and that was the way it should be. And Josh was smarter than he thought. Any nagging feelings of doubt, any issues he had with Josh's character or intentions were not based on anything articulable or objective. He knew his bad feelings came from a little jealousy. The truth was, Nash also felt relieved. He didn't even mind, too much, when she stopped coming in altogether. He knew that time would make all his twinges fade and eventually go. He knew this because he'd had to let go of things before, as everyone did. It was sad to admit it, but forgetting was a slow, gradual liberation. But knowing this about himself also proved that at some level you don't completely forget the things you endure. They just fade until it almost seems as though they happened to someone else.

He would get used to not seeing her in the store. And later, when he saw them walking together on the street, he reassured himself that it was a good thing for her, and maybe it really was.

Without Mouths

SOME DAYS Henry thought exclusively of the evening to come. He would walk around the city, doing his upkeep on his buildings, blinking in the sun, and he would tremble with dread.

He could manage, most days, to redirect and distract. Five weeks went by, and he got nothing. They have finally left for good, he thought, then stopped, retracted that. He had become fervent in his superstitions. Every thought, every move seemed to require a countergesture just in case.

He lay on his bed and nothing came. He rigorously avoided dark thoughts. He watched television. He dropped into sleep, or at least a tossed, soporific stupor, and then he woke with a start to an extra-loud infomercial, his shoulders mangled into the couch, his throat parched.

He felt fear at a distance first, and then more intensely as it had a gaming, even playful approach. Don't look at the clock. Just turn off the set and go back to sleep.

But as he got up off the couch, he glanced at the wall clock:

3:00 a.m. He couldn't find the remote, so he pushed the power button directly on the television. The room abruptly went silent. He felt a creep of adrenaline as he listened into the night. He tried to laugh it off—just don't start listening for things.

He felt his heart beating faster. He felt the silence of the house overcome by a multitude of tiny midnight sounds, just like how the dark outside will fade as your eyes get used to it until gradually you can see the thousand stars, the trees, and the moon shadows on the ground. He heard the hum of his refrigerator kick in. He heard the rain tack against windowpanes and roof. He heard the furnace die down.

He woke again with another start at dawn. He felt relief: not only could he not remember any dream of any color but there was the blessed weak sun and all the glorious diffused light of a Northwest sunrise. He lay back on his pillow feeling at a great distance from all his worried ruminations during the night. Then, gradually, almost imperceptibly, he felt an odd breeze—a tropical, slow heat blow languidly across his face.

Shit.

Henry is in a narrow street. He smells nothing of the palm trees he passes, nothing of the hot pavement he walks on. He smells instead a monolithic bludgeon of a smell: an oily-yet-astringent, froggy formaldehyde smell. He turns in to a doorway. It is the Saigon hospital. But it is Ho Chi Minh City now, and he is there for a reason.

He walks down a corridor to a special division. It is quiet. He pushes open a swinging door, and he steps inside.

The smell of formaldehyde is acute now; he puts his hand to his face to no avail. He sees, in shadows at first, then more clearly, rows of large glass containers. There must be two hundred of them. Then his eyes adjust. He sees the forms suspended in fluid. Flimsy, fetal, tiny beings. The doubled forms with one body half-grown into the other. Faces without mouths. Limbs without digits. The formaldehyde smell continues, and the bodies have a translucent cast in the bottles. There is no constant among these catastrophes except why they are here, in these jars, and what they signify.

When Henry stopped he wasn't puking, or even crying. He stared at the sunlight in the room. What can sunlight do for me? He knew, if not today, or in a month, he would again smell that viscous formaldehyde in his nose and throat, right in the light of day.

What else frightens Henry:

> *Chloropicrin gas smells of apple blossoms.*
> *Hydrogen cyanide agent smells of toasted almonds.*

and

> *Asphyxiants, vesicants, lacrimants.*

and

> *The things that must be answered for are without end.*

I'm with the Bandwidth

"JUST MAKE yourself at home." They had been together for a few weeks, but things moved slowly. This was the first time Miranda had been invited to his house (actually his parents' house). Josh went straight to his computers. He owned two gleaming flat-screen monitors with protoplasmic, translucent gray-blue casings and sleek, silent keyboards, ergonomically contoured in the middle. He had no mess, no clutter. No loose papers.

"I like keyboards that click," she said. He looked at the screen. He seldom touched the mouse but used everything on programmed key command.

"I don't like squishy keyboards," she continued. He checked his e-mail. It looked like he had about two hundred messages. He opened one from the list and scanned it quickly. It was strange that Josh lived in suburban splendor in Bellevue. He stayed a couple of nights with her in the city, sleeping over but still not having sex (not completely anyway, which was somehow mutually acceptable to both of them though they didn't speak of it). She didn't mind that he didn't stay much past dawn. Or that he preferred his room at his parents' house.

"Let me just reply to this. Give me a minute."

"Too soft and squishy . . ." Miranda turned away from him. She couldn't really be surprised by anything Josh did—he was deliberately full of surprises, which naturally became anything but surprise.

She had to admit that when she finally got here she felt a pang of longing for spotless suburbia. After she stepped over yet another kid at the Black House. Or just the odor from the fridge. And Josh's house was the highest realization of suburban splendor she had ever seen. His room was very large. Past the desk and entryway a carpeted step led down to the area where the bed was. The room was done in shades of gunmetal gray-blue. Sleek and spotless. No pictures of Che, no volumes of Noam Chomsky. In the corner of the sunken area, a large double bed, neatly made, and beyond it two door-sized windows that led to what looked like a balcony. Above the bed, a skylight. To the right a door to his private bathroom. This was the sort of contemporary home in which there were at least as many bathrooms as bedrooms.

"Okay, done." He turned to her on his swivel seat. He reached in a drawer and pulled out a small bag of pot. He started to roll a joint.

"You just keep it in your desk, out in the open?"

Josh smiled. "Oh yes. They would never look in my drawers without my permission."

Miranda shook her head.

"I mean, does this look like the room of a pot-smoking loser?" he asked.

"No, it doesn't even look like the room of a human being."

"That is lesson number one. You control what people believe

to be true about you. All of it is subject to manipulation. You can avoid interference very easily. Most people are quite shallow about their judgments. Even parents." Why, Miranda thought, does everyone think I need lessons all the time?

He sat on the floor by the balcony, careful to blow the smoke out the open door. She noticed a small symbol affixed to the wall above his desk. Slightly to the left of the monitors. It was a small linocut print of a cat, stylized in futurist blocky black-and-white. The sabot cat, the anarchist symbol for sabotage. It looked creepy and unsettling here among the titanium laptops and infrared mouses.

She sat on the floor beside him and took a hit. The long light of the fading sun crept into the room as they smoked, making the metal grays almost rosy silver, glittering and glowing with reflected warmth.

Josh also had a tiny tattoo of the sabot cat on his chest. Miranda noticed it every time she undid the buttons on his shirt, revealing the smooth, nearly hairless chest, the white, clear skin and the small tattoo, sharp and black. It impressed her and reassured her. He had been this way for a while. He was committed. This was how Miranda measured commitment: the will to etch permanently your beliefs in skin. Here he was, in a development of three-car garages, cathedral ceilings and fifteen rooms, here he was with his two hundred e-mails and his clinically precise manipulations, already in possession of a genuine secret life. She thought of these things as she pulled him toward his bed.

Skin so milky and smooth it reminded her of marble statues, or melamine plastic plates, or ultramodern computer casings. He began some nice kissing on her stomach, just grazing her bra-clad breasts, edging around them with tantalizing restraint. His lips were coral pink and very soft. His mouth looked slightly swollen from rubbing her skin—he was almost girlish, pretty. He didn't seem at all like her, with her sudden curves and subtle scents. She felt randomly colored, with tan lines and freckles, a bruise, a bump, a broken capillary. They tangled for hours on the bed, it seemed, with clothes loosened but not quite off, and long, deep kisses that unnerved Miranda at first but then made her want more and more. She drifted in and out in the darkening room, no music, no talk, just his generous mouth and his hands stroking her lower back, or her long hair, which even she had to admit probably felt nice to touch.

She did not yet love Josh. Not yet. But.

He was the real thing, wasn't he? A serious person, a tactician, an expert. A certainist. He gave her his jacket and led her out on the balcony. From there they climbed on the roof, where the lone tree by the house gave a modicum of cover. It was hardly dark with all the ambient light from the streetlamps and pouring out through sliding glass "entertainment" doors. And tastefully lit pools, in the contemporary style, not seventies aqua-blue but a dark, econatural moss blue-green, with monument-style lighting. And here they lay back on the roof and smoked again. She ached and wanted to climb against him. Instead they lay shoulder to shoulder, nearly touching, staring at the sky. Josh told her of all the actions he had done, and then he laid out his future targets. And why.

She stared into the suburban night from their secret perch and listened.

Miranda messed with the radio. It had a search button on it, so it found a strong signal, stayed for a few seconds, then went on to the next strong signal.

"You'll never get the college stations with that search button," Josh said.

"I hate bad reception."

"All the alternative stations have weak signals, though."

"I have to pee." They had taken Interstate 5 until they reached Ashland, Oregon. From there they went west to coastal Route One. Taking this detour was her idea. Miranda liked Route One. It was a highway, not a freeway, and you could see the difference in the surrounding areas. You could see redwoods and coastal views. Run-down old logger towns that seemed more a part of Oregon than California. Fields after fields of grapevines. Sad motels built with tree tourists in mind. The kitschy tunnel made in the base of an enormous ancient redwood so you can drive your car through and marvel at the size. She liked the lonely creaking of the trees when you walked under them, and their size. Not because big things impressed her per se but because she felt humbled and finally had a perspective of her own life in the history of the world. She felt a grasp of the spiritual, something hard for her to feel normally, walking along Fifteenth Avenue, or talking to her friends, or brushing her teeth. She loved knowing these trees would outlive her. And how tiny her life was, a blink of the universe. It comforted her, she didn't feel insignificant, just part of something long and large and beyond her grasp. The world beyond her life and desires. It was then she felt a largeness of spirit and a generosity.

"There isn't anywhere to go to the bathroom. If we took the interstate we could go to a rest stop," Josh said and looked at his watch. Miranda switched off the radio.

"Why did you turn it off?"

"There's a cafe. I'm hungry anyway."

"There has to be at least one public station we can pick up." It was Josh's plan to drive down to Alphadelphia. She insisted on Highway One even though it added at least three hours to the trip. She was curious about Alphadelphia. She was curious about who actually lived there. When first inaugurated by its corporate underwriter, Allegecom, it was everywhere in the news. Allegecom—the massive corporate entity that contained everything from pharmaceuticals (through its offshoot Phero-tek) to genetically modifying seeds with coordinated, matching pesticides (through its biotech arm, Versagro)—was taking an unprecedented foray into developing and running an entire community. Then the press attention abruptly stopped, as it always did, and no one mentioned it again. So how many years had it been?

"Five years. Population is now five thousand people." Origi-nally, three people applied for every open spot. She remembered hearing about what criteria were applied. How people tried to buy their way in. The stringent rules of Allegecom.

"That's targeted capacity. The size that allows maximum diversity with minimum alienation."

"Five thousand exactly."

"Just enough people to keep you from going stir-crazy and inbred but not so many that you don't feel surrounded by famil-iar faces. As determined by a precise social scientific program, developed by Allegecom's team of crack human perfectionists."

Josh had it all down. He had been turned on to the Alphadel-phia kick by one of the anarchist groups he subscribed to online. It was on a list of targets. It seemed on the five-year anniversary of Alphadelphia, Allegecom had great public relations claims to make, great payoff for its hard work and considerable expense, in its social experiment, the First Self-Sustaining Techtopia in America. And they would announce plans for another, improved community on the East Coast. The perfect target for an action, but Miranda hadn't heard what the action might be, or maybe Josh hadn't figured it out yet.

There wasn't, finally, much to see. Houses and cul-de-sacs. Lots of trees and consistent, intensely modern architecture. Hor-izontal homes of glass and metal. South-facing and integrated into the indigenous but cultivated foliage. Miranda didn't think it looked bad at all.

"It's not nostalgic or overly homogenized," she said.

"It is just a gated tract development with a veneer of innovation. It is shallow and insidious and grotesque. A parody of a community," Josh said. "Sustainable, ha." He scrutinized the promo pamphlet he had in his hand. On the cover it said

Allegecom:
Building Communities That Tread Lightly
but Beautifully on the Earth

They didn't come up with anything particularly subversive to do to Alphadelphia. But over the next few months Josh did concoct an elaborate parasite to hijack the recruitment page for Allegecom's new community. At first glance the site looked exactly the same, but Josh inserted parody throughout. He changed the site subtitle from Green World to Greed World and revealed every counterpoint to the ecotopia they claimed to be creating and were heavily marketing. If users clicked on the little red wagon icon, which was where Allegecom discussed its community service projects, they were directed to a link about a lawsuit that a community of ten thousand in Central America was bringing against the biotech arm of the company. It showed pictures of sick animals and children, and then the company's promotional material on the various pesticides and genetically altered seed sources to match, along with statistics of money made in third world countries by Allegecom. These sorts of hijackings and parodies weren't illegal. Not yet. But they hovered in some middle ground, acknowledged by all concerned as soon-to-be-illegal activity.

In December Josh even made *The New York Times*. The Styles section did a piece on political hackers and included a description of Josh's latest attack on Allegecom: The Corporate History Icon (a funny little anthropomorphized sprouted seed) on the Commitment & Community page took you to a Josh-hosted site describing how although Allegecom Pharmaceuticals marketed a plethora of antidepressants and antianxiety medications, it used to market dioxin to the Pentagon under its now defunct proto-pesticide division, Terrayield. It cited evidence that the research, development and marketing of dioxin continued despite the fact that their internal experiments had shown teratogenic and carcinogenic effects since the 1940s. You could then click on a little skull and crossbones icon to get the whole sad saga of Agent Orange and how hard it was to sue a now defunct, disappeared arm of the corporation. All divisions and subdivisions have separate identities, each with distinct liabilities.

After twelve days Allegecom took all of Josh's work down. But not before a lot of people saw it and a lot of papers reported on it. The *Times* article not only revealed Josh as the author but even showed a picture of Josh at his computer, looking angular and cool, decidedly unhackerish. Miranda thought talking to a reporter was a little reckless. Josh was practically begging to get busted.

"Guess what?" Josh smiled and closed his eyes as he lay back on his bed. They were in the clean and perfect house. More and more they stayed there instead of at the Black House. Josh preferred it. More privacy. Fewer fleas.

"What?"

"Allegecom's personnel department wrote me a letter."

"Why?"

"Next month they want to fly me out to New York to meet with Leslie Winters, the project director for their new community."

Miranda laughed and shook her head. "You're kidding."

"I think they want to offer me a job. New tactic—instead of prosecuting me, hire me. Sort of like promoting a union organizer to management."

"Did you tell them to fuck off?"

"No. Are you kidding? This is a great opportunity to see Allegecom from the inside." He sat up and squeezed her hand. "Don't you want to come with me?"

Sure.

Visitors

HENRY WANTED to go out for a beer with Nash. They walked down the street to the salty British-style pub and sat in one of the back booths. Henry looked a little shaky. He smoked with his inhaler on the table. He wiped sweat from his forehead with the back of his hand.

"What's wrong? You look like you haven't slept," Nash said.

Henry turned his head and took a quick look over his shoulder. "Look, I need to talk to you."

"Okay."

"I mean, some of the shit I'm going to tell you, I don't know."

"It's cool."

"I don't care at this point." Henry took a long swallow of beer. "I sometimes have these dreams—but not exactly—waking nightmares."

"Like night terrors," Nash said.

"Yeah, but baroque, elongated, all-sense trances."

"Like what?"

"Like really detailed hallucinations of spraying Agent Orange all over jungles and riverbanks. Spraying villages."

"That's horrible."

"I'm dropping white phosphorus and napalm bombs. I can see it—smell it burning through skin. My skin, too." Henry looked down at the table. "One nasty one I had—glass jars filled with formaldehyde and these fetal disasters. I see these faces and wake with these near smells still in my hair, and odd, off tastes in my mouth."

Nash watched Henry stub out the cigarette. His breathing was getting heavier and shorter.

"Have you ever heard of anything like that—incongruous, inexplicable odors? Unexplained smells can be profoundly disturbing—I tried to find out about it," Henry said.

"They're hallucinations, just like hearing things or seeing things," Nash said.

"The dead bodies of saints don't smell like decay, you know. They smell like roses and perfume. They call it the odor of sanctity."

"So what?"

"This is like the opposite of that—awful smells for evil things."

Henry's hand shook as he took out another cigarette and lit it. He inhaled and then started to sniff. He grabbed a bar napkin off the table and wiped his nose and forehead.

"God, that's a hell of a thing," Nash said. "You must have had some tour. No wonder you have this kind of trauma all these years later."

Henry was nodding and then stopped, looking straight at Nash. "What are you talking about?"

"What happened to you. In Vietnam."

"Nash, certainly something has been happening to me, but I was not in Vietnam."

"Post-traumatic stress. Very common in vets—"

"I was 4-F for my hearing. I have never been to Vietnam."

Nash watched Henry take another swig on a beer.

"What? You weren't in combat?" he said.

Henry shook his head and swallowed.

"I wasn't even hard of hearing. I faked out the test. It was the easiest test to fake, you just hesitate when they give you the graduated sounds, you wait a few seconds until you indicate you have heard something. The funny thing was that I ended up actually losing my hearing in one ear almost to the exact extent I faked it. You know—if you are out of sight, I don't get much of what you say. Funny."

"I'm stunned."

"And I kind of feel like I deserve it. I knew all about that war, and I never did a thing to stop it. I made sure my ass was safe, and then I drank my way through those years. And I knew it was wrong. I didn't do anything. And ever since I have paid and paid."

"What do you mean?" Nash said.

"I mean I started getting symptoms a few years after the war ended. Of dioxin exposure, although I didn't know what it was yet. I started researching about the war, and what we did there. I got rashes and asthma. I read everything I could. Then, about three years ago, I started in with these night and day terrors. The symptoms got much worse: insomnia, shaking, acute respiratory problems."

"Are you getting help for this?"

"I've taken Nepenthex for years. And lately Blythin. They are designed specifically for combat-related post-traumatic stress disorder."

"Henry, did you tell them you aren't a vet?"

"They didn't ask me. They said I have severe PTSD."

"But it's different, it isn't related to experience."

"But it is—I can't explain, but these memories I have, these proxy memories, they are real."

"Real memories . . ."

"Of things people have experienced. I'm certain. But that is not what I want to talk to you about."

"You certainly have real physical symptoms."

"The point is that up until now, I have only had dreams about combat. Last night was different." Henry glanced behind him again and then leaned in toward Nash.

"It was also during the Vietnam War. But I was not a soldier, or at least not in the military. I was organizing to blow up houses. Big summer homes of some high-level corporate executives. I was working in someone's empty home, setting explosives. The house workers had been warned to leave, I guess, because it seemed empty of humans. It did have family pictures and furniture and beds. Teacups and board games. I saw it all blown to bits. Some board member of Monsanto or General Electric or Dow Chemical. To protest against the war."

"Really? But I guess it sort of makes sense. In a nonsense kind of way."

"But."

"What?"

Henry put his hand on the table and leaned toward Nash. "It wasn't me, that's the weird thing," Henry said.

"*That's* the weird part? That it wasn't you?"

"It was you. In this dream, I was you. I was in your head, seeing through your eyes, but it was unmistakably you."

Nash shook his head and then let out a short laugh. "Well, it was a dream, wasn't it?" Nash said. "An immaterial, unreal, fantastic dream. You read about this stuff and then you dream about it. It's a projection."

Henry rubbed his bloodshot eyes.

"Not a memory or experience," Nash said.

PART FIVE

1973–1980

Bellatrix

THE BUS LEFT Berry and Caroline ten miles west of Little Falls. They waited for three hours as drivers from the broken-down Erie Canal industrial towns sped past the two freak chicks hitchhiking. Caroline had asked Berry to help her dye and cut her hair. A new look for a new place, she told her. After they dyed it (a so-called auburn, an unfortunate synthetic beet tone), Caroline pulled her hair up and tied it in a topknot. Berry said cutting the topknot off would instantly give her a shag haircut, just like Jane Fonda in *Klute*. Caroline pulled some strands at the nape of her neck out to keep the back a little longer and then let Berry hack away at the ponytail. With some struggle it was cut through, leaving an uneven, layered, but undeniably shaggy hairdo. Berry left her hair as it was, curly and long, but let Caroline pile it up in a loose bun. Berry's nose and upper lip were still swollen, but Caroline helped her cover the bruises with makeup.

"You want to make a good impression, don't you?"

"I guess."

Caroline looked in the mirror at every rest stop. Her hair looked awful, but she certainly looked different. She put on a crocheted floppy hat, large-framed sunglasses, opaque lipstick, and decided not to care too much. Eventually, walking and hitching, they made it up into Herkimer County, a swath of sparsely populated farmland hills that rose up from the Mohawk River, part nineteenth-century ghost town industrial, part bucolic country utopia, green and almost obscenely lush and dense. They stopped at the New Harmon General Store, picking up two six-packs of beer, a sack of rice and a large jar of peanut butter. Caroline took out her county map.

"We just follow Hurricane Brook north, stick to the left bank, and we should be there in two hours."

"I have to carry this beer for two hours?" Berry said. She shook her head and then took two beers out and handed one to Caroline.

Eventually they came to a dirt trail. There was a sign at the foot that said,

No visitors. No tourists. No exceptions.

Then another sign under it, apparently hammered onto it later, read,

This means you, freak!

They ignored these injunctions and continued on the path. A couple of hundred yards up the trail, another sign,

Keep out!

with another addendum sign; this one read,

Whose sister are you?

Caroline couldn't tell if the question was addressed to the inter-
lopers coming up the trail or was a response from them.

At last they saw the woods open up to a clearing. Glinting in
the sun was a dome composed of multifaceted pieces of hard-
enameled metal, all different colors—most shiny, some rusted at
the edges, some primer matte—welded somewhat sloppily at
their interstices to create a large, ragged futuristic dwelling. A
painted sign said,

Harbinger Hut, Version Two

"Turn around, both of you. Slowly." From behind them. They
turned slowly toward the voice. A woman with a rifle and a yellow white-chick ersatz Afro faced them, barrel pointing. She
wore what looked to Caroline like a Brownie uniform, including
the kneesocks but without the sash and the badges. Her large
army boots somehow emphasized rather than disguised the
shapeliness of her long legs.

Berry started laughing. Caroline squeezed her arm hard to
make her stop.

"What are you doing here? Can't you read? This is a closed
community. We got no room for new members."

"Yeah, so we gathered," Berry said. "So much for communal
spirit—"

"Look, fat chick, look at this in my hand and shut up. This
isn't a commune, it is a community of women."

Berry's mouth dropped open, and she began laughing even
harder.

"Hey, it's okay. We're here by invitation. We are here to see
Mother Goose," Caroline said.

"You know her? She knows you're coming?"

"Not directly, but yeah, she knows we are coming."

She lowered the gun. Flashed a two-fingered V at them and waved them toward the dome.

"Sorry. I have to be vigilant in the summer or we get overrun with every speed freak and junkie moocher the city can spew our way. They come and piss in your streams and you're supposed to mop their brows and nurse their strung-out, parasitic hearts until the whole place becomes a flophouse, you know, Bowery in the foothills, right?"

She stopped at the entrance to the dome. "I'm Jill, by the way. Hill Jill, I watch the perimeter. Come on in and I'll get you some food."

"We brought beer."

"Not allowed."

Berry looked at Caroline and raised an eyebrow.

"So let's get it inside and drink it quick," Jill said.

Hill Jill's dome was as comfortable and airily spacious inside as an omnitriangulated polyhedral dwelling could be. It had a rose-stained, translucent resin skylight, handmade simple wood furniture and a wood-burning cookstove. There were macramé decorations and many brightly colored yarn god's eyes strung from the ceiling. The dome apparently also ran on electricity: Jill used a small refrigerator and a state-of-the-art, vinyl-veneer-encased hi-fi stereo system surrounded by stacks of records. Her platform bed was covered in Indian blankets, and an entire "wall" was hugged by a curved bookshelf full of books. Caroline could see books on Eastern religion and the requisite copy of the *Whole Earth Catalog*. Several panels of scratched and cloudy Plexiglas embedded in the sides of the dome served as the only windows. Through the Plexiglas they could see the hills and woods beyond the trail.

"Nice space in here," said Caroline.

"I built it myself out of abandoned car parts. Reclaimed from the refuse of industrial society. Everyone builds her own house. You can't stay if you don't."

"Are they all domes like this?"

Hill Jill shrugged and slammed the bottle cap off the beer on the edge of the cookstove.

"Some are. There are your usual Buckminster Fuller dome freaks up here. You can just follow a recipe and build a home out of junk. Put a little resin sealant on the seams, caulk it with tar. Some of us are more elaborate. I'm tied in to the grid with electricity. I used fiberglass insulation, PVC pipe. Plastic sealants. I have a well with running water. But every woman does her own thing."

"They let you decide, huh?" said Berry.

"Technology will set you free."

"You could spend all day hauling buckets of water. Or keeping a fire going," Caroline said, flipping open a beer.

"Exactly. Technology to eliminate drudgery. We are right in the midst of hardscrabble nation, twenty below in winter. I am no primitivist."

"What's this community called?" Berry asked. Jill ignored Berry and continued sipping her beer. Berry repeated her question.

Jill glanced at her finally and smirked. "This is Total Bitch Ranch, sister, Full-Tilt Pussy Ridge. This is High Daddy Farm, you dig? Heretic Homestead, Come-Down Campus, Hepatitis Hill."

"C'mon."

Jill cocked her head and gave Berry a slow once-over.

"Classified, sorry. Drink up and then we'll go up to El Dorado."

Berry started to flip through the LPs leaning in a stack by the stereo. There were several Ohio Players albums that featured cover photos of a black woman with a shaved head and a bored expression in various states of bondage. One of these albums opened to a gatefold of the nearly naked woman in a studded collar wielding a large leather whip.

"What is this?" Berry held up another album using two fingers, as if the record smelled bad. This cover photo showed a black woman buried up to her neck in dirt, her mouth open in a scream, her huge Afro framing her head. Crooked letters spelled out *Maggot Brain*.

"Well, it isn't Joni Mitchell, is it?" Hill Jill said, taking the record from her. Jill turned on the stereo and put the needle down. The distorted guitar and funky rhythms of Funkadelic blared out in badass dissonance. A voice intoned cryptic nonsense about the earth mother. But then, slowly, mournfully, from some far-off place, a long, emotional guitar solo sent stingingly beautiful waves of sound into the room. The guitar sound elongated and contracted for second after second. They all sat and listened, and Jill closed her eyes, making it clear she wanted silence and respect for her music. The music evoked an underlying loneliness that at first made Caroline sad and then started creeping her out. It occurred to her that the guitar solo might go on forever. Berry stared at the cover and killed another beer. At long last the guitar resolved itself back into a sort of melody and the track ended, the whole thing segueing seamlessly into some sexed-up, dark funk.

After they finished three more beers, Jill decided it was time to go, and they started the walk from the perimeter toward what was called the common house. Along the way, Caroline saw dwellings of various and unusual construction. None of them was in sight distance of any other. Sometimes this meant artful placement of shrubberies and ditches. Other times it meant long walks between paths. Some of the dwellings were like Jill's, variations on dome construction, multiseamed hemispheres. One was a log cabin, rough hewn. There were adobe, cavelike buildings; simple, flimsy thatched huts; rammed-earth-brick houses covered in plaster; even a clapboard saltbox painted white like something from a Christmas card. There were pole-construction, barnlike, prefab homes, gnome-type tree houses, and straw-bale-earth igloos. At each one, artful touches seemed to be added for beauty or whimsy: stained glass set in plastered walls, leaking, unfinished. Mosaic patterns made in rough masonry. One even had turrets and minarets. Another had an actual moat. Caroline had heard about communes like this, seen the pictures in magazines. Up on the hill she saw other dwellings built into the earth, some of them jutting oddly to accommodate trees or boulders. These houses were like submarines, or sci-fi movies. Two distinct categories could be discerned despite all the various details: either simple modest shelters, such as tepees, corrugated-tin sheds and mud huts; or high-tech conceptual houses with recycled industrial waste, pod rooms, pressed plastic and synthetic particleboard construction.

"That one over there is Hesperides' house. It is all found refuge, rescued and liberated materials from abandoned factories in Utica and old farmhouses along the hills. She calls it Cake Corners. She's part of the tech-yeses, like me. Over on the other side you have the tech-nos. They are strictly no running water or electricity. Self-consciously primitive, Rousseauian idealists. They cook and wash in one common space and share everything."

"Sounds groovy to me," Berry said.

"Yeah, some of us did that scene before and learned our lesson. That's why we call it Hepatitis Hill. Me, Mother G and some of the others are followers of Hygeia."

Both women just looked blankly at Jill.

"You know—running water, clean flush toilets, septic tanks and hot showers."

"Oh yeah, right on." Caroline smiled. Berry shrugged.

....

"Do you move to the rural sect because you believe in the per-fectibility of human interaction? Or is it an escape, an expression of deep misanthropy?" Right away Mother Goose started giving them her set-piece commune rap. She had met them at the path and was leading them to the common house. Berry squeezed Caroline's arm when she saw where they were headed. A huge clapboard building, painted brown-purple with brightest pink detailing. It was a simple rectangle shape with a gambrel roof and a perfectly intact stone foundation. Each window contained twelve small panes of old glass above and below each sash.

"It was built in the 1840s by two renegade New Harmon Community women. Really. Not purple originally. White, of course. And built to imitate the original Shaker buildings of the 1790s. You've heard of it, New Harmon Community? They named the local town after it. This land has a history of radical alternative community. Christian extremists who thought private property was the root of all evil. We are talking complex mar-riage, total communal and shared living, including the raising of children. There is even an archive of their papers and journals at the town library. The rednecks that run the town have no clue what New Harmon Community was—if they knew, they'd probably change the name."

Mother G was an older woman, heavyset and sturdy. She wore her gray-streaked hair back in a bun, with a plain muslin blouse and skirt. She seemed every inch the religious reformer, unmade up and defiantly plain. The furthest thing, Caroline thought, from sexy. She felt garish in her hat and glasses. Caro-line glanced at Berry, who appeared becomingly wide-eyed. It was funny to see them face-to-face, both large and fair, but Berry dripping with panels of diaphanous fairy materials and her ten-drils of angel hair; Mother G, neat and tucked.

"You see, I am an empiricist. Out here we can try for some precision, eliminate variables."

"Such as?" Berry asked.

"Well, men, for one obvious thing," Jill said. Mother G looked at her. Jill scowled.

"You cannot base a community on subtraction, on mere opposition. It becomes reactionary and escapist. Cryptofascist. And people can fixate on the most sensational aspects of what is a much more subtle and sophisticated vision. Nevertheless"— and here Mother G paused and took in Berry's swollen lip and Caroline's odd hair color—"you are here for your own reasons, and I can offer some refuge, at least temporarily."

"Great."

"But if you want to stay more than a week, you have to petition for membership. No tourists, no freeloaders," said Jill.

"We would invite you to partake in the governance of the community as well as its work," said Mother G.

Mother G lived in the main house in a small private room. She put Berry and Caroline up in the dormitory on the third floor. There was a bathroom with a large claw-foot tub, and rows of perfectly aligned and spotless single beds. Built-in shelves lined the walls, along with peg boards to hang clothes and brooms. The first rule they learned—one of many—was nothing on the floor. There were drawers for shoes, and the brooms hanging from pegs were meant to be used. Nothing on the floor so everything could be swept clean.

Next Berry and Caroline were introduced to the work wheel, which assigned each woman in the community work credits for jobs of her choosing. Everyone, no matter how long she had been here, had to obtain a certain number of work credits each week. Jobs that people hated, such as cleaning the stables or washing the toilets, were assigned more work credits. Things people liked, such as baking pies or collecting eggs, were assigned fewer credits, until jobs had equal appeal and everything eventually had a volunteer. Unfortunately, it also meant that everyone did everything, instead of people doing what they excelled at. So although someone with Caroline's experience and talents in the kitchen should be cooking and cooking often, the wheel offered no more labor credits to her than to Berry, who was an awful cook.

"This model is not perfect, but it is the most egalitarian way to structure things, I think. It's an experiment. Each way of organizing creates its own repercussions. Simple things, like organizing work, can have dramatic social effect. We may, at a later point, encourage people who excel at something to do more of it, but then we will end up with people born to clean toilets who never get to do the good jobs. So at the cost of efficiency and quality, we have an extremely high level of fairness and equality," said Mother G to Caroline over a breakfast of fruit preserves and sourdough bread.

Caroline enjoyed the possibilities of the community. She even liked the element of no men. Berry showed less enthusiasm. She spent her days up on the tech-nos' ridge, smoking pot or hanging out in the sweat lodge. She found the tech-yes industriousness exhausting and a little suspect. She preferred to have fewer amenities at less effort. But she still slept at the dormitory with Caroline and did the labor assigned her on the wheel. After their first week ended, Caroline and Berry told Mother G they would stay and wanted to petition for membership.

Mother G explained that if you wanted to stay you eventually had to build your own house, and not in view of anyone else's house. You could participate in community meals and decision making as long as you participated in the work wheel. If you wanted to fend for yourself, like some of the tech-nos, you could opt out of the labor credits.

Caroline learned that most of the women had dropped out from the Harvard Classics Department, where Mother G used to teach. Others were design and architecture heads from MIT. She also discovered that Mother G was the financial benefactor of the community. It would take years for actual self-sufficiency to develop, so she'd put up the money to buy the land and initial equipment. Many of the women were veterans of other communes, usually defunct, that had open-door policies and absolute freedom. These became overrun with drug addicts and social outcasts. This place was to be a revision of previous communities. Mother G wanted to have a space where basic cultural assumptions could be challenged. Such as what women were like without men. And whether we could escape the cultural paradigms we were raised with. She restored the old Shaker-style house, paid the taxes and often bought supplies for the community. Although they grew vegetables and kept chickens and cows, they were not anywhere near self-supporting. So in a sense Mother G was deeply in charge, and this too could not be escaped, no matter how many work credits she clocked in.

But Caroline liked her. And she liked the place despite its contradictions. She liked the cloistered effect, the way each woman reinvented herself. No one admitted to their past lives here. No one wanted to cop to anything but the moment and the future. It was the perfect place for someone like her, wasn't it?

Temporary Like Achilles

AFTER NEARLY two months, Caroline and Berry still hadn't built their own house. Instead Berry managed to convince the cloistered women on the hill to let her move in with them. But she took frequent breaks—after a few days huddled with the tech-nos (open-fire cooking, barefoot basic farming, infrequent bathing, spell casting) she escaped to the tech-yeses (hi-fi players, refined sugar, clean water, Band-Aids, tampons). Caroline still saw her most days, in her floppy hat and granny dress, when Caroline decided she wanted a moment of sotto voce commentary or just an unspoken collusion of outsider feeling. Caroline still didn't feel entirely comfortable at the commune. She had been living at the dormitory as discreetly as possible—certainly she should have moved out by now. But building a house seemed a big commitment for someone in her position.

After collecting her weekly work assignment, Caroline met Berry on the trail, and they took a walk out beyond the edge of the commune. They sat eating sandwiches on some rocks by the stream. Caroline turned on Mother G's portable radio. The Beach Boys' song "Good Vibrations" came on. Caroline turned up the volume, and the song played up into the hills around them.

"This was *the* song my junior year at high school. That fake end, when it segues into this whole other sounding song but still is connected, somehow, to the old one—that blew my mind." Caroline talked as she braided Berry's hair. She just began combing it and braiding it without asking Berry. Otherwise Berry would start to get dreadlock mats and knots that were impossible to remove. Berry didn't seem to care one way or the other.

"This song is all right."

"This is a great song," Caroline said.

"Thing about the Beach Boys, it's not that they're too corny or whatever. I don't mind that. But they are completely not sexy—"

"Yes, that's true—"

"Utterly sexless, even. Unless you are twelve years old."

"That's not the point."

"What else could be the point?"

"Loneliness. Longing. The sadness that leaks through all that enforced sunny cheer. It's heartbreaking."

Berry shrugged. "This is a cool song."

"It's in the sound, not the words. It's the way you feel, or rather the feeling you get. Like slightly off, rancid America, you know?"

Berry turned to her and smiled. Her blond braids glittered in the sun. "When you move somewhere new, it's good to have someone or something from your past there with you, reminding you of who you are, don't you think?" she said.

I don't know where but she sends me there

"Listen to the harmonies. Why is it that harmonies can give you chills? Why do they please so deeply?"

"Like it is so easy to lose track of yourself, in a way, if you go somewhere new," Berry said, her voice choking a little bit. She laughed at the sound.

"Are you feeling nostalgic?"

"Emotional, maybe. What do you expect with all the free-floating estrogen around here, right?"

Caroline tied the long braids with leather laces. She got up and brushed tiny pebbles from the backs of her bare thighs. It was cold already. As soon as the sun went down it got cold in these old mountains. Berry got up, and the two of them walked slowly down the path. As they approached the community from the north, Caroline glimpsed the common house through the trees. For the first time she thought Mother G's house looked beautiful, particularly with the gentle diffusion of the dusk light making the purple paint a nearly unnoticeable natural brown. Usually the flush clapboard and lack of adornment seemed too plain to her. No flourishes in the returns at the edges, no fluid, fanciful lines, nothing for its own sake at all. No embellishments to discover in a lintel or in a dormer. Not a hint of whimsy in a molding or a cornice. But now, when she glimpsed it through the trees, she noticed its symmetry. Its economy and its balance. The harmony of the lines of the perfectly straight clapboards and the mullion lines between windowpanes. Repetition and order. The sturdiness of it. And the beauty of it, quiet, modest. Even, perhaps, despite itself. But there was a slight pretense in all this simplicity, though, wasn't there? It was just as deliberate, just as constructed as the most ornate Victorian house; just as contrived as the elaborate and distinctive Greek Revival houses that dotted the surrounding countryside. Its absence of style was never that, was it? Just as contrived as the simple, reduced culture of the commune. Nature had nothing to do with any of it. Artifacts, all of us, no matter how deep in the woods.

"The tech-nos will be gone in another month. They spend their winter in the Southwest," Berry said.

"No kidding," Caroline said. "That's funny. I'll bet this whole place gets halved in the winter. They get stacks of snow up here."

Caroline reached the end of the path first. Berry ran to catch up to her and swung an arm around her shoulders.

"What are you thinking?" Berry said.

"What am I thinking at this moment? I'm thinking I wouldn't mind a beer and some men."

"Really? 'Cause that is completely what I am thinking."

"No kidding. You?"

"Shut up. Look, I mean today. Let's go take a break. We can hitch down to Little Falls and stay in a motel overnight," Berry said, clapping her hands together.

"And eat some hamburgers and smoke and go to a bar."

"Candy bars."

"Men."

"TV and newspapers and—"

"Men."

"Yeah."

Neither of them had been farther than the tiny town of New Harmon since they arrived. Caroline thought of it: men. Young and dumb. Old and mysterious. Unshaved faces. Whiskers, what it feels like to kiss a man with whiskers. The prickle of it. Handsome, square-jawed men with short haircuts. Beer bellies. Large hands. Some men had gnarled veins that poked out from the muscles of their arms. An arm that fit around her waist. Some men, Bobby for instance, could reach an arm around her when she lay beneath him, lifting her gently to him by her midsection. They were all like him, and yet none of them could compare at all. But still, having not seen any men for so long did make her giddy and almost delirious with anticipation. Surely that wasn't the intended effect of a women's community?

Clothes changed, money in pockets, the two women walked the long trail to the road and hitchhiked to New Harmon. They waited and hitched a few more miles. They waited and hitched some more until they reached Little Falls. The Big Town. They ate dinner in a small Italian cafe on Main Street. Berry was thinner and tanner than when they'd first arrived in New York. Caroline could see that now. She hadn't sat across from Berry and really looked at her the way other people might. Berry ate and spoke and drank all at the same time and in the same way—fast. They were receiving what seemed to Caroline an excessive amount of attention. Both of them felt a little overexcited, and this feeling radiated from them. As they left the restaurant, the people at the other tables stared at them. They both wore dirty jeans and gauze blouses with angel sleeves and tiny embroidered designs. Berry had sewn them out of scarves. The bottoms of the blouses came to points in the front and the back, but the sides were cut high, so if you reached an arm up, a flash of waist peeked out. Caroline's red hair dye was fading and starting to grow out. She wrapped a scarf around the roots and tied it by the nape of her neck, the ties hanging down, gypsy-style. She wore large hoop earrings that, along with the dangling scarf tips, brushed her neck and tickled her whenever she turned her head. When they got outside, Berry undid her braid and pulled her curls loose.

"Do I look okay?"

Caroline nodded. "That choker looks good with your hair down. You look like a fallen Gibson girl. You look really great."

Berry rolled her eyes.

"Like a former lady who has been shipwrecked and still clings to a few scraps of her past gentility."

"All right already."

They shared a hand-rolled cigarette, herbal in taste and sweet in scent. Caroline felt suddenly very happy.

An older man slowly walked by, staring at Berry from her legs to her neck.

They walked to the edge of the Mohawk River. Several bars were situated on a sort of barge between the river and the canal. All of them were dives, but one called the Waterfront had loud music and some traffic in and out. They went in, and Caroline immediately noticed two men drinking at a table. Their long hair reached well below their shoulders and looked incongruous with their tan work boots and mashed-up carpenter hands. Since she had arrived in New York, she'd noticed more and more of the shit-kicking truck-driver types let their hair grow long. It was no longer a sign of grooviness. Good old boys, rednecks and freaks became hard to tell apart. They all even smoked pot. The bar was full of similar men, but these two were the best prospects. For the first time Caroline had no problem thinking of sex as something abstract that she could want, independent of someone, and then find a man to fulfill her want, instead of the other way around. Sex floated around her. It seemed mystical, magical. The last person she was with was Bobby. She knew that this would have nothing to do with that.

Berry went to the bar to get drinks. Caroline watched the two men sitting by themselves. They talked and sipped beer. Occasionally they would look up at the room but not with the focused determination of men on the prowl. She watched them for only a minute, then she turned away. She looked back again and caught the men staring at her. She examined her hands and smiled to herself.

Berry returned with two schooners of dark beer. "Let's stick together tonight. Maybe find two guys already hanging out, if we can."

Caroline barely turned toward the two men, and Berry gave a once-over to the whole room to check out who Caroline indicated.

"Like those two," Berry said, turning back to Caroline.

"Maybe." Caroline glanced at the men again. Neither was actually very good looking, but they also weren't unattractive. The men leaned back in their chairs and sipped at their beers and smoked.

The driving riff of a Creedence Clearwater Revival song came on over the speakers.

"We could just get high with them and see how we feel," Caroline said. "Or we can get a motel room. I mean just us, if you want." She realized then, in the course of speaking her last sentence and with a sigh of relief, that the thought of the unencumbered sex was enough really; she was almost ready to call it a night. She suspected that this was a real difference between men and women. How easy it was for her to live with the unrealized fantasy, already imagining the reality to be more complicated than sexy. The dynamics, for instance. They might both be more attracted to Berry, and they would be subtle about it (or not), but she would still pick up on it somehow. She would be with the disappointed one. Or up close they might not smell or taste good. Or they would do or say something hopelessly sad or corny. And then she would be stuck in some compromised position with these flawed fantasies. What were the chances they would not disappoint?

Now The Band was playing "The Night They Drove Old Dixie Down."

Besides, so much of what seemed fun about the idea was feeling the desire of someone else for her. Because being wanted was an essential part of her desire. Having to deal with some man's disappointment, no matter how faint, felt way too depressing.

That was what they looked like, these two men, like the studiously unscrubbed and unglamorous members of The Band. With the big, shaggy Civil War sideburns. What were they called? Muttonchops.

"We'll see," Berry said and held up her beer to Caroline. They tapped their glasses together and then took two foamy sips. She could feel, to the depths of her body and without even looking around, the stares of the two men. Caroline watched Berry glance toward the two men, who had now stopped smoking and seemed fully occupied with looking at them, half-smiling, one tilting his chair all the way back and the other leaning into his elbows on the table.

"Wow," Berry said. She took a long swig of beer, and then Caroline looked past Berry's shoulder, in the opposite direction of the men, and noticed what hung on the wall behind Berry.

The Rolling Stones' "Tumbling Dice" started next, with its big raunch gospel chorus up front before the lead kicked in, and Berry sang along with the ohs of the female backup singers—except they were really front-up singers at this point—shaking her head back and forth, then switching to singing with the lead vocal when that kicked in, messing up the words.

The wall behind Berry was decorated with posters from the Wild West. A desperado-outlaw theme halfheartedly accomplished with Jesse James and Billy the Kid wanted posters. Caroline noticed a black-and-white poster that said "FBI Most Wanted" over a large picture of the Weather Underground siren Bernardine Dohrn. She was in a leather miniskirt and knee-high boots. It showed her fingerprints and vital stats just like a real FBI poster, but surely doctored to feature an alluring body shot of Dohrn instead of a mug shot. Caroline had seen the body shot before, of course, it was one of the reasons some women distrusted Dohrn, the way she seemed to play into the porno of outlaw chick with great legs. But she did look great, didn't she? But Caroline was not thinking long about Dohrn because she soon noticed other, smaller FBI wanted posters. These were not altered but actual tear sheets, like at the post office. Some were covered over partially and hard to read. At Bernardine's left toe she could see a poster of another woman fugitive, whom Caroline took several breathless seconds to realize was her, Mary Whittaker, a.k.a. Freya. It was, after all, her high school photograph, a photo five years old and not a picture she particularly cared for. But it looked remarkably like her. Anyone who saw it, particularly with her sitting right beside it or under it, would easily recognize her. Naturally no one was actually looking at the wall except Caroline, who felt her mouth slowly fall open.

"What is it?" Berry said.

Caroline shook her head and forced herself to turn her gaze back to Berry at the table. "Nothing."

Berry glanced over her shoulder at the wall behind her and then back at Caroline. "What?"

"I don't feel very good." A completely true statement.

"You don't?"

"Let's leave."

"Why?"

"Can we just go and get a motel or something? Can we just get out of here?" she said.

"What about the Allman Brothers over there?"

"Forget them. C'mon."

They got a room in a small, clean motel with prints of the Erie Canal on the wall. Berry flipped on the TV. Caroline went to the bathroom and closed the door. She splashed water on her face. She let the water run and took several deep breaths, staring in the mirror. She looked like herself, no question about it. Everyone could see it, would see it, the whole town, the whole world. But would anyone notice her picture, so upstaged by dangerous Dohrn's eye-enchanting legs?

They put the brown quilted bedspread on the floor in front of the TV. They sat cross-legged on it and smoked a joint. Caroline could feel her body slowly relax into the night. They watched Johnny Carson and then the late movie. They ate M&M's candies one after the other and chased them with bottles of beer. And they talked to each other, or Berry talked and Caroline listened. Berry told her she didn't want to spend the winter at the commune.

"Where do you want to go?" Caroline asked.

"You mean where do *we* want to go. I'm taking you with me."

Caroline smiled and let Berry stroke her hair. She loved Berry, she did. She cared for her, she trusted her. And then Caroline made her mistake, or walked into it, or let it happen:

"What happened in the bar? Why did you look so upset? Were you thinking about Bobby?"

"Sort of."

Berry looked at her, waiting. Sometimes you are expected to give something to people. It is hard to resist. Sometimes you might even trust people.

"Look, I haven't been completely honest with you about my past. I want to be honest with you. I trust you. But what I tell you has to be a secret forever," Caroline heard herself say. She sounded stern, even harsh.

Berry sat up, intent. "What! What is it?" she said.

"This is really serious."

"I will never tell, I swear. I know what it is, though—"

"Listen—"

"You're Bernardine Dohrn." Berry laughed.

Caroline shook her head and looked at her hands. Later she would recall this moment and consider what had transpired. Everyone will swear never to tell and mean it. No one can resist, or very few people can resist, the chance to learn a secret. The question was, did Caroline, in her need to tell someone, think to explain to Berry what would potentially be at stake for Berry if she kept Caroline's secret? Caroline didn't think enough about it then, but she often thought about it later, after it was too late.

Caroline told her, Berry heard her.

That night Berry bathed Caroline in the warmth of acceptance and intimacy. Even, perhaps, admiration. But as Caroline tried to fall asleep, the relief of confidence faded. The fear set in. A person who knew your secrets stayed part of your life forever. She would always have to be connected to Berry.

When Caroline woke the next morning, it all came back to her. She watched Berry sleep and felt profound regret. Berry was as kind and benign and loyal as they came, but she had a big mouth, she would slip up, she would get drunk and tell a boyfriend. Caroline watched her sleep and sort of hated her, hated all her flaws and weaknesses.

They ate breakfast in silence. Caroline tried not to panic, and then she gave up.

"Look, Berry, what I told you last night, we should never, ever speak of it, no matter what." They sat across from each other in a diner booth, and although no one else was anywhere near them, Caroline spoke in an angry whisper.

"He made you do it, didn't he? Men are always getting caught up in violence," Berry said. She poured syrup over a mound of pancakes and butter.

Caroline took a deep breath. And then, from somewhere it came, this feeling she had not had since before she went underground. She felt outrage and anger, a chemical burn.

"That's not it, not by a long shot. I'll tell you once. One time. Then no more questions, right?" Caroline stared into Berry's face.

Berry stopped eating.

"It wasn't his idea, it was my idea." She paused, pleased for a second at saying it. She wished she could leave it at that, and she already felt weary of trying to explain herself. But she continued. "I'd had enough of demonstrating against the war. We'd all had our fill of it—years of it. It changed nothing. I wanted to actively oppose. Not protest, some form of symbolic speech or gesture. We wanted tangible, unequivocal action. It was not necessarily the right tactic. I will say this, though, I was sure it was right at the time. I had to do something, I had to put myself at risk, personally. I had to meet the enormity of what they were doing with something equal to it. There was no end. They were sending troops home but with such bad faith; they knew that would placate the antiwar movement, but then they stepped up the bombing. They had no intention of not continuing. Napalm, someone makes that, you know? Someone sits in an R and D lab and thinks, Let's make it burn, but hey, let's add plastic so it will also stick. But look, they just jump in the water, so let's add phosphorus so it burns underwater, burns through to bone. So people on the board of Dow or Monsanto or GE decide that this is a good way to make money, and they are so removed from the consequences. These men are at such remove they could help prolong it, a year, two years, and is it right that that should cost them nothing? We are invisible to them. How smug they were, ignoring us. I wanted them to feel some consequence, pay some price for the terrible things they did for pride or power or profit."

"Okay, I know."

"And it wasn't intended to be violent. It was just destructive. Of stuff. For a purpose. Like the Berrigan brothers said, some property doesn't have a right to exist."

Berry began to cry over her pancakes and syrup, clutching her fork.

"Intentions do matter. They make all the difference . . ."

Caroline felt the words fail her, and her face felt hot, and then she realized she was crying too.

"Why are *you* crying?" Caroline said, wiping at her eyes.

"It was a brave thing, honestly, I think it was a brave thing," Berry said.

"It doesn't matter what you think. I didn't do it for you." Caroline still felt angry at her, which made no sense. Then she inhaled and made herself look placidly at Berry. "I'm so sorry you have to know. I shouldn't have told you."

"I can't really believe it, to be honest with you. It hasn't sunk in, you know, that you're this entirely other person than what I thought." Berry reached her hand across the table and touched Caroline's arm. "But I think I understand, though. Really. Look at the bright side, at least the president is getting his now. He's stepped on his own cock, hasn't he? The war's ending, and now he's going down too."

"Yeah, but it doesn't feel the way you thought it would, does it?" Caroline said. She pulled her hand out from under Berry's. "It just feels like everything has gone to shit."

They hitchhiked back to Hepatitis Hill. They didn't, in fact, speak of it again, nor incidentally did they speak of where "they" would be going next.

Caroline knew that she would have to leave soon. She knew that the FBI would get to the communes, and they already knew her alias probably. She would have to leave in the night, and go somewhere far away and change her name again. And when the FBI came, maybe Berry would talk or maybe she wouldn't. But Caroline would be long gone by then.

Caroline hid in the woods and headed for the highway as soon as she saw them. She kept some emergency money for just this instance. Because from the minute she spoke to Berry she knew it would happen, and sooner rather than later. She saw the men in their suits, the sedan. She did not know if Berry would tell them anything. Berry would either betray her or suffer. And Caroline would not stick around to find out. She walked with speed past trees and rocks and old broken fences. She bushwhacked until she found a road, and then she looked for a ride.

The day had begun the same as many other days. She woke up in the common house at dawn. She went outside to start laundry duty, which she liked. The morning was cold and clean—the air smelled sweet with burning wood. Already people were up and cooking. She grabbed a pile of towels to fold and sat on a stone in the early morning sun. She watched the camp come to life from a distance. She could see, through the tree branches and the red and yellow leaves, the women from the tech-nos coming down the hill in their wimples and robes like medieval nuns. They were theatrical in their reinvention. Reinvention as choice, as pride.

Watching them, Caroline realized her time was over. Before the feds showed up, before the sedan, she felt it in her bones. Living in the woods made you believe in intuition. She could never be a carefree reinventor. She lived more like a woman in a doomed affair. As days, then weeks and months eventually went by, the accumulation of time made things not deeper, or better, or safer, but more dangerous, more doomed. Eventually the day would come when consecutive events could not help but be traced, ruminated upon, dwelt upon, all leading to her, or to him. One weak link, from one weak moment. An overlooked detail, or a mistakenly trusted person—Mel, say, or Berry. All things led to her *because all things led to her*. The truth wanted to be told; this was the force of facts versus will and luck. Facts always win because they are simply always, and they will outlast everything.

She left because she didn't belong there. These women dreamt of utopia, but what else did they have to do? Caroline had lots of things to do: Run. Hide.

Dusk approached by the time she made it to the road that would eventually get her a hitch to the highways. She felt calm in her escape and didn't mind waiting for a ride, walking roadside. Another cloudless, cold fall day, the sun setting and throwing long shadows across groomed meadows, specific and detailed near tree trunks and telephone poles, and then stretched out to such abstraction that it took a minute to determine which shadow belonged to which object; the world divided into the bright—

sun-facing, gloriously illuminated in gold-brown light—and the shadowed—darkened and indefinite, as murky as the future, and as mysterious. She didn't get a ride for hours, and she walked through expanses of fields ending in two-block hamlets, the clusters of houses creating swathes of cold darkness across the roadside.

She hadn't seen them talk to Berry. She didn't see Berry point at her work station, tears in her eyes. In truth she didn't even see men in suits, or the dark, late-model sedan. She just felt it and didn't look back. She disappeared.

She hitchhiked west, and fourteen months after her invention, she would leave Caroline out on the road somewhere and think of another person to be. She was supposed to meet up with Bobby on New Year's Eve, in L.A. By then she would be someone new. *If you don't hear from me, we'll meet at the end of next year at the Blue Cantina in Venice Beach.* That gave her six weeks or so.

She stopped first in a small farming town in Pennsylvania. She lasted only a week at a rooming house. She stayed in bed for three days straight. The sheets were clean and pressed, but they scratched her skin and had an undersmell of detergent and mold. They seemed to hold dampness deep within them, and she couldn't rest. She couldn't find a job. She quickly approached broke. She even ate dinner at the church soup kitchen.

She forced herself back on the road, again hitching. Anywhere west. She thought she could work somewhere for a couple of weeks and get enough money for a bus to L.A.

She stuck to the highway and walked in the direction she was headed as she hitched. She had a system. She refused any rides with two men, or with men in pickups, or with men with pinwheel, Benzedrine eyes. It was getting dark, and she decided to accept a ride from a man in a beige Pontiac Le Mans. This seemed a good bet—he had a woman with him. Caroline sat in the back, and the three of them traveled in silence for many miles. She noted, discreetly, that the woman was far too young, really, to be his wife. But she also noted the man's clean, conservatively cut clothes. His pressed, collared shirt. His short, combed-back hair. She trusted getting a ride from a semi-establishment type. A regular middle-class guy who obeyed the law. The young girl, however, was not dressed neatly. She wore cutoff, tight, faded jeans. She sat with her feet up on the dashboard. The soles of her bare feet were black with dirt. She looked younger than Caroline. The girl wiggled in her seat and didn't speak. After a while, she took out rolling papers and began to deftly roll a joint. She wound it in her fingers and neatly licked it down. She pulled out the car lighter and lit up, all of which surprised Caroline. Then the girl passed it to him, and they shared the smoke. They didn't offer it to Caroline at first, then the girl gestured the joint toward her as she inhaled. Caroline shook her head no and looked out the window. There was a menace to the offer, a sort of chaos to the exchange, when the license of drugs was divorced from any familiar context. The joint had been appropriated by anyone, or by the mainstream, for baser, meaner purpose. Appropriated as another way to get fucked up and do what you want. Not liberation but mere licentiousness. Why not? Was there anything inherently groovy in a drug?

They continued for a few miles in silence. Caroline considered the possibility that she should escape, but then she shrugged it off. Everyone gave off freaky vibes toward her, she just needed to stay calm. She sat and waited until the man turned the car off the road to the shrub-concealed shoulder. He got out of the front seat, and the girl edged over to the driver's seat. All of this happened quickly and with no words uttered. The area was deserted, and before Caroline got herself together to run for the bushes and take her chances in the middle of nowhere, the girl pulled out into the road and the man with the short, neatly combed hair sat in the back with her. Caroline saw the girl glance in the rearview mirror at them: the slightly bored, lascivious look finally sent Caroline's adrenaline into her chest and limbs. The girl smirked a bit at Caroline's eye contact and hit the gas as the man reached for her in the backseat. Caroline pushed him away, but he just pushed her down on the seat. He was not smirking but serious as he pulled her T-shirt up and held it. She shrieked, and he covered her mouth with his forearm. He used his other hand to pin both her arms over her head and held both her wrists tightly with his hand. He didn't say a word, in fact he had a vacant calm about him. He took his other arm away from her mouth and moved it down to his pants. Caroline didn't scream but took advantage of the moment to push herself hard to get out from under his body. He brought the back of his hand up fast in a smack under her chin, jarring her head and neck. Her jaw felt fragile under the blow. She stopped moving. She watched him reach his hand down below his waist, his maneuvering and hitching out. She could taste her own blood where her teeth had hit her tongue. She felt him yank the elastic top of her skirt down and then pull it up. Her underwear was maybe ripped off or pushed aside. She couldn't tell. She didn't struggle and lay there at a distance from the moment; it happened, and she was as absent as she could be. She did think about not wanting to be beaten or killed. And would not think of him thrusting at her or feel him inside her. She could will that. She did think for a moment of the girl watching in the rearview mirror, and it made her gasp. Then she regained herself and willed herself immobile and totally withdrawn. It worked. It ended quickly after all. And in his disgust at the end, he pulled away from her with a shove but did not hurt her further. The girl pulled over, and they left her by the side of the road. The whole incident took less than fifteen minutes.

Almost instantly her feeling came back. She felt as achy as if she had been run over. She straightened out her clothes. Bruises would soon appear. Then she felt—and this was truly the worst of it—his mess ooze out of her, into what remained of her under-pants. She pushed with her muscles until she got it all out of her, then pulled her panties off, under her skirt, by the side of the road. She wiped herself as efficiently and discreetly as possible with the damp cotton. She felt a deep humiliation holding her underwear in her hand and not knowing what to do next. She shrugged her shoulder up and pushed her face against her short sleeve to wipe the tears out of her hot eyes. She discarded the soiled underpants by the side of the road. She no longer had her rucksack of clothes and few belongings. That was still in the car with them. She had thirty dollars in one of her shoes and that was it.

She sat for a while on a rock at the edge of the road. She stopped crying. Then she thought: *It never happened*. She would never speak of it, or let herself think of it, ever. She was quite certain that you could change your past, change the facts, by will alone. Only memory makes it real. So eliminate the memory. And if it was also true that there were occasions when she couldn't control where her mind went—a dream, a cold sweat at an unexpected moment, an odor that would suddenly betray her—time would improve it. Time lessens everything—the good things you desperately want to remember, and the awful things you need to forget. Eventually all will be equally faint. This was one thing her second life had taught her about how humans endure.

It was at this point—and not later, when the meeting with Bobby at their agreed-upon rendezvous point didn't happen—that she began to inhabit her new life as her only life.

Dead Infants

SHE MADE IT to a friendly, unhip, stranded desert town just over the border from Arizona. Nova, California, population three thousand. It was, despite the best efforts of fifty years of laissez-faire development, a pretty town. It sat on a mesa and looked at desert and mountains. She rented a room with a name she made up on the spot. She spent her last few dollars on hair dye—light brown to match her roots. Leaning close to the mirror, she put on several coats of mascara and some pink lipstick. She patted concealer over the bruise on her chin and finished with face powder that looked a shade too pale. She pulled her newly dyed hair up and piled it on the crown of her head. Then she pinned a wide headband in front of the piled hair.

She landed a waitress job in a diner the very first afternoon she looked. She felt a surge of confidence and safety. The counterculture didn't exist here. She could have her own hair color and she could have a "public" job. In the vast expanse of this country, who was she to stand out?

Every morning she got up at five. She went to the diner and got ready for the breakfast rush. It was over by eight thirty, and then they would have a long cigarette break and get ready for the lunch rush at eleven thirty. They were busy, which made the time pass quickly. At two she would be exhausted and nearly done with her work. Ready for another cigarette, a change of clothes, and then a beer or a Seven & Seven. The girls all drank Seven & Seven or Canadian Club and Coke.

The next day they would show up, laughing about hangovers and throat clearing behind their fists over cigarettes and coffee. They stacked scratched yellow molded-plastic glasses for water. They refilled ketchup bottles and saltshakers. The quarters and dimes added up to a surprising amount of money. She liked the midmorning coffee break: one lit cigarette after another, and endless cups of weak coffee from thick mugs with permanent stains in the bottoms. It took three packets of sugar and two containers of half-and-half for the coffee to taste of anything. They wiped old, sticky syrup from plastic dispensers with wet cotton rags. They swept the floor and sprayed Windex on the Formica counter (Formica is a decorative laminate made of paper and melamine resin—she couldn't help but hear Bobby's voice. But it pleased her that she remembered), then there was yet another cigarette break, and a round of cleaning plastic menus until they signed out at three. Sometimes in the heat of the rush they would move within inches of each other—reach and duck at the exact right moment without saying a word. She felt an adrenaline lift getting it done when five things needed to be done all at once. Being able to do this in the face of chaos gave her a tangible confidence she hadn't felt before. It was satisfying—a confidence that she wore in her hips.

She wasn't exactly like these women, it was true, but she was close enough.

These were not "liberated" women. They wore orange-toned

Pan-Cake makeup and push-up bras. They all watched their figures (and used that word, *figure*) and never wore anything but inexpensive, synthetic clothes. They didn't discuss the issue of vaginal versus clitoral orgasms or debate the inherent oppression of intercourse. But they spoke often of sex and men—all of them were divorced or supporting someone who cheated on them. They wore awful orange-tan stockings and took care of their kids by themselves. They smoked and drank and didn't mind their lives until they had one too many Seven & Sevens. Then they burst into tears at the prospect of forty more years of the same jobs and the same men, but with less pretty faces and more painful backs.

They weren't all that different from the consciousness-raising women or from her.

She liked it, and within days she felt she could pass for one of them. She was getting good at this, she really was. It was funny—she thought of it like that, but she *was* one of them. After all, who were they, exactly?

Anyone can start a new life, even in a small town. Everyone moves so much these days. You get a divorce, you move and start over. Try it. See how little people ask about you. See how little people listen. Or, more precisely, think about how little you really know about the people you know. Where they were born, for instance. Have you met their parents? Or siblings? There was a time, maybe, when just being new in a town made you seem suspect. Because you were suspect—people didn't have any way to verify you were who you said you were. And why did you have to leave where you came from? But there is a long history (seldom spoken of in the gloriously amnesiac everyday) in America, and in a democracy, of starting over. It was almost an imperative, wasn't it? America was founded, of course, by people who invented new lives, who wanted nothing more than to jettison the weight of all that history, all that burden and all that memory of Europe. That was one form of freedom. Freedom from memory and history and accounting. Even if an endless series of beginnings tended to reduce everything to shallow repetition and eliminate any possibility of profound experience, it certainly served her, at this moment, in this place.

New Year's Eve, 1973. She sat at the bar and waited for her friend Betsy to return from the bathroom. They had already drunk many cocktails and were probably going to go to a party with Betsy's boyfriend and his buddy. Or they would stay at the bar all night and listen to the bartender, Jack, in his early thirties and with the indifferent, slightly crawly sexiness of Bruce Dern, but with more muscles and less darkness. He doted on them but only ever spoke in a deadpan that the women found increasingly hysterical. He would do just as well as a party, and they would not have to worry about fresh drinks or melted ice at midnight.

It was true that she could have driven to L.A. She could have covered a few shifts at work, borrowed Betsy's car and been in Venice in five hours. It was also true that, despite her drinks and Jack's dry humor, she did think about whether Bobby had turned up at the designated place and was waiting for her right now. But she was pretty sure he wouldn't have shown. She could not bear going there, all that way, to be let down by him. She would rather sit here and still have the possibility that he might have shown rather than the certainty of disappointment. It was 1974, and she celebrated with her new friends and began the unthinking of it. She tried not to think about the dream she'd had the night before. She didn't believe in premonitions, of course, but she had started to feel uneasy. All the paranoia came back. Her ID here was not at all secure—she had been way too careless about that, again. And there, at the edges of the forced festivities of this night, among her new friends, she knew she would be leaving this place also—definitely and soon.

She told people she had to go back East and take care of her ailing mother. She had five hundred dollars saved, and by spring she finally reached the West Coast. She would get an airtight ID, and she would be safer in a big city. She moved randomly from place to place on the outskirts of L.A. These were the days of pale-beneath-the-tan partying, roller skates and halter tops. And harder, meaner drugs. It was as if someone had taken the aura of the counterculture and extracted every decent aspiration. What was left was the easy liberation of sex and drugs. Was this a function of Southern California, or was every place as weary as this now? Surely the sunshine and beach made the boardwalk a magnet for every marginal person in America. Southern California was full of off-the-grid illegals: draft dodgers, ex-cons, undocumented workers. It was exactly what she wanted. Here she could disappear into the everyday. She could stay far from the rads.

She drank beer and smoked pot all the time. She walked on the beach and had short relationships with men who lived off her.

Only one thing gave her purpose: she needed a new identity, not one made up but one that could be built on. It was a project. She scoured microfilm in the local libraries until she found a baby's obituary. She needed a person with a birth certificate who had never applied for a Social Security number. She needed a baby who had died in a different county from where she was born, so no cross-reference was made with the death certificate. (Bobby described this method as straight out of *Day of the Jackal,* and why not?) She could easily obtain a copy of the birth certificate, and from there she could get fake "unfake" and untraceable ID. She could get a real Social Security number, a real driver's license and even a real passport. She methodically built her documents. That was her main achievement of those L.A. years: a safe, airtight identity. She became the dead infant Louise Barrot.

Louise, I am Louise. It felt different taking someone else's name instead of making one up. It was a deeper, meaner lie, somehow. The morbid origin of the name did affect her. Sometimes, though she knew this wasn't what she should be thinking about, she thought of the baby Louise. She thought of the parents watching their baby in the hospital as she struggled to breathe, of her tiny, froggy legs and purple, balled fists. She even kept a copy of the infant's obituary.

It took a year to build her new identity and assemble all the paperwork. After that, she had less to occupy her. One year turned into four. She cooked at a cafe in Marina del Rey. She rented a small apartment near the pier in Santa Monica. On her days off, Louise walked along the boardwalk or down Fourth Street. Some days she actually forgot where she was headed but kept walking anyway. On one occasion a man coming from the opposite direction walked straight into her. He didn't stop but kept walking. His nonreaction to their collision bewildered her. She stood there, unmoving, staring at his back as he walked away. And then, maybe a week later, the same thing happened again. A woman walked toward her on the sidewalk in front of Ralphs supermarket. She had the sort of unseeing stare that people wear in public. She didn't sidestep when she got to Louise but walked into her, smacking her shoulder. Again, the woman didn't stop walking or say anything to her. She kept going. This time Louise felt less disturbed. She almost laughed instead. Louise thought, It's finally happened. I'm invisible.

She went on this way. Not visible really. A vapor.

If you don't read the paper, time doesn't move forward.

But she could see it in her hands—veins more visible beneath the skin—time passed. She didn't read the news, but she kept the TV on all the time.

Raid. Kills bugs dead.
Aim. Fights cavities.
Oxydol. A better clean.

Then she met August. With his heavy, handsome face and very long black hair, which he kept pulled back in a tidy ponytail. He smelled slightly of coconut (which she later realized was suntan lotion) and strongly of tobacco. He bought her drinks and spoke to her in measured, soft tones. Gentle even. She didn't mind his attention at all; in fact, what she felt was overwhelming gratitude. Who was she but a "speck in the cosmos"?

August kept a clean apartment. He owned a nice stereo and a new, large TV. He didn't seem to care one way or another about who was president. He wanted her around all the time. She settled into cooking for him and the daily repetitions of an ordinary life. Laundry. Cleaning. Shopping. Why shouldn't she enjoy being taken care of a little? The character of those first years as Louise was a swift and steady decrease in possibilities. But wasn't that true of everyone? As time went by, wasn't every life a kind of narrowing, a steady relinquishing of possibilities?

PART SIX

Spring 1999

Ordnance

NASH FOUND Henry by the Incendiary Devices section of the Tactics bookshelf. He stood there until Henry looked up. Nash pulled Henry's hand away until he could see the pamphlet Henry was reading. It was an ecoterrorist broadside titled "Using Explosives to Eliminate and Discourage Outdoor Advertising." Nash grabbed it out of his hand.

"Can I have a word?"

"Of course," Henry said. He followed Nash toward the back office, which was really just a large closet filled with books, invoices and catalogs. Henry sat on the only chair, and Nash leaned on the desk.

"I'll get right to it. I don't think climbing buildings in the middle of the night is such a great idea, you know?"

"Neither do I," Henry said.

Nash smiled and folded his arms across his chest. "I know you've been destroying those billboards."

"But those boards are ads for Nepenthex, which is made by Pherotek—"

"Yeah, I know. I figured that out, finally. They are part of Allegecom, which is the same company that put dioxin in everything from PVC pipes to Agent Orange."

"That put dioxin in Agent Orange and kept it in for years even when they knew it affected humans. Even when they could have made it without dioxin, like Agent Blue. And these bastards also made various incendiary munitions, as I'm sure you are aware."

"Naturally. A lot of companies made munitions."

"Antipersonnel ordnance—"

"Yep. Designed to destroy humans and keep property intact. Check."

"But these guys"—Henry's voice got quite loud at this point—"they make the antidepressant that was prescribed for me specifically for the depression I have due to dioxin and combat trauma. It was actually designed to treat combat stress trauma, which they caused in the first place."

Nash laughed, shaking his head.

"That would be very ironic, Henry, except for one thing: you were never exposed to Agent Orange or combat of any kind. Furthermore, and perhaps what's even more important, no one knows why you are tearing down billboards. It is an illegible act. It changes nothing. And whatever else you are contemplating—"

"That corporate entity and its billboards are morally bankrupt," Henry said. "That billboard is pornographic and offends decency."

There was a knock. Sissy called from outside the door.

"Nash? There is no one watching the store."

"Where's Roland?"

"He's gone."

"I'll be right out. Christ." Nash put his hand on Henry's arm.

"I'm not unsympathetic, you know. I've no problem with property destruction per se. There is nothing sacred about property, particularly this sort. And although I think it would be nice, I also don't think the gesture has to mean anything to anyone but you, or that it has to change anything for it to be worth doing."

"You noticed, though, didn't you? And they noticed. They had to replace their ad, didn't they? Twice now." Henry smiled.

"But it is dangerous," Nash said. "And not just because you are an old, sick guy who shouldn't be rappelling down buildings in the middle of the night. There is the possibility that destroying something changes you in unexpected ways. It's channeling your worst dark self. It can inspire a wanton side, it can thrill and titillate. How can I put this? I think it's cruddy for the soul. I think it makes you into a dick."

Nash moved to the door. Henry put out his arm and stopped him.

"But I feel better. It makes the symptoms abate."

"What do you mean?"

"I was exposed, in effect, or I am exposed, by whatever means. And I do take their pills. It is my irony and my insult. And when I destroy their signs—with a fierce but just heart, I swear—I feel better. I can actually have peaceful sleep."

"Just don't get carried away," Nash said. "You've made your point."

"It's about my dignity."

"Gotcha."

"I feel restored by it."

"But maybe . . ." Nash spoke while leaving the room. Henry followed him.

"Maybe what?" Henry said.

"Maybe it is the night ops on the billboard. Maybe you are right. Or maybe it's their antidepressant that is making you feel better. Maybe it's the Nepenthex."

Jason's Journal

HER WHOLE life has become suspect. Not just the fact that she admitted to being in California dive bars with dissipated rock stars. Or her evasions about her life pre-1980s. No relatives, no friends, no mention of anything. But that's not all—there are other issues once you start thinking on it. Once you have it in your head that someone close to you is hiding something, everything is suspect.

For example:

Last night she said something that struck me as odd. She and I were watching the news together. I got bored and went to my room. I scratched out a school essay in about thirty minutes. It's all so easy, it is just a joke. Then I went online to the Cabin Essence site, which is where I find my bootlegs. I was deep in conversation with a guy in Alabama who posted a bunch of stuff about a tape of the complete "Good Vibrations" sessions (which seems to me a song of such oddness and complexity that I could spend months parsing it and unpacking it) when I heard a knock at the door. I knew it was my mother, and I shouted at her but she couldn't hear me because I was playing the music loud. I lowered it and hollered "What?" in an exasperated tone. She didn't answer but knocked again. I got up and opened the door. She stood there with a pale, slight smile, clutching her sweater sleeves, which are always too long so she plays with them, half-burying her hands in them. It occurs to me she does this deliberately to emphasize how petite, how tiny, how frail she is. As if she can't buy sweaters in the proper size.

"Yeah?" I said with exaggerated inflection. I did not want to encourage her.

"Jason."

"What is it, Mom? I'm doing a paper for class." She nodded and then looked around my room a bit. She doesn't get to come in very often. I keep it clean, and she stays out, at least I think she does. I turned the music way down. I didn't want to spark any recovered memories about her glorious old days hanging out with Dennis Wilson.

"What is it about?"

"What?"

"Your paper for class."

I shrugged. I didn't know where this was going. I don't have much patience for her these days. I want her to stay out of my way, ask no questions. She doesn't understand that this is just the way it goes for mothers and sons in these years. It's not her, it is just the not-her of her that I want, I want nothing from her except for her not to ask me things or stand in my doorway with a pale, sad look on her face, clutching at her sweater sleeves.

"Don't you have a class tonight?" I said. She teaches her adult cooking classes. She tutors illiterate adults. She mentors under-privileged children. It is not like she has nothing to do but talk to me. She nodded.

"I made you some dinner, it's in the fridge." She just stood there. I gave up.

"It's about Alger Hiss, HUAC, that stuff."

"That's great," she said. "That's very interesting."

Oh, Christ, I shouldn't have said anything, but she wanted something, and I just didn't have the heart to say nothing. Now she was going to want more.

"So what do you think?" she said.

"About what?" I asked.

"Did he do it?"

"Did Hiss do it?" I said.

She nodded.

"Of course Hiss did it. No one disputes that anymore."

"It's generally known, you're saying."

"He did it all right."

"Well, thank God that's cleared up. All this time I've been wondering." She said this earnestly, and there was a pause, and then she began to laugh. And I laughed. Which was surprising. She finally turned to leave. Then she stopped and looked back at me.

"Why, though?"

"Why what?" I asked.

"Why would Hiss do it?"

"Who knows? He certainly didn't make any money from it. I guess because he believed it was the right thing to do."

"So why are you writing about the Hiss case, it being generally known and all?" She was quite serious again, not laughing. I looked at her, and I don't know why I said this, but I did.

"I'm curious about him. The fact that he spied isn't so remarkable. Or even that he was in a position to lose so much privilege. I find that sort of admirable if misguided. What I find amazing is how he lied his entire life. How well he lied. If it wasn't for the facts, it would be quite convincing. How does a person manage to not crack his entire life? Not even on his deathbed?"

She stood there, and she looked right at me, an open-eyed look.

"I mean if something is worth doing, shouldn't you admit doing it? Shouldn't you take responsibility for your actions?"

She looked a bit startled. "Maybe other people would suffer if he confessed it," she said.

"Maybe. Or maybe he regretted it."

"That's very possible."

"Or maybe he was a coward," I said.

And then it passed, she was backing up a bit, then moving down the hall.

"I made some chicken quesadillas. You just have to heat them up."

"That's great, thanks."

She turned away. But I stayed in my doorway a moment more.

"I wonder, you know, about whether his wife knew the truth. Or his friends."

She stopped again and looked at me. "And what conclusion have you come to?" she asked.

"No one knew the truth. He didn't even know anymore, maybe. To live that long with it, you must have to convince yourself it never really happened. Don't you think?"

She shook her head and shrugged. She looked weary and old and far away. "I don't know," she finally said. We were weirdly awkward, not our usual awkward. She said, "You're a bright kid, aren't you?"

My mother is a stranger. And she is strange. I am not sure at all what she thinks or feels about anything. And it's funny because she should be wondering about me, not the other way around. I should be thinking about rock-and-roll and girls and drugs. Not why she gets so fuzzy and confused sometimes.

I retreated to Gage's house. He was on some kind of one-night George Clinton–Funkadelic kick. Which meant we had to listen also to P-Funk All Stars and Parliament, and every tributary that leads to and from these bands. What other albums they were session musicians on, what songs of theirs were covered by other people. He put on *Maggot Brain* from 1971, an admittedly awesome album. The cover alone—an Afroed black-power chick screaming and buried up to her neck in sand. And smokin' psychedelic funk, very heavy and druggy sounding, with a swell of flange and fuzz at the edges. It had a creepy menace about it still, particularly a drop-dead sad and lovely extended guitar solo on the first song. Gage naturally whipped out a joint. I can't smoke, it doesn't make me feel good. It makes me confused and overly deliberate. But I smoked anyhow, and the music became claustrophobic and frightening.

"You know what this music sounds like?" Gage said.

"What?"

"It sounds like his mother just died."

I looked sideways at Gage. What did he mean by that? What was his point? The wail of guitar got longer, more extended and further from the melody. Did it go on forever? Could it please just return? It was all too dark for me, so I begged off and went back to my place to listen to *Pet Sounds* (the original mono version on vinyl). I put on the old-fashioned headphones with the oversized foam-filled ear cushions and lay on the floor. And I let the Beach Boys' choir voices wash under and over me until I was in a gloriously unfractured universe of exquisite, naïve beauty.

Sometimes I think I am in love with my own youth. I do not want to go forward, I always want to be carelessly lost in this music. I never want to get sick of it, and I never, ever, want to outgrow this or anything. I certainly don't need to know anything more about her.

La Chinoise

NASH HADN'T seen Miranda in several months. He had heard rumors that Miranda was moving east with Josh, or had already moved east. She finally resurfaced for a meeting of the Last Wave Cinema Collective, one of Prairie Fire's underground art and ecto-provo groups. Nash didn't organize the group, but he let the participants show their films and collect what they could at the door. The unfortunate thing, in Nash's view, was how lousy most of the work ended up being, how boring: painfully didactic and too often satiric in the most shallow way— just the sort of satire that reinforced oppressive American cultural hegemony rather than challenging it. Nash figured bad films, particularly bad attempts at political or subversive statements, were so unappealing they were not just sad and depressing but counter-revolutionary, reactionary, practically on the payroll of status quo America. He gave no—absolutely no—credit for "heart in right place" or "attempting with limited resources." He felt insulted by lousy films.

But tonight Nash found himself doubly irritated and unable to resist glancing over at Josh sitting there next to Miranda. The lights were lowered, and someone showed a video of two G.I. Joe dolls, one dressed like Saddam Hussein, the other, Michael Jackson. It was a nonstarter, a stoner's idea of social critique. Afterward, the "filmmaker" held a forum.

"So, any comments? Obviously, this is just a rough cut. We are going to get ten minutes together, then hit the festivals, get some backers to put up money for digital animation, Avid, Pro-Tools and Flash formatting." He wore wire-framed, narrow oval glasses low on the bridge of his nose and his black hair long and spiked straight up in sticky, unmoving finger pulls. A tattoo of an overwrought ivy strand riddled with viciously drawn thorns started at his neck, disappeared under his shirt until it reached his forearm, then wound painfully to encircle the delicate bones of his wrist. It looked as if a killer plant had crawled under his clothes and was stealing around his limbs to strangle and devour him. Nash found the tattoo distracting, and he couldn't really even look at the kid after a time.

"I think that doll stuff is played out. I remember seeing Barbie doll reenactments of historical events back in the early '90s," said Sissy, looking very sober with two neat, tight braids and precision-cut bangs. Oversized vintage aviator-shaped glasses overwhelmed her face and would have evoked low-budget porn movies if the lenses had a sunset tint, but since they were clear glass and obviously prescription, they seemed more like something a middle-aged serial killer would wear. Nash realized this was precisely the look she was trying to achieve, and he couldn't help taking some pride in the fact that he could "get" it. Because most of the kids recognized her as a writer for the more underground of the local weekly magazines, when she spoke they regarded her as an absolute authority. Of course she only had a music column, but still, she was attached to the media, so everyone treated her as if she might bestow some instant fame on any one of them. There was nothing these kids respected like media connections.

"The copyright infringement stuff with Mattel or Hasbro that inevitably happens with any Barbie or G.I. Joe reference is also sort of pointless. No one is going to let you show the thing publicly, but you can naturally put the cease-and-desist letter in your press packet and try to get some cred that way, I suppose. But it has to get a lot of notoriety to overcome the fact that it won't really be seen."

Josh raised his hand.

"Actually, have any of you heard of the '60s filmmaker Bobby Desoto?" he said. "Desoto made a series of films from 1968 to 1972. Many are on Super Eight, and some of them use dolls, or clay figures, in hand-done stop-action. They look amazing: beautiful in their own right, with that Lotte Reiniger sort of primitive-intricate animation, pinhole lighting and paper effects, but also with these very funny absurd political voice-overs, like *La Chinoise,* Godard's film with the speeches about the Vietcong recited in flat, singsong tones by French beauties in miniskirts. Where the tone is such that you are never sure if the extreme didacticism is being satirized or espoused. It is both. Mix Godard with Gumby and Georges Méliès, that's what Desoto's films are like." Josh smiled at the group of perplexed but nonchalant cineastes staring at him.

"Desoto clearly was way ahead on all of this. Including copyright stuff. He made several films out of other films and news clips. He looped and sampled found clips, juxtaposed things for various effects. A prankster, as well. He also did some straightforward documentary stuff, not nearly as successful as the other things. He even got Jean-Pierre Léaud to narrate one of them, half in French and half in highly accented, rough English."

"Are his films available on video?" a girl asked.

"No, but there is this sort of neo-Luddite group, the Format-ters?" Some of the people nodded. "They are all about retro for-matting. They preserve and disseminate stuff in its original format, like eight-millimeter, Super Eight or sixteen-millimeter film. Vinyl records, eight-track tapes, even laser discs. As long as it is obsolete, it's included. No digital remastering or video trans-ferring. You can also buy projectors from them. Anyway, they deal largely in bootleg stuff, so it is semi-illegal. All the Desoto stuff is bootlegged."

"So the artist doesn't get any money for it?" asked Miranda.

"Well, Desoto, as it happens, was involved in some terror-ism, bombings related to weapons manufacturers, I think, toward the end of the Vietnam War, and he went underground. He is still a fugitive. So there is no way for him to get any money."

Nash glanced in Josh's direction, and then he raised his right hand with his index finger and middle finger together and extended. A reluctant gesture. Josh nodded at him.

"So, how did you find this neo-Luddite bootlegger group?" Nash asked.

"On their website," Josh said and then smiled widely at Nash.

"Naturally," Nash said, "on their neo-Luddite website."

"There are actually quite a few of those. They are finally not really antitech. They are kind of tech fetishists in a way. When you think about it."

"The Formatters, huh?"

"Desoto was a genius."

Nash shrugged. "Sounds to me like they just value whatever is obscure and difficult to access. Obscuristas. Seems elitist."

After the group meeting was over and everyone had left, Miranda reappeared, either not having left at all or returning. Nash did the inventory. This meant a clipboard and a title count of all the books on the shelves. It meant counting all the backup books in boxes. It also meant reshelving the books the kids put in the wrong place. He did this once a month, working all night. He liked it, usually—concentrating but not thinking. Making order. He listened to his music—Thelonious Monk tonight. Miranda watched him work until he finally paused.

"I've missed having you around," he said.

"I've been in New York. I'm moving there, actually."

"I heard about that. Great. That's great."

They both nodded at each other. Coleman Hawkins blew down the last verse of "Ruby, My Dear."

"Can I help you do inventory?" she asked.

Nash shook his head.

"Can I hang out for a while?"

"Of course."

She watched him mark his clipboard. After ten minutes or so, she took out one of her hash-laced cigarettes and lit up.

"Smoking in the store?" he said. She just laughed and inhaled, holding the smoke in her lungs. She held the joint out to him. He walked over and took it from her.

"You still bite your nails," he said. He took a drag. She sat down on the floor and crossed her legs.

"I should put that nasty nail polish on, the stuff that tastes awful, so I won't bite them." She pulled him next to her. He sat on the floor and took another drag.

The hash made the music expand and deepen around them. Nash found the intensity almost unbearable. The music wasn't meant to be background.

"Are you upset about something?" she said.

He handed her what remained of the hash cigarette.

"I'm moving with that guy, Josh. He went to my high school, you know."

"I'm not—"

"I don't mean you are upset about me and Josh, I just meant you seemed upset about something—"

"I didn't know you went to high school together."

"—and then I said that about me and Josh next because it was on my mind."

There was a long, piano-filled pause between them. Nash laughed, nervously. He stood up. "I have to finish inventory. Unfortunately, my concentration is so fragile I can't talk and count. And with the hash, I may yet drool all over the books."

Miranda nodded but didn't move or get up to leave.

"And that crap cinema pseudo meta-provo group has got to go," he said, mostly to himself and his clipboard.

"I thought they were ecto-provo."

"That has no meaning, you realize that, don't you? Still, that's probably the best thing about them," Nash said.

"You don't like Josh, do you?" she said.

"He is a very bright guy. A little overenamored of his finely calibrated sensibility perhaps, and maybe also contrary for its own sake, and definitely more cynical than he could possibly have the right to be. But, all in all a sharp kid."

"You don't like him."

Nash smiled at her as he marked something on his clipboard.

"We are moving to New York for a project Josh is working on. Top secret. I think it will be cool."

She started to say more, but as Nash began silently mouthing his count, she stopped herself.

"No, I don't like Josh," he said, but she probably didn't hear, because she was already out the door. After he realized Miranda was gone, Nash sat for a minute. He leaned back and lay on the bench by the bookshelves. He closed his eyes and listened to the music.

PART SEVEN

1982–1999

Rules of Engagement

IT WASN'T THAT she no longer loved Augie. She felt increasing affection for him. It wasn't that she found him repellent in any way. Objectively she would watch him from across the room when he went to get another beer from the bar. He was pleasing in a gentle-bear way. Nice muscles covered by an easygoing layer of soft fat. No edges, no offenses. But somehow the initial excitement of sleeping with him left with no warning. It didn't wane or dwindle. It just disappeared for her altogether.

She liked him, his hair, his large eyes, his bumped-up hands, his open face. She thought he smelled just fine—not at all bad. Sometimes she noticed his breath, but not too often. That was not it. There was nothing specific in his person that offended her or put her off. Everything was fine, even pleasing. So why then did she suddenly have no desire for him? He still desired her. He wanted lots of sex, and she complied as much as she could. But sometimes he took so long, and her generosity would fray. She would catch herself thinking, Come on. And he would nearly come but not quite. He'd want to switch positions. And the thing of it was Louise knew she could never betray her impatience. She couldn't say "hurry up" because that didn't help at all. No, the best thing was to feign enthusiasm, to act as turned on and enthusiastic as possible to peak his desire and make him come. But it was a fine line: if she feigned too much enthusiasm, he might try to hold back longer, to prolong her enjoyment. Often she flicked her tongue at his ear suddenly, or whispered a hushed cliché to him at a crucial moment. She knew to stroke his back but not in too distracting a way. It wasn't that she minded his being inside her, but the artifice and the effort required, that was tough. He relaxed after and looked at her in adoration. He didn't know, did he? She was ashamed and terrified to think that he might know. But maybe he didn't. She had become so good at arousing him, at the micro-modulations that worked his desire. She had paid attention, it was true, but just not for the reasons he believed.

Would it be better to be honest? He used to try, quite often, to get her to come. He was not bad at it. He would slip down beneath the sheets and stay there until it was done. He seemed to enjoy himself—perhaps feigning for the same reasons she did, perhaps not. She didn't fake orgasms. No reason to. When he used his mouth she could have them quite easily. Sometimes so intense and shaky that she couldn't believe they came from within her. But it still didn't matter. She also did this for him. She didn't really care if she had the orgasm. She would just as soon have gone to sleep. Because in a way an orgasm is mostly a physical thing, which doesn't necessarily have to do with desire. Desire was more complex: a desperation and a need you felt before, an imagining and then a realizing during. It required mind and body. Her body was just fine. Her imagination—well, it failed her most of the time.

She wondered if she felt this way because she still longed for

Bobby. Because she still, after all these years, remembered his smell, his taste, his touch. Mostly she remembered wanting him deeply. She could also still remember when she had wanted Augie badly. But her desire for Bobby continued, that was the difference. And there was the question: Did she still want Bobby because things didn't have time to dwindle and disappear the way they did with Augie? Or was it just different, did she just love Bobby more? If she'd met Augie first, would she pine for him? It occurred to her that her shutdown, her unfeeling state, could not last indefinitely. He would catch on, or she would grow too impatient, and it would be over.

Sometimes when she lay on her bed, she considered that there was no longer any point in not giving herself up. She knew she could dwindle only so long and then she would turn herself in after she had made the freedom part of her life as lifeless as any incarceration could possibly be. "There's no escape." Yes, but not for the reasons you might think.

When August reached for her, she would order herself to think of her early times with him. The rainy afternoon she visited him at his job site, a large country house. He took her hand and led her into the woods behind the building. Despite the rain, they leaned against a tree, kissing and pulling at clothes. He yanked and adjusted her and then she was on him, both of them clothed and aching for it. She could remember all these moments in her head; she could not remember them in her body. She could not get them to live in her skin, between her legs and then to a shivery platform of interior nerves, forcing the tiniest of anticipatory contractions, the floor of her muscles already quivering. She could not conjure that.

She knew she should change her life. She felt herself to be in such a diminished, subtracted state. It even occurred to her that it might be the name itself—Louise Barrot. She believed taking the name of a dead infant had colored all her possibilities, tinted everything with morbidity. She knew also that the dead infant took on more significance for other reasons. Her underground status had convoluted all context—the fact that she could change her identity so completely changed the very possibility of engagement, or precluded the possibility of real engagement. She regarded everything and everyone from a distance, both ephemeral and abstract.

After a few months of dustiness that progressed into a low-grade disgust for her life with Augie, he began to speak to her about their future with great specificity. Amazingly, Augie had developed a real attachment to her. But it just made her feel trapped, circumscribed, desperate. People with real freedom never do really "free" things, like reinvent themselves, leave lives behind, change everything. Only trapped, desperate people did that. It took such coldness and will. She thought of it constantly. Rephrased it to see if she could find some comfort in it. Not *go to jail*. But *surrender*. *Resurface*. That sounded good, as though she had been drowning underground. She could *yield, retire, repent*.

She could see her family again. But she would have to go to trial. She would have to convince them she was innocent, which she wasn't. Repentant? Perhaps. Regretful? Definitely. Or she could make a speech, say she wasn't sorry, say she'd do it again if she had her life to live over. And then she would certainly go to jail for a long time. Especially if she didn't give any information about the others, which of course she could never, ever do.

But could she even take a stand? Because the truth of it was she wasn't sure of the tactics they had chosen, or of the consequences. There wasn't moral clarity. The truth was she even doubted the intentions, the motivations. This was tragic, a great, terrible tragedy, to do something so clearly full of consequence, so irreparable, and then to have such foundational doubt.

She would stare at the rain outside their bedroom window and recite the narrative of what had happened. She considered, as accurately as she could bear, what exactly she, or they, had done and why.

Bobby had taken convincing, hadn't he? He wanted to make his movies and leave it at that. He was frightened of action. And she convinced him. It was mostly her, wasn't it?

Bobby had shown the group the latest of his "protest" films. These were meant to be polemical propaganda pieces. Credited to the SAFE collective, the film really was made solely by Bobby. They sat on the floor, four of them, in the dark, as he ran the projector.

The glare of the sun on the street in unforgiving Kodacolor. An old man leaves his house. He walks to his car. Cut to the same old man walking on the street. He squints at the sun. He is unaware of being filmed. He is outside a monolithic International-style building. He enters, and the door closes behind him. We see again, the same thing, in excruciating real time, the old man walk to his car. We see him leave in the morning, squint in the sun. The camera is stalking him. The third time through the filmmaker appears, or a man one supposes is the filmmaker. He approaches the old man with a hand mike.

"Excuse me, Dr. Fieser?"

The old man looks at him and scowls. He shakes his head.

"Can I ask you a question?"

The old man speeds up.

"Why would you invent napalm? Why?"

The old man stops and turns to the filmmaker. He stares at the microphone and then speaks.

"I am a scientist. I solve problems. I don't ask what use they are put to. That is not my job. That is the politician's job."

"What domestic use did you imagine jellied gasoline could possibly have?"

"I am not responsible. Leave me alone." The man stumbles and

tries to escape into his house. *The camera follows, and you can see his face as the filmmaker shouts at him from off camera.*

"Pauling refused to make the bomb."

The old man is trying the door to his house. He is fumbling the keys. Still, the filmmaker is talking.

"Do you think the employees of the Topf Corporation in Wiesbaden in Germany during the war should have asked why they needed to develop hydrocyanic acid in increasingly large quantities? Should they have betrayed any curiosity about why their employer was building larger and larger crematoriums for the government? Do you think these Germans had an obligation to ask, What for?"

The filmmaker follows the old man in close-up and is upon him at his door. He thrusts a Life *magazine in his face. It has the famous photo of a girl running. She is naked and in agony. Napalm is searing her skin.*

The old man glances at the photo. "Yes, I've seen that picture. It is terrible."

The old man glances down at his retrieved keys in his hands and pauses. Finally he looks up at the camera. The camera stays on his face for several minutes. It is a weary, defeated face. He doesn't respond but turns at last back to the keys, unlocks the door and enters his house.

The film shows various ordinary details of the house: The wreath surrounding the door knocker. The woven welcome mat. The glow encased in a rectangle of plastic for the doorbell. The neatly trimmed lawn that edges several flower beds. The oval slates making a footpath. Some garden gloves. Then the film ends.

There was a brief pause as the film click-clicked until the projector was rethreaded and the film rewound. Their friend Will spoke.

"You make us pity him."

Bobby turned off the projector and flipped the lights back on. He shrugged.

"He looks haunted, pathetic, old," Mary said.

"He is haunted, pathetic, old."

"But he bears responsibility for atrocities, and he won't admit it. He doesn't even desire our sympathy. You hold the camera on him. You dwell on his shakiness. You let his humanity play on us," Mary said.

"Yeah, you seem like a tiresome asshole, a bully, and he seems like a victim," Will said.

"That's the truth. I showed the truth. The truth is complicated. More complicated than we would like," Bobby said.

"But are you creating a polemic, a tool, or are you on some ego-artist trip?" Will said.

"Your film makes things complicated, and that doesn't inspire action, that inspires despair," Mary said. "Besides, who says that's the truth? That's sentimentality. If he is blameless, then who do we assign blame to? Aren't all individuals human? Can't you portray Nixon and Kissinger as lonely, misguided men leading lives underwritten by existential desperation? Is that what the world needs right now? Empathy for all the powerful, careless old men?" Mary became angry as she spoke.

"I see your point," Bobby said.

Later, by themselves, he brought it up. "I feel outrage. I feel anger. But I am undone by sadness. When I am behind the camera, I feel a desire to understand and empathize. To undercut my own points. The truth is, that's when it becomes interesting."

Mary nodded, but she didn't really listen. She was waiting for her chance to speak.

"You have to decide," she said. "You are describing the pursuit of art. Maybe it is a way to make you feel more comfortable in the world. Maybe it is beauty, or even integrity. But meanwhile that is a privilege. A privilege we enjoy at what cost? People are dying and can't afford that kind of empathy for all sides. Do you think the warmongers and fascists and corporate munitions suppliers waste time feeling empathy? Do they second-guess themselves?"

Bobby leaned back and put his head on her lap. He looked up at her as she continued.

"The question is, do we want to leave action to the brutes of the world? This is the moment to decide. There are some inherent problems built into acting. It lacks perfection. But I believe we must fight back, or we will feel shame all our lives. We, the privileged, are more obligated. It is a moral duty to do something, however imperfect."

She stopped. She put her hand in his hair.

"If we don't do something, all our lives we will feel regret."

Two days later, just as she began to relent, Bobby came to her with a plan. And the home and second-home addresses of all the board members from all the relevant corps: Dow Chemical, Monsanto, General Dynamics, Westinghouse, Raytheon, DuPont, Honeywell, IBM and Valence Chemical. He carefully worked out the timing, the execution, the communiqués to the press.

But now Mary developed doubts. She started to wonder if he had been right in the first place, that denying the complexity of the world made you as bad as they are. Even if you do act, you may be guilty of the wrong motive—vanity, or self-righteousness. Or maybe you will pick the wrong tactic. Perhaps your analysis was incorrect. You could be making things worse, more polarized. And finally, maybe they shouldn't relinquish their purchase on the humanity of everyone. Maybe that was the very moral line that saved them from becoming the people they despised and judged. She could argue it either way, with equal conviction. But there was no point in discussing it again. She knew he wasn't looking back. He was now a force in motion. She watched as everything came together. And then she helped everything come together. This was the power of a couple—their doubts occurred at different times and canceled each other out, making them much more fearless as a pair than they would ever be on their own. And that's how a life changes—it could go either way, and then it just goes one way.

A week after Louise had decided to turn herself in and six months after she had abruptly lost her desire for Augie, she discovered she was pregnant.

Revolutionary Acts

THEY BOUGHT a house in deepest middle-class suburbia.
It was a split-level. On a cul-de-sac. In a development with other
very similar houses. The streets were clean and empty. The house
had lots of room, and nothing was broken. It was a clean, safe
place. When Louise opened the front door and picked up the
paper, she could've been in any state from California to Connecticut. As it happened, August had moved them to Washington State
just before the birth. Louise remembered at last feeling a distance
from smudgy mimeographed broadsides, leaky faucets, and windows that didn't stay open unless you propped sticks under them.
She lived in skylighted, pachysandra-edged comfort, and she was
nine months pregnant.

Her thin body stayed thin, but her belly grew and stretched .
beyond her wildest imaginings. She felt passive beneath it—that
taut belly led, and she followed. This was the most specific her
body had ever felt. She didn't feel peaceful or beatific. Nothing
as typical as that. She felt her life further reduced to maneuvers

and negotiation. Very concrete, physical challenges. Getting out of bed sideways. Bending at the knees to put something in the garbage compactor. This precise body ordered her thoughts. I have to pee. I have to move my leg because it hurts. I have to eat.

And it prescribed what she couldn't do: She couldn't get drunk and find some random person to sleep with. She couldn't run away and change her name and therefore her life—she would still be a nine-months-pregnant woman wherever she went and whatever her name was. And she couldn't stop it—the barreling of her life toward this new life. So each day she made herself toast and eggs. Each day she watched the TV. She cleaned the house and looked at catalogs. She paid the bills and cooked dinner. When Augie came home, she traded foot rubs with him. She fed him the dinner she had cooked. And she washed dishes, occasionally stopping to prop a hand against her middle back. Augie would ask if he could help her, and she would stoically reply no.

In the final weeks before the birth, she enjoyed cooking and freezing as much food as possible. This was maybe a typical pregnant woman thing to do: prepare for the days ahead with reheatable casseroles and lasagnas. Louise applied a slightly inappropriate energy to these cooking endeavors. Augie bought a freestanding Sub-Zero freezer for her, and she overwhelmed it with individually wrapped and marked meals. Either a baby or a nuclear winter was coming—in either case, they would not starve. The frenzied cooking of those last few weeks was the most satisfying time of her life so far. It had a twisted optimism. It included a future, which was something she hadn't seen before. Louise abandoned all thoughts of turning herself in. She had to be who she was for quite a while. She at last had no choice. The baby anchored her, finally, in her world. When she gave birth to Jason, she finally found something she believed time would not ever betray or dwindle. The feeling she had for her son was sentimental, it was frightening, it was unimpeachable. It was self-negating and beyond love. It was an ungentle feeling, this baby love.

Jason was a demanding child. Before him, the most profound feeling she had had was an all-points loneliness. This loneliness was so profound as to be almost abstract: she felt distance from her distance. There was nothing abstract in Jason's need for her. It was desperate and constant and loud.

Louise had felt—for so long—hopelessly different from everyone else. She realized that her despair came from not being truly known by anyone. She understood the animal need to be recognized, to be familiar to others. Her anonymity was what colored her unhappiness, and it only worsened over time. The fear abated, the paranoia, the nightmares. Even the violence, the act, the failure—all of these faded with time. But her loneliness, the crucial difficulty of her underground life, had grown ever deeper and colder—inescapable.

So was it any surprise that the event that changed her life was Jason? Here was a creature to love and look after in some authentic, permanent way. More than that, he was her obligation. If she turned herself in, who would take care of Jason? Could she abandon him when clearly he required her specific looking after? It was her body that fed him, and her voice that soothed him. Having Jason was either the best thing she ever did or the most selfish. It was certainly the second act in a life that had been entirely circumscribed by her first act, with all the same complications of being both selfless and selfish. Both.

She discovered a whole new set of fears. She watched him breathe at night in his crib. She wondered if his breath would stop as randomly and mysteriously as it seemed to have started. She feared his fragility. She feared losing him. But she recognized these feelings as what any mother felt anywhere. Any one of us could have bad luck. Any one of us could lose a baby. No mother could be truly secure or certain. We could all get sick and die. We could have broken, deformed babies. We couldn't control how the child was treated by the world. Or the man. This enumeration of fears comforted her. Calmed her. She was no longer a unique being in a unique position. It wasn't just her— to be a human is to be perpetually insecure, always edging on death, chaos, the uncontrollable. Being a mother made this apparent. And you get this small window where you can give your child a feeling of unconditional security, no matter how much fear you feel. In creating this sanctuary for your child, you feel comforted in your own anxiety.

She now viewed the world in a different context. We all can and will be overwhelmed in the middle of the night by the given. And seeing how it is all so fraught and doomed, why not take the greatest risks? Louise felt a cosmic calm as she held her baby and promised to protect him for as long as she could. Giving birth for her was a revolutionary act. How could she embrace uncertainty more profoundly?

She held Jason under her chin and breathed the scent of his soft hair. To close her eyes and inhale gave her enormous pleasure. It was a kind of bliss that made her thoughtless and tearful.

One day, when he is old enough to take care of himself, I will sit him down and tell him all about my life. I will turn myself in and do my time. He will understand.

Occasionally, over the years, she would ask herself, Does he still need me? Is it time yet? And it wasn't simple, because he would always need her.

When August had his accident, she saw the effect it had on her son. In the eight years following August's death, Jason rarely mentioned his father. He never once asked any questions about his death. It was as if August had never existed. More than ever this made her believe it was not yet time for her to act.

Louise observed her son these days, and he was his own person. Just not an adult. Some near-adult. Jason was soft and doughy. He hardly looked at her anymore. At dinner, he read. The rest of the time he was in his room. If she spoke to him, he displayed such weary indifference. If she touched his shoulder, he flinched. Occasionally, she caught him smiling with her. Other times he stared at her with intense scrutiny. She didn't mind when he said sharp, even cutting things to her. She was instead pleased that he had wit and intelligence. But most times it was clear he regarded her as a source of annoyance, if not embarrassment.

Even so, she couldn't turn herself in yet. Not only could she not tell him yet (soon, maybe) but there was at long last another compelling reason to stay out of jail. She would miss Jason unstoppingly.

PART EIGHT

2000

Ergonomica

"OUR VISION is a totally intentional community designed by Allegecom for franchising and profit. We will build on what was learned in our first community: green and self-sustaining, but not too. No gray water or too much trouble. Nothing primitive. Green for what is seen. Feel-good relief. Diverse, but not too. Different kinds of people but all with the same desires and goals—to be deliberately there. A gated community, naturally. Communal, but not really. No elimination of private property, for God's sake. No shared lawn mowers or water heaters.

"What I am saying is we have the opportunity to make money on certain back-to-the-earth desires, for alternatives to suburbia. People who are alienated by malls and material bombardment. We can give them what they desire. We can take that spirit and exploit it for a franchisable experience if we truly understand it. People want a nostalgic, knowingly referenced community experience. But they don't really want anything truly alternative.

They don't want a wife-sharing, Manson-esque, un-American, no-property communalism.

"We have chosen a site five hours north of New York City. Technology allows a postsuburban environment. Let's call it a radiant posturbia. We don't need proximity to cities. We are wired. The land we are looking at is near New Harmon, New York. One of those deserted, dying places that will grant us huge tax incentives if we build there. It is rural and beautiful but totally depressed and cheap. Moreover, it has a history of alternative community. In the nineteenth century it had a community of Christian socialists. In the early '70s it was a women-only commune. Now it will continue its history as alternative to the city, to crime, to pollution.

"A commune and a corporate community are not all that different. A corporation is merely a commune with different values. But like a commune, everything is organized around a collusion of interests. It creates an inside and an outside. And let's not forget, all communities are exclusive. By definition you exclude all that is outside the community. A corporation has rights and privileges that are distinct from its individual owners', just as a commune has collective interests that supersede each individual's interests. Both allow groups of people to act in concert but without consequence.

"Organizations eliminate personal responsibility. That is their purpose. And isn't that what we want? Isn't that a relief? So here is my vision for Allegecom as communard:

"Green for what is seen. What does that mean? We want an antidepressant environment. We are interested in the ecology of ease. In other words, we do what is environmentally correct unless it causes any discomfort. Green community, sure, but wired to the hilt—high speed and totally high tech. Free-access homes, built-in hardware and everything tied in to the Allegecom interface to be tracked for marketing purposes. This will also afford people maximal purchasing opportunities. No out-in-the-country deprivation here. Our motto will be 'Local community, global convenience.' The logo will use an Arts and Crafts font. The website will be designed to attract the nostalgic. We build archaic-looking icons on our site. We give them a retro inter-face—things that look old but act new. We fetishize the details.

"Then we make franchises of our radiant posturbia.

"We market meaningful community, privatize it, copyright it, trademark it. We build emotional attachment to our logo and to brand-specific experiences.

"Ultimately we make prefab communities that never feel syn-thetic or mass-produced. It will be the corporate village that will make money on the desire to escape corporate hegemony. We want to attract the people who hate Wal-Mart. So if we give them the feel of something alternative and unique but execute and con-trol it according to Allegecom's strict guidelines for optimum per-formance and return, and of course happiness, everyone wins."

Josh sat down. The others at the meeting politely clapped.

Tourists

MIRANDA HÁD to have one of the large whole wheat scones from the Mercury bakery. It was one scone, a single thing, and yet it was as big as your outstretched hand, as big as your head. It was a loaf of a scone. With a sort of inhalable relief and pleasure, she got her mouth around the first bite. And black, strong coffee—this was part of it. Yes, a scone, particularly a wheat one, was a dry, crumbly endeavor. So the coffee, its bracing, tannic liquidity, was an essential component of this particular pleasure. She was at it and already dreading the end of her little feast, already on first bite lamenting the diminishing mass of the thing. She felt a nearly existential sadness that her hunger could be so earthy and present but its satisfaction so abstract and impossible to accomplish.

Someone stood by her table. She looked up, an enormous bite shoved in her mouth. It was Nash, and she felt a blush of self-consciousness over the slab in her mouth. But it was at that exact moment she finally reconciled herself to the fact that she did indeed still have feelings for Nash. She realized he was one of the main reasons she felt so homesick for Seattle.

He smiled and offered a little wave. She took a gulp of her coffee. She tried to chew discreetly, politely, quickly, so she could speak. But there is no elegant way to chew a large chunk of dry, flaky scone no matter how much coffee you chase it with. What was worse was the coffee was just a tiny bit too hot for this gesture, too hot to be gulped carelessly, and so she gagged a little, inhaled a piece of pastry, and her eyes bugged and watered as she pushed her way through, crumbs spewing slightly.

"Take your time," Nash said. He waited. "That's really quite a monster of a pastry you got there."

She nodded. The swallowing accomplished. "I love these scones. I sometimes used to walk all the way across town just to get one. I am a glutton of the first order. You know what I like most about them?" she said.

"Their size."

"Yes, their glorious, single-serving, one-portion, huge size. It's terrible. But I'm depressed, and well, that's what I feel like."

"A little gluttony is charming."

"Maybe. But it isn't something I really wanted to explore at length with anyone this morning." Miranda stopped eating the scone. It no longer interested her. She needed a private suite somewhere where she could consume her pastry in peace. Now, well, too late. She sipped her coffee.

"I'm sorry. I was just walking by and saw you."

"No, I'm glad, sit."

"Are you sure?"

"I'm happy to see you."

"You're visiting?"

"I've been back for a week now. We're staying downtown. The Ace." Miranda smiled, slightly embarrassed. "Josh wanted to stay at a hotel."

"So how is Josh?" Nash said.

She studied him for a moment. He was quite bald. But he had a good face, a nice-looking head. He would look better if he just shaved all his hair off, or if he cut it very, very short. "I have been meaning to call you, or come by the bookstore," she said.

"I know."

"He's fine."

"What has he been up to?"

"I'm not sure, he doesn't tell me. I don't really ask, actually." She sipped her coffee.

"You look very good. Disaffection suits a woman," Nash said.

"He works for Allegecom."

"Your face has thinned out, despite the monster muffins. You look very sharp and intimidating."

"Scones. It is a scone."

"Right, sorry. Allegecom, that's peculiar."

"Full-time. He works quite hard, in the website-research whatever department. I think." She started to laugh. She really didn't know what Josh did. And that made Josh seem grown-up and old. Older, somehow, than even Nash.

"He watches a lot of TV. He has to monitor the culture, you know."

"Of course," Nash said.

"He took me to the wax museum last month." Miranda finished the last of her coffee and hated the fact. "Madame Tussaud's, I'm not kidding. Have you ever been to one?"

"No," he said. His halfhearted, slight smile.

"Well, the line was a half-hour wait, on a weekday. And it cost nineteen dollars to get in."

"Is this Josh culturally slumming? Is he there to sneer at people? Can't he get enough of that watching daytime TV?" Nash said, suddenly annoyed.

"You really don't like Josh, do you?" she said. "I thought that too, but he really wanted to see the wax museum. It is pretty insane, I mean as an indicator of things, as a barometer, or whatever. See, you go through these rooms and there is no pretense made to it illustrating history, or whatever. It is all wax celebrities. Even the historical figures are more celebrity than anything else. That's the whole point: if you don't really know what a person looks like, you're not going to really be impressed with the verisimilitude of a wax likeness, are you? I mean, are you going to be impressed by a wax depiction of Diderot or Princess Diana?"

Miranda started back on her scone and then realized eating it would complicate telling her story. "But here's the thing, all these wax figures, you know, Oprah and Madonna and Cher, they are not in some glass diorama, apart from you. Here is the crux of it, here is why people wait on line to get in: the wax figures are all around you and among you. So people can take pictures with their arms around Nicole Kidman's waist, or put a two-fingered antenna behind the head of Giuliani. Or put a hand on Diane Sawyer's upper thigh. People are allowed to touch, to walk among, to desecrate these lofty beings. See how short and helpless they are, smiling and unmoving? And although you can't actually damage the things, you can do whatever else you please, and it was something, the minions loose among the celebrity dolls. There is a real air of hostility toward these creatures, people put real energy into these feelings. It was a sick scene."

"It's so good to see you," Nash said.

"We were appalled, fascinated, freaked out. We understood, though. And no one else seemed to think it odd, which was maybe the most disturbing thing about it."

"I really don't like Josh."

"He took a photo of me embracing Castro," Miranda said.

....

Miranda returned to her hotel. Josh sat at his computer and didn't say anything when she came in. The room was dark. The TV and the computer gave off the only light.

"Did you go out at all today?" she said.

"I have a lot of work to do."

"Like what?"

Josh sighed and turned to her. "We're launching the website for Ergonomica, and I had to make sure everything works."

"Really? Making sure it can't be hacked?"

Josh turned back to his computer. "Something like that."

Sometimes her own boyfriend gave her the creeps.

Jason's Journal

WHEN YOU finally figure it out, it seems you knew it all along.

I hadn't given any of it any thought for quite a while. Not true, of course. I thought about it all the time, but I hadn't actually made any progress on it. Gage wanted to watch VH1's *Lost Videos*. As a rule I try to avoid VH1. This despite the fact that they have, particularly in their classic rock and California rock specials, a nice fixation on all things Beach Boys. Naturally, I find this nostalgia embarrassing. But Gage was shameless. He was over his '70s thing, and now he had fixated on late-'60s American psychedelia, specifically the band Love. You may remember Love. Classic candidates for obsession: forgotten but once quite known. Several hits and a great, dated, specific sound. And *two* African-American members. And we are talking 1966. Most important, Love was led by a neglected, self-destructive genius who is currently rotting in jail. Arthur Lee scared the shit out of the hippies; he was an angry black punk who called his band

Love and then played as though he hated everyone. He used hard drugs and finally got busted in the '80s on a concealed-weapon charge. Gage seemed to find this element most fascinating. Admittedly, I like Love. Their attitude, their look and their badass freak sound, simultaneously baroque and garage. Not at all groovy or flowery—it was tough and new and kicked hard.

Of course, if Gage was interested in black proto-psych rock-and-roll, you'd think he might be into Hendrix. I mean we lived in Seattle—Hendrix is a native son, a local hero. And he died tragically. And no one dressed cooler, ever. Ahh—but you haven't been paying attention. The very fact that Hendrix is a near god here makes him an impossible choice for Gage's devotion. No, Love's Arthur Lee was it—both first (which counts) and forgotten (which really counts).

Anyway, I went over to Gage's to watch "California Classic Rock: The Lost and Forgotten." I agreed, knowing that even VH1 might still have something I'd want to see. Like the infamous *Lost Love Movie*. Which I had never heard of, but I pretended I had.

"That was made in '68, right?" I said.

"No, I think '69, actually. After the decline had set in."

"I never saw it. I heard about it," I said.

"Apparently the bootlegged copies are floating around again. I saw it for sale once, and I should have bought a copy while I had the chance."

Shortly into the part of the program about the great bands of L.A. in the late '60s, they went into the story of Love. Love discovered the Doors and Hendrix. Love never toured, which is why they never got as big. And Love took so many psychedelic drugs that they finally disbanded because none of them could even play their instruments anymore. And oh yeah, there is an underground film about them, known as the *Lost Love Movie*. While the voice-over glossed on the film briefly, they didn't show a video clip. They showed two black-and-white stills. One was of

Arthur Lee in sunglasses on a bench in a park. The angle was quite low. He leaned back on the bench with his thumbs hooked through his belt loops and his legs spread. He wore wide-wale cords and a wide belt. Then they showed another still. This still was shown for maybe six seconds. A long time. I don't remember what the voice-over said. But the photo depicted three people on a ledge next to the freeway. The person closest to the camera was Arthur Lee, in the same pants and glasses. The person to the right, the farthest away from the camera, was another Love band member (although as I recall he was technically no longer in the band by '69), Bryan MacLean. Also in sunglasses. But the person in the middle, the person between them, was not a band member and not wearing sunglasses. Despite the graininess of a still garnered from a video of an old film, I could see that this person was unmistakably my mother. A younger, prettier version of the woman I live with every day.

I gasped and quickly coughed to cover it. I stared at Gage. He was barely paying attention and clearly had not noticed.

"Bogus. Just show the fucking film, don't talk about it. Let's turn it off."

"No, it's almost over," I said. I wanted to see the credits. No mention of the film or film stills.

After I got home from Gage's, did I storm into my mother's room, demanding to hear all about her life as a California groupie? No, I didn't. Because I know, absolutely, that that isn't the story. That there is a bigger secret, something that makes my mother the sort of odd person she is. I know, somehow, what it is. I just can't quite name it yet.

No, after I got home from Gage's, I went to work on the Internet. I went to the site most likely to sell copies of the film: www.undergroundmedia.com, where a year earlier I had in fact purchased a very distant-generation bootleg DVD copy of *Eat the Document* (the notorious never-released documentary about

Dylan's '66 gone-electric tour). They said the *Lost Love Movie* was not available. I kept trolling around until I finally found a site that listed the film. It was part of the neo-Luddite Web ring and only sold original-format items: Super 8 films, 16-millimeter film, reel-to-reel audio. They said they no longer had it. But they directed me to someone else who archived a site devoted to outlaws. I discovered the *Lost Love Movie* was made by Bobby Desoto, who made several underground films as part of a collective before they set off a series of bombs to protest the war and went underground in the early '70s.

I started to feel physically ill, nauseated, but I couldn't grasp it all yet.

Desoto is still at large, as well as others from his bombing and film-making collective, so naturally people are interested in him.

Now I was starting to fit it together. It all fit together.

The guy from the website finally agreed to sell me a copy of the Super 8 and 16-millimeter films made by the collective. But he said he was an Original Formatter and refused to transfer it to video on principle; in fact, he made me swear I would never transfer it to video, so I had to get that done somewhere else. I bought not only the *Lost Love Movie* but all the Bobby Desoto he had, three films. And when I finally had the transfer, all contained on a VHS tape with a blank label, I locked my door and settled in for a look.

Here's exactly what I saw:

FILM 1:

A black screen. "Love" appears, in flowing, fat, cartoony script. This is Super 8. There is a sound track. No music, but people talking, out of sync with the images. Not slightly out of sync but deliberately off, not even close. There are scenes of an interview where you hear nothing but cars going by, then scenes in the park where you hear the interview. It was kind of cool, actually. And then a freeway scene, sort of cliché L.A. stuff, but there, briefly, is my mother. She has long, straight brown hair center-parted and pulled flat and smooth behind her ears. She wears those round, oversized John Lennon glasses. She is smiling and then seems to ask Lee some questions, but all you hear is music (the gorgeous opening riff from "Alone Again Or"—a song from '67, not '69, but never mind). Lee mouths an answer to her questions, and then there is a close-up of my mother's face. She looks, well, playful. She laughs, then glances off camera—a shy, flirty move. She's having fun. Then it cuts to the band playing, but now you hear the interview, and I hear my mother's voice say, "What do you call it, your type of music?" And then Lee answers, "Love, baby, can't you feel it?" and then the remarkable sound of my mother's laugh. Then it ends. The credits list the names of the band members; Desoto's art collective, Soft Art Film Elastic, or SAFE; and the interviewer, apparently my mother—Mary Whittaker.

FILM 2:

A stop-action animation film, silent, again Super 8, made with G.I. Joe dolls. And doctored Barbie dolls. Intercut with army films, recruiting films, corporate in-house films. Artifacts, found clips, stolen and recontextualized. I think I have heard of this film. A rather silly send-up of corporate militarism, but well made, and hey—the first, perhaps, of its kind?

FILM 3:

This film is noted as the last, 1972. It is 16 millimeter, I think. It is called "The Scientist." It shows an old man being hounded obnoxiously by this dick one assumes must be Desoto. The film cuts to a speedy montage of some shots of corporate headquarters signs: Dow, Monsanto, General Dynamics, Westinghouse, Raytheon, Magnavox, Honeywell and Valence. Not the subtlest film I ever saw. Again, credited to the collective SAFE (but now it stood for Soft Art Film Efflux). And again, under the listed members of the collective: Mary Whittaker.

I don't really know what to make of this. I have to find out more about the collective and Desoto. And Mary Whittaker.

Tracers

NASH HEARD someone approach from behind as he locked up Prairie Fire. He turned cautiously. Miranda stood there, somewhat winded, hair loose around her shoulders. It was cold, and her breath made little mists in front of her open mouth. He smiled at her and pocketed his keys. She put her hand on his arm and looked up at him.

"What does Miranda want from me?" Nash said. He liked saying her name. She just stood there looking at him. Both of them waited, and then Nash leaned over and kissed her. She pulled herself closer to him and the kiss—harder than he expected, actually—until their lips slid apart and the one kiss became small, slow, breathy kisses on neck and ears. Slow, but urgent still. Nash breathed for a moment into her long hair; he held himself against the skin just below her ear and paused there. Miranda clutched at him. He couldn't feel much of anything through his wool peacoat, but he pressed against her anyway. She then tried to pull back for a second full kiss, but he wanted to stay where he was, where he was breathing through her hair, his hands now on both sides of her head. She smelled, variously, of stale, all-night cigarettes; something citrus and dried; flowers also, or perfume oil. Something else too, a vegetal brightness, not decayed but living, a woman-skin musk, barely there.

She took his hand and walked him back to his house, no longer smiling, and then she stopped suddenly on the stairs leading up to his doorway. She didn't turn around but stood there in front of him. He stepped up and pressed against her back and legs. She leaned back into him.

This is the best moment I will ever have, he thought, but it was already over, they were on their way up the stairs. She undressed quickly. It was cold, and she got under the covers, leaving just her panties on. Then she reached under the sheets and took those off and tossed them on her pants and blouse on the floor.

This is the best moment I will ever have.

This is great good luck.

Nash felt the same thing again as he sat by the window early the next morning and watched the sun come up. He looked at Miranda asleep in his bed. Her hair was in her face, and he could just see her lips and nose. He watched her stir, push the hair out of her closed eyes and then sink back into sleep. He sipped some water. The worn oak floor reflected light, the sky brightened from deep blue to light blue and Miranda finally pulled herself up on the bed, smiling.

Miranda had been at a bar in Belltown with Sissy. At ten o'clock she decided to take a walk up Pike Street, over the freeway, and up to Fifteenth Avenue. She made it there just as Nash was locking up. She thought of a funny thing to say, but when he turned around she just smiled. He seemed so surprised. Then almost resigned when she put her hand on his arm. She didn't expect that he would kiss her, but as he did she realized why she was there. She held his head and kissed him again. She was cold, and she felt the warmth of his body. She decided they should continue indoors. Partially she was cold, and partially she couldn't help thinking of Josh, or Josh's friends, seeing them on the street.

She practically dragged him up the steps, so quickly was she moving; then she stopped abruptly near the top so Nash almost crashed into her. She didn't turn around when she felt him behind her but leaned back, gently, into him. She liked this long body pause, the tease of it. Something you can barely stand to do.

She began to pull off her clothes. She felt him looking at her, and she wasn't embarrassed. She felt young and lovely, which was something she didn't often feel, certainly not with Josh. But don't, don't think of Josh now. And she didn't.

They moved awkwardly. His arm in her face, she banged her head at one point. "Sorry." "Sorry." The condom was a disaster, it was on, but oh, how it felt. After a while they gave it up—which is what people do, because it feels worth it—then pauses, whispers, adjustments. Calibrations.

Despite the confused and awkward coupling, it was still painfully exciting. Miranda felt that if it went too smoothly it would mean it didn't matter as much. She thought this during, and she then decided to stop for a moment and just hold him close, kissing him slowly. She pushed against him and stopped "trying" to do anything except feel his breathing and his weight next to her. She let him move her to her side, facing him and leaning back on the bed. He placed a hand across her and rested it on her middle back; then he moved it slowly to the indent of her waist, then down the curve of her hip, and very, very softly along the edges of her thighs. She moved her legs slightly apart, and he barely touched her inner thighs. He traced his hand lightly up to her stomach, and he looked at her, unsmiling. She stopped smiling too, and let him touch her. That could have lasted hours, the gentle touching, the close faces, the kisses. Eventually, they did the beginning part again, not awkward at all, but easy, easy. And somehow without warning they both slipped into a deep, calm sleep. When she woke up he was watching her. It felt nice. She beamed at him.

"I'm too old for you," he said.

She stopped smiling. "I know," she said.

Miranda waited for Josh at the brand-new lo-fi coffee bar on Broadway. Espresso and cappuccino had become so ubiquitous in the city that nearly every block featured an espresso cart, or a coffee kiosk, or a cappuccino counter. The trend was so overly elaborated that the details of consumption became parsed and specific; there were conventions and argot. Cappuccinos could be "wet"—meaning made with not just foam but a little steamed milk. There were macchiatos and lattes, and a thousand variations on beans and brewing. Naturally it didn't take long for the coolest, newest coffee bars to defiantly serve only drip coffee. In retro, normal-sized cups. Eventually, perhaps, it would be instant coffee. She drank the watery brew and read the paper. She felt excited and high from hardly sleeping. Her skin glowed from kissing a man with some stubble on his face. Her chest was a little red as well, as if she had hives or a rash. It's weird how when you first sleep with someone it is almost like your bodies are allergic to each other. She felt absurdly pleased, and then she watched for Josh. As soon as she saw him, she would put thoughts of Nash aside, just deliberately unthink them.

The left wall of the shop was covered with underground magazines and newspapers. All those promising titles: *Angry Girl* and *Bitch*. *Slits & Tits* and *Heroic Heretic*. All these fierce chick zines that claimed to be überfeminist but sounded like S & M porno magazines. Liberation, apparently, had to be appropriation, with double A batteries and a double D bra; pert Betty Paige bangs and no apologies.

She noticed Josh walking slowly toward the coffee bar. He wore a sports coat, corduroy with elbow patches. These days it was either that or the cable-knit cardigan. He looked like a Midwestern professor lately, less young prep and more middle-aged uncle. She found it a bit affected, not that clever. But Josh was a very affected, very formal guy, no matter what he wore. He caught her eye and barely acknowledged her as he approached. He did have such remove. That part wasn't affected. That part just was. It was enormously alluring to her for reasons she didn't care to fathom.

"How's Sissy?"

"Great. We had fun." She had told him she was spending the night with Sissy. Which was really the plan, until she just decided otherwise. Josh sat and took a sip of her coffee. He frowned a bit.

"Where did you guys go last night?" He didn't look at her but at the newspaper he had in his hand.

"Here and there," she said.

"Right," he said and opened the paper. He was reading *The Wall Street Journal*.

Together they walked through the ever-expanding ultrahip retail center. Miranda hated it. It was a mall but not called a mall; it was really postmall, a series of attached indoor stores with the sensibility of independent boutiques. Whether they were corporate chains or not (many were owned by corporate chains), they appeared quirky and eccentric. There was a tattoo emporium. A store for DJs, with underground twelve-inch dance records, turntables with slip mats, and metal-braced "coffin" boxes for carrying the records to the clubs. A cineplex showed foreign and independent films. Even an art museum in the basement with video installations. The centerpiece was a large, trendy clothing store called Suburban Guerrilla.

Josh and Miranda wandered into the store, lost and mesmerized in the low-intensity way only an airless retail space can induce.

"The Gruen effect," Josh said.

"What?"

"When you become narcotized by the retail array, when you enter the shopping soma, the enticement overload."

Miranda nodded vaguely.

"I've been studying it. How the placement of doors and windows can manipulate psychological states. The very architecture makes you feel small and submissive. Victor Gruen was the first to recognize that if you are forced through a series of shops before you find the poorly marked exit, and if you hear music of a certain tempo, and if the lighting is right, you will reach the disassociative state in which you will be vulnerable to suggestion. You will feel the urge, or desire, for impulse purchases."

"Really," Miranda said, wandering absently toward a table piled with books, candles, shirts and throw rugs, all done in the same three shades of green-blue. She examined a rack of clothes. There were fake vintage dresses with bohemian patches. Gauze and macramé peasant dresses. Lace-trimmed camisoles next to a poster of Carole King's 1971 *Tapestry* album. Angel sleeves and high-heeled boots. Clogs and granny glasses, but also tube tops, denim short-short cutoffs, roller skates. And finally a whole rack of fat, colorful, striped clip suspenders next to long-sleeved sweatshirts with puffy satin rainbows sewed on them, circa 1976.

Josh picked up a reissue of the *Silver Surfer* comic book from a table piled with puka-shell necklaces just like David Cassidy used to wear in the '70s. He walked past the selection of graphic novellas to Miranda, who was looking at an earth-art display. A huge poster of Smithson's *Spiral Jetty* hung overhead, and underneath were books on contemporary environmental art and land art of the '70s. There was a DVD on Andrew Goldsworthy, and leaf-patterned bike messenger bags as well as vintage Greenpeace buttons and some vinyl Jackson Browne records in plastic sleeves.

"It's not just the Gruen effect, you know. It's the way everything is no longer organized by category but by subject. By theme, everything is tied together by associations of theme," Miranda said.

"Yes. On the Internet one thing leads to another in this nonlinear, associative way. Increasingly the world will imitate the Internet in how it processes information. Like Allegecom opening its drug superstore in imitation of its hugely successful retail website. The first physical store to spin off a website. Brilliant."

But Miranda wasn't listening. She was distracted by one last themed section. The walls were covered in black, and the clothes on the display racks were all black. There were books on anarchy and radical environmentalism. Big coffee table anthologies. But there were also triangle-shaped black scarves for sale—just like the ones the anarchist blac bloc kids used when they busted windows at Niketown and Starbucks last year. Just like on TV.

"Jesus," Miranda said. Josh came over with a big smirk on his face. He picked up a calendar with "Paris '68" on the cover, and each month featured a different Situationist graffito. There were posters for Godard's *Le Petit Soldat* and the remaster of *The Battle of Algiers* and a booklet of Weather Underground communiqués. A datebook with a cover photo of Bernardine Dohrn in a miniskirt holding a fist in the air. A vinyl shower curtain with a drawing of Subcomandante Marcos, and a note attached explaining the sales helped the Chiapas Zapatista movement. Ripped and safety-pinned clothes arranged in piles by boxes of vintage Doc Marten boots. And from a lacquered faux milk crate, Miranda pulled out little silk-screened patches meant to be pinned to shirts (never sewn!) that said "Sabotage" and "Anarchy," exactly like the homemade patches the kids on the street wore. One even said "D.I.Y." (Do It Yourself). She looked at Josh. "This is totally appalling."

He smiled broadly. "This is the purity of capitalism. There is no judgment about content. You have to marvel at its elasticity, its lack of moral need, its honesty. It is the great leveler—all can be and will be commodified. Besides, what's wrong with Emma Goldman being sold at the mall as a cool accessory? It is still Emma Goldman, isn't it?"

"A confused context is the essence of alienation," Miranda said.

"Who said that?"

"I did. I think," Miranda said. She picked up a deck of playing cards. "New Left Series." Each card had a different photo on the front, biography on the reverse. Dave Dellinger. Mario Savio. Abbie Hoffman. Mark Rudd.

"But you're looking at it all wrong. See, capitalism can exploit your desire and exploit your need to subvert its exploitation of your desire. It revives—reinforces—itself on the blood of its critics and their critique. It embraces contradictions. It revels in irony."

"No, that isn't irony," Miranda said. "That's just cynicism. And it doesn't contain contradictions. It just reduces everything to market value. It is simplistic and reductive. The irony is there for you because you are alienated from it but still live in it. The irony is yours, not the system's." Miranda looked sideways at Josh. "Or you used to be alienated from it but still live in it. Now you seem to revel in it."

The "New Left" playing cards even came with instructions for a game to play using them,

Storm the Dean's Office:
Watch out—if you put the wrong cards together,
there is a sectarian meltdown!

"Let's take your little friend irony for one moment," Josh said. "Irony can be the most subversive of stances. It has the potential to undermine and even to redress the hypocrisy and falseness of the culture. But that has become the favorite mode of the new corporate generation. Every ad you see. Even Republicans use irony now. So that leaves the earnest stance you love to use—so tedious, so"—Josh paused—"shrill and feminine," he continued. "But guess what? It doesn't matter. Not irony or earnestness or all the stuff in between—the earnest irony or ironic earnestness— can ever touch the perfect, all-powerful, underlying system."

"That's a very shallow reading of things. There is still a lot you can do to upset things. You are just talking yourself into something." She turned over the deck of cards—$19.95.

"My treat," Josh said.

"I don't want them."

"Well then, how about the Movement Rebels, Outlaws and Fugitives playing cards?" Miranda shook her head. "I'm getting them for you. I insist." Josh took out a gold corporate American Express card and went to the register.

"When did you get that credit card?" she said.

He handed her the package. "You aren't actually surprised, are you?"

"Actually, I am."

"I got it with my promotion," Josh said.

"I didn't know you got promoted."

"Didn't I tell you? I think I must have told you. They loved my ideas for the franchised alternative community. I'm in charge of the whole thing."

They reached the edge of the mall. The rain was pouring down on Broadway.

"I don't have an umbrella," she said.

"You can use my jacket. My car is parked three blocks down."

"No."

"Don't be silly."

"No, I don't need it."

"Okay," Josh said. "I'll get the car and bring it around. Just wait here." Miranda stared at the rain. She watched him hurry down the street. What did she expect?

They drove across the freeway overpass on Eastlake hill. The city looked quiet and deserted, while the freeway was backed up beneath them. Miranda stared out the window. Josh kept looking over at her.

"I'm not going back to New York with you," she said.

He started to laugh. "It is true that I enjoy making money, I won't deny it. Thing is, I feel the same. I don't think I am a materialistic person, you know. I never wanted stuff."

She leaned her head against the window. Conversations in cars are the strangest, because you don't look at each other even though you are sitting close enough to touch.

"What it comes down to is I just don't want to look at other people's garbage my whole life. There is always garbage blowing around the street outside our apartment. Life is too short. All I want is a clean, quiet place. Beauty and order and peace. If Allegecom contributes—as it most certainly does—to the world's degradation, undermining, at least in a global sense, order and peace, as well as multiplying garbage, and—let's face it—suffering, then it also mitigates, quite directly, my own contact with garbage and suffering."

Miranda didn't respond. She opened the pack of "Outlaw" playing cards. They were even worse than the other pack. On the front of each card was the photo of a person or the logo of a group. On the back were stats and facts about them done just like baseball cards. There were RAF/Baader-Meinhof cards, Red Brigade cards, as well as cards with individuals: David Gilbert. Katherine Power. Eldridge Cleaver. Miranda flipped through them absently. She stopped at a young man with long, curly hair and sunglasses. He had a familiar quality. She read the back. Bobby Desoto. Alt filmmaker and underground activist. Founded a collective, SAFE (Secret Attack Fear Effort), which allegedly planted bombs at the summer homes of corporate board members. Still at large. Miranda paused, then turned the card over. She stared at the mouth. That crooked smile. Of course. Of course.

"What are you looking at?"

"Nothing," she said. "These cards are disgusting for so many reasons. If you can't even see that—"

"Fine. Give them to me then."

"No."

"C'mon." He took them out of her hand and put them in his jacket pocket. She stared out the window, arms crossed.

He reached over to her.

"Do not. I don't like it," she said.

He stopped the car in front of their hotel on Second Avenue.

"You're wrong, you know," Josh said, taking out the playing cards and waving them at her.

"What?"

"When you said a confused context causes alienation. But altering the context—appropriation—is subversive. Even liberating. Walter Benjamin said that about a thousand years ago."

Miranda shook her head. "He was talking about art, not people." She gestured wearily at the playing cards. "Those are human beings. Human beings do not need to be appropriated."

Augury

NASH WALKED up John Street to a small bungalow-style house. The eaves hung far out beyond the edge of the porch. The curtains on the large front-facing window were drawn. He knocked. No answer.

"Henry?" he said. "Can I come in?"

"Yep."

Nash entered the dark house. It took a moment for his eyes to adjust. Henry lay on the couch in his flannel bathrobe. A throw with a Seahawks insignia covered his lower body. His feet poked out from under the blanket. The toenails were thick and yellow colored. His crosshatched skin at his ankles looked dry and tired. In the end, feet and hands don't lie. They're the oldest parts of a body.

"I brought some beer," Nash said. Henry waved his all-knuckle hand at him to bring it over. Henry had lost so much weight since Nash last saw him. His head looked oversized. Gray stubble covered his chin and neck. Nash popped open two bottles, then sat opposite Henry, in a rocking chair, sipping.

"I look like I'm dying, huh?" Henry said.

"What did your doctor say?"

Henry shrugged. "We can try this or that, but what it comes down to is it is in my bones. How much deeper can it get than the marrow of your bones?"

"I can't believe it."

"Death by hubris."

"What do you mean, death by hubris?"

"Dioxin. Defoliant. We thought we could kill everything that grows and there wouldn't be human consequences."

Nash cocked his head, started to speak, stopped. Henry watched a sports channel with the mute on. Kids jumped off cliffs with parachutes and snowboards. The editing was very chopped up and fast. Henry finished his beer and lit a cigarette.

"So what now?" Nash said. Henry pressed the TV remote control. The channels flicked by in silence.

"Should I go?" Nash said.

"No, no. I like your company."

Nash looked around. He started to pick up newspapers and empty glasses. He emptied one full ashtray into another.

"Don't do that either."

Nash sighed and put the stuff down on the kitchen counter. He dumped the ashes into the garbage and brought the clean ashtray to Henry.

"I thought you said the billboard stuff was making you better," Nash said.

"It did. It got rid of the dreams. But the cancer was in my bones a long time ago. I just didn't realize."

Nash stared at the TV.

"What?" Henry said.

"Maybe it's just a coincidence, you know?"

"That I got non-Hodgkin's? That's what people exposed to dioxin get."

"But."

"I got sick due to dioxin exposure from Agent Orange. This is the truth, Nash, and you will have to work your mind around it. This is how my life makes sense. This is how my life signifies something."

"Okay."

"I want you to think about it the way I'm telling you to. It's important for you, trust me."

Henry leaned back into his pillows.

"The dreams, in fact, have returned. But they are no longer violent and chaotic. They are peaceful and chaotic. Sometimes I see the faces of dead children. Sometimes I see soldiers. But I don't resist it like I used to. It doesn't frighten me."

Henry closed his eyes. He seemed about to drift off. Nash watched him breathe. He could hear the trouble in the exhalations. Henry's eyes opened with a start. He found Nash and looked relieved.

"I understand everything now. Even you."

"Oh yeah?"

Nash watched the papery skin on Henry's eyelids. The eyes twitched slightly. There were dark purple shadows in the creases. The whites of his eyes were not bright. A very fragile affair, an eye.

"I know you tried to take a full swing at it. That's not shameful. I'm glad for you," Henry said. Then he seemed to fall asleep. Nash pressed his fingers over his own eyelids and rested his head in his palms. He listened to Henry's noisy sleep sounds. Henry slept, his face placid and calm, arm over head, in what looked like a repose of surrender. The room did not smell of roses or incense. Or even of ethereal apple blossoms. It smelled of sweat and urine and beer. This almost surprised Nash. And then he got up and walked to the door.

"Nash?" Henry called out.

"Yeah?" Nash said.

"It's back up, you know."

"I didn't want to say anything." Nash had walked by the bill-board earlier in the week. For months nothing was there, and then a Nepenthex ad appeared overnight.

"Bigger than fucking ever," Henry said.

Jason's Journal

My mother is not only, not merely, my mother. She's a revolutionary. She's a fugitive. She's a liar. She's a killer.

Consolation

Henry woke to damp sheets. He felt his sweat, and he felt icy cold. He took a deep breath and let himself slip back into sleep.

Phosgene gas smells of newly mown hay.
Lewisite gas smells of geraniums.

PART NINE

Contrapasso

JASON SLAMMED doors and locked them. He shot Louise intense, searching looks that he quickly covered with blank mid-distance stares.

This wasn't the usual indifference, but then what was usual? She resisted her impulse to push his hair back from his forehead. He was in an awkward stage, slightly pudgy and spotty. She didn't mind if he shrugged her off when she put an arm around him. She couldn't comfort him through his adolescence, but she could stay out of his way. She believed that if she didn't interfere, her talented, brilliant son would get everything he needed from the world. She also knew that the day would come when he would find her out, but she refused to think about it. Two weeks of his schizoid scrutiny unnerved her. When he finally confronted her, it shouldn't have been a surprise.

Jason sat down to dinner. He did not watch the TV or read his book. In fact, he didn't eat. He just stared at her, and suddenly she knew what was coming. She caught her breath—after all this time, she was astonished it was finally upon her.

"I watched *America's Most Wanted* yesterday," he said.

It was really happening, wasn't it?

"The show was all about this woman who was a terrorist in the '70s. She is still at large."

Louise felt it physically creeping up on her, making her hands shake. There is an unreality to a moment you have been anticipating your whole life. And then the moment happens and you're still there, breathing. She felt such relief. An amazing calm overtook her.

"There wasn't any show," she said, quietly.

"Her name was Mary Whittaker, and they showed a picture of her."

"There wasn't a show," she said.

"She was part of a collective that blew up three summer houses of corporate board members—munitions producers, I suppose, I don't remember. In any case, there was the last bombing when something went wrong—or did it go wrong?"

"You know about that?"

"On *America's Most Wanted* they showed a picture of Martha Malcolm—"

Louise shook her head. To hear that name come out of her son's mouth.

"How did you find out?"

"I'm telling you about the TV show," Jason.

"There wasn't a TV show, stop saying that," she said.

"There was," he said.

"You're lying," she said.

Jason started to laugh.

"I'm lying, huh? That's fucking rich," he said. "Why don't you look at me, Mom?" He glared at her, his face red and angry.

"You shouldn't judge something you don't know about," she said.

Jason put his hand under his plate and flipped it off the table. It crashed on the floor. Jason squeezed his hands into tight fists. Louise stared at the plate. And then something happened. He started to cry. Louise hadn't seen her son cry since he was a toddler.

"I was going to tell you one day. I can tell you about it now. If you want to hear about it, I will tell you," she said.

He wiped his eyes.

"You can't look at what we did in a vacuum. This immoral war was going on and on. And whatever we did, we thought it would help scare them into ending that war sooner."

"Yeah, how'd that work out for you? Didn't that war last like nine years?" Jason said.

"It doesn't only matter if we succeed in our intentions. It matters what our intentions were. We wanted to do something. There had been years of peaceful efforts. Things escalated. It was an act of desperation."

Jason nodded.

"You must believe that we never intended to hurt anyone. That was a terrible consequence that we never desired or sought. Which doesn't excuse it, but maybe it makes it more understandable to you."

"It must have crossed your mind, the risks you were taking, and not just with your own lives. But that doesn't even matter to me. Whatever. I mean, I can easily buy that you were foolish enough not to realize how inevitable it was that planting bombs would lead to killing somebody. I just can't believe you lied to me all these years about who you are."

"I planned to tell you when you were old enough. When I was ready to turn myself in. The last thing I would ever want is for you to have to keep my secret."

"You want to turn yourself in? After all these years?" His tone had changed slightly. He sounded surprised.

"I'm so sorry. About all of it. But yes, I plan to turn myself in as soon as possible."

She gripped her hands in her lap and waited for the withering speech that would come next.

"Did my father even know the truth?"

She shook her head.

"It's amazing," he said.

"It sounds amazing. Most of the time it was just everyday. Except no experience was ever one hundred percent what it was. There was always this extra thing, this underlying doom."

She started to pick up the spilled plate and food. "I'll clean it," he said.

When he finished he sat down across from her. She took her pipe out and started to smoke. She held it out to him, and he ignored her offer.

"It was something, though, what you did. You had guts, really, I never would have guessed," he said.

"It was a huge miscalculation. A huge mistake."

"At least you did something. What a world that must have been where ordinary people actually did things. Things that affected, however tangentially, history."

She tried to think of what to say next. But she couldn't speak. She felt such a huge sense of relief. She felt so grateful to her son. How did she get such a break after everything else? She reached her hand out to touch him.

"Jesus, don't get carried away." He shrugged her off. "I haven't forgiven you for lying my entire life."

She laughed.

"I'm glad you think that's funny," he said.

"No, I just think you're funny. You really are very funny. I'm not ever funny, am I?"

"Oh yeah. Here's something that will make you laugh," he said. He handed her a piece of paper with a phone number on it.

"What is it?"

"Bobby Desoto's number. His name is Nash Davis, now. In another thrilling twist of fate, he lives not very far from here."

She clutched the piece of paper. She hadn't expected this at all.

"How did you find him?"

"I tried different possibilities. Finally I used the acronym from the film collective. There were a few American references to SAFE on the Internet, but one stood out. It was for an anarchy board that posted something for the Prairie Fire bookstore. I investigated this SAFE and discovered it stood for Scratch Artists for Effacement. It is a notorious meta-prankster group that semi doesn't exist. That just reeked of Desoto to me. This guy Nash Davis organizes events at Prairie Fire. So I called him. Bingo."

"You really are smart," she said.

"Don't get carried away."

Louise remembered every detail of the day she first met Bobby. He kept filming her at a protest at the draft board. He followed her around until she finally told him to stop. She recognized him. She'd been at a happening where they showed some of his movies. He agreed to stop filming her if she would get some Chinese food with him.

After they ate he took her to the Valence Chemical building downtown. He walked her down the hall, pulling her by the hand. He opened the doors marked "Private." He was gleeful and fearless as they went from room to room. He also seemed to know where everything was. He pulled her into an empty room full of file cabinets. He glanced at her, opened a couple of drawers and threw several stacks of files in the metal wastebasket. He lit them on fire with his Zippo lighter and pulled her out of the room laughing. He tried another door. It was locked. He looked up and down the hall, then took out a metal tool and jimmied the door open. He pushed her inside and closed the door. It was dark, and he leaned her against the wall and kissed her.

"I'm showing off for you. Aren't you impressed?"

"Very," she said. Then he kissed her again. Later that night he would confess that his father was the head of the Research and Development Department at Valence Chemical. He hadn't told any of his movement friends about his family. His father practically invented (or at least developed) applications for several synthetic polymers: polystyrene and polyvinyl chloride. This was part of a revolution of industrial thermoplastics. Nash's father pioneered plastics that were used to make stable film stock, long-playing records, PVC piping, water beds and—inevitably—various kinds of munitions: plastic fragmentation mines as well as particularly vicious plasticized gasoline and white phosphorus bombs that made—as they detonated and burned with a relentless, stubborn, chemical stink—the most beautiful, white, elegant-but-brisant smoke trails.

After that, they stayed together every single night until they went underground.

The bar in Belltown had seen a series of better days. It was attached to an old hotel, which way back when had captivated the hip youth of the music scene. They moved on, leaving the bar and hotel to budget European travelers, who then gave way to the single-room-occupancy crowd. Louise waved the cigarette smoke away as she entered. It was still light outside, and this was not the sort of place that worked at all during the day. But it was deserted, and she understood why Bobby had chosen it.

She saw him at a booth in the back. She was shocked to discover that, beyond his looking old and frail, or in spite of it, he was unmistakably Bobby, and she felt the same as she had twenty-eight years earlier: the air felt thin, and her whole metabolism quaked at the sight of him. She closed her eyes at the inner flutter, and it pleased her to feel it, it really did. Then she of course started to cry. Bobby stood up as she approached. He reached for her hand, and she pulled back, out of reach.

After a minute she sat down. Bobby grasped her hand before she had a chance to stop him.

"It's all right," he said.

She said nothing, pulled her hand away and pressed both palms to her eyes. She inhaled. She took a paper napkin and pressed it to her face. She raised her hand at the bartender.

"Some bourbon. That one," she said, pointing to a bottle.

"Two," Nash said.

"I'm turning myself in," she said.

Nash drank his bourbon.

"I wanted to let you know. I won't say anything about you, of course, but I thought I ought to warn you just the same since Jason got in touch with you so recently."

"I had a feeling you were going to tell me that," Nash said.

"They may figure it out anyway, but they won't hear it from me," she said. She looked away, but she could feel him watching her.

"It feels exactly the same being with you. It is just the way I remember it," he said.

"Yes." She forced a swallow.

"It doesn't matter," he said.

"What?"

"I don't care if they find me," he said.

"What do you mean you don't care?"

He pushed his empty glass toward the center of the table. "I decided about ten years back I wouldn't hide from them anymore. I would just do my thing, inconspicuous and law-abiding but not hidden and paranoid. I tread lightly, sure, but no more running away, no more name changing, no more cold sweats in the night. I just do my thing and accept that sooner or later they'll figure it out. Jesus, your son figured it out in like a week. So I will just go on until the day, which will seem like all the others, that I am finally apprehended."

"I get it," she said.

"*Apprehended,* though, that's the word, which is seized and taken, a much more accurate word than *arrested,* which means stopped. Because things don't stop at the arrest, do they? They begin there with a whole world of trials and lawyers and then the plodding consecution of those endless, circumscribed, uniform days," he said.

She exhaled. She felt so weary.

"Are you really prepared for all of that?" he said.

"What you describe isn't so different from my current life. But if you know they'll get you, why not turn yourself in, make a better deal?"

"No way. I will sit in my little bare room forever, but no way will I volunteer to sit in their little bare room. I just won't make my so-called freedom a prison by trying to evade them. I did that for too many years, and I won't live like that." Nash sounded as though he was about to launch into something, but then he stopped. "But, of course, you know exactly what I'm talking about."

"Goddamn it," she said, lowering her voice. "It would have been so much"—she didn't want to cry again—"so much easier if I knew someone else in the same position. If we could have talked even once."

A few more people trickled into the bar. Louise started to get up to leave. "I have to go."

"Wait," Nash said. She stopped. "Listen, you should tell them about me. You can get a better deal if you tell them," he said.

"I can't do that."

"Yes you can. You want to spend time with your son again, don't you? Be part of his life. Because that is what we are talking about. You tell them it was my idea. You tell them you didn't realize what you were doing. Mary, take advantage."

"No."

"I owe it to you," he said.

"No you don't."

"I want to owe it to you."

She was starting to feel dizzy. "I thought you always blamed me for what happened."

"Never. I knew how it would go. I knew someone was going to end up dead," Nash said. Someone sat in the booth next to theirs. Nash leaned toward her a bit and spoke in a low voice. "There was a moment, a very clear moment, when I knew not only that it might happen but that it would definitely happen. And I was still willing to do it. And not because I really believed we would change anything for the better. I did it as a testament to my own certainty, as a test of my conviction. I needed to prove to myself I could go all the way."

"I didn't realize we could kill someone," Louise said.

"Let me ask you something. If we had killed one of the targets, one of the board guys who knowingly developed land mines or antipersonnel devices, dioxin poisons or napalm. If we had taken out someone like that instead of a housekeeper, how would you feel about it?"

"It would feel no different. It still would have cost everything and probably changed nothing. Nothing for the better, anyway."

"I'm not so sure. I'm more culpable, see? You are excused. I am not."

She rubbed her eyes. She felt totally drained.

"So turn me in," he said.

"You sound like you want me to do it."

....

"There was no answer."

"Try again."

"I let it ring and ring."

"Maybe you dialed the wrong number."

"No, but I'll try it again." Louise remembered exactly how it all went down. She remembered how Bobby took a deep breath and then picked up the receiver.

"There's no time," he said. He looked at his watch.

"How much time is left?" Tamsin said.

"Thirty minutes," Bobby said.

"Jesus Christ."

"Maybe she already left," Bobby said.

"She might be vacuuming and not hear it," Mary said.

"Jesus, oh shit," Tamsin said.

"We have to call the police," Mary said.

"Yeah, I'm doing that," Bobby said. He grabbed his jacket.

"Where are you going?"

"I'm going to use the pay phone on Eighth Street. You keep trying that number."

"Hurry up!" shouted Tamsin.

Bobby looked at her, then spoke to Mary. "I'll be back soon. Everything will be fine. Don't panic."

"Yeah."

He ran out.

Tamsin started muttering. "I knew this would happen. Oh God."

"Nothing has happened. Let's keep trying the line." Mary dialed and waited. A busy signal. She held it out so Tamsin could hear it. She redialed. The repetitive signal sound.

"I think the phone might be off the hook." She looked at her watch. Time just kept going forward. Everything kept going forward. The moment approached. Tamsin was crying.

"Maybe she left."

"No, the phone is busy." How can this be happening?

Bobby came back.

"Okay, people, let's get it together. We split up. Listen to the news. If everything is okay, we meet at the farmhouse and stay there until things cool out."

"And if things didn't go okay?" Mary said.

"We do what we discussed we'd do. What we have to do." Bobby grabbed Mary's hand. Tamsin was at the door, leaving. "Tamsin!"

"What?"

"Be cool. Don't panic."

She nodded. Then she left.

Bobby shook his head. "Shit, I knew it." He pulled their bags from under the bed and looked around. He started to quickly pack.

"It's going to be okay, isn't it? The police got there in time, right?"

"I'm going to make some phone calls and get some money," he said. "I'll be back in a couple of hours. Get ready."

She listened to the radio and emptied the apartment of any evidence of them. She wiped rubbing alcohol on every surface. There wasn't any news.

When Bobby walked in later, he didn't say anything. She knew instantly—his face was white. He was sweating.

"Oh no," she said.

"I'll drop you at Grand Central, and then I'll go to Port Authority," he said. He spoke in a flat, low voice.

She couldn't speak.

"Are you ready?"

She nodded.

"No talking in the cab, okay?" He picked up their bags.

The cab ride went so fast. Why was everything moving so fast?

At the station he kissed her. After he left, she walked quickly to the women's room, closed herself in a stall, bent over the toilet and waited to be sick.

Louise watched the news as always. More KGB files had been opened and made public. The files revealed several previously unknown British and American agents. She watched the press descend on a petite, ancient lady. Under a code name, she had spied for decades, all the while living the life of a modest civil servant. The cameras hounded this lady in her lace collar and barrette-clipped hair. Why? They Wanted to Know: Why and What and How. She told them she had no regrets.

"How much did they pay you?" they asked.

"I did not want money. I'm not sure the younger generation understands. I'm not sure they accept it. We wanted the Soviets to be on equal footing with the West. We wanted them to have a chance. We believed in it. It was what we thought was right."

"Yes, but how much money did you get?"

She just shook her head.

"Aren't you sorry for what you did?"

Louise turned off the TV. She really was going to do it. She was going to turn herself in. And no one would understand. It didn't matter at all.

Last Things

AFTER HENRY died, Nash wanted to do something to their ad, a tribute of some kind. But he put it off and never got around to it. He even avoided driving past the billboard on Second Avenue for a while. He just didn't have it in him anymore. The will to do it. He was tired.

He drove a lot these days. Henry had left him his car. And the bookstore. Nash couldn't refuse, but he sort of cursed Henry as he drove. He drove sometimes at night when he couldn't sleep. Which was pretty often. He missed Henry, he really did. And now and then he thought of Miranda. He knew she didn't go back to New York, but he never saw her. And he thought about other things, too. Like *when* and *how,* which were questions he hadn't thought about in years.

About two months after Henry died, Nash was driving home from the University District to Capitol Hill. It was a rainy evening, and the roads were deserted. Nash listened to talk radio. At the top of the hour they announced the news headlines. A newly released study linked the antianxiety drug Nepenthex with non-Hodgkin's lymphoma. Not only was there a connection between cancer and Nepenthex but the university scientists doing the original FDA test reports had covered up possible carcinogenic evidence. Several of these scientists admitted to getting large grants from Allegecom, the corporation that owns Nepenthex. They denied any conflict of interest. The FDA was temporarily banning sales of Nepenthex. Allegecom was seeking an injunction to stop the ban.

Nash headed straight on Second Avenue. Why not? It was a lonely, dark night. He could find some way to trash that vinyl billboard. He wasn't going to climb the face of the building, but he should be able to spill paint down from the roof. He'd kept the five gallons of latex paint in his trunk for weeks. He would do it. He owed it to Henry.

His mouth started to get dry. He could easily be caught and arrested, but he had nothing to lose at this point, nothing.

The building with the board came into view. But instead of the luminous pink letters and sculpted pills, a black face loomed. A huge skull and crossbones obscured the ad. When Nash got closer, he could see it was a vinyl overlay designed specifically for the board. The names Blythin and Nepenthex were visible, and Pherotek, as well as one luminous pill. But the skull and crossbones loomed above them. And above the skull was the legend in cutout letters: WHO IS RESPONSIBLE?

Nash stopped his car in front of the billboard. It was fantastic. Perfectly done. And so quickly. Better than the feeble gesture he had considered. He got out of the car and stood in the middle of the deserted street in the rain. The board defacement was signed. He could see a small tag on the vinyl face. SAFE, it said. He couldn't believe it at first. Then he laughed. Someone had finally jacked his acronym. Someone smart.

Nash drove home, all the while trying to guess what SAFE

now stood for. Maybe Some Angel Future Ecclesia. Or Safe Appropriations for Ever.

Nash woke up early, made his bed, his toast and his coffee. He ate as he sat near the window, wearing his bathrobe. He watched the first sunlight streaming in, catching the shine on the wood floors, warming him as he finished eating. It was a lovely morning.

He heard a vehement knock at his front door. He quickly got up and started to dress. He put on a sweater. He bent over and tied his hiking boots. He put on his peacoat and his watch cap. More knocking and talking.

He stuck a pen in the spiral of his notebook and tucked it in his large welt coat pocket. He opened the front door. Two men stood in the doorway in suits and overcoats. The Cascades loomed in the distance behind the men. The mountain peaks were clearly visible and, he finally had to admit, gorgeous. One of the men reached into his coat.

"What took you so long?" Nash said.

She pressed the buzzer. The wooden fence was over six feet tall. A woman's voice answered.

"It's Jeanie Morris for Mrs. Benton."

"She's not at home."

"She's expecting me. I have an envelope to drop off for her." Mary clutched the small envelope in one hand, and in the other she held a purse. Tiny drops of sweat collected on her upper lip despite the chilly wind blowing off the ocean. The door buzzed, and she walked into the heavily landscaped courtyard. The house was new but built to resemble a Victorian shingle-style beach bungalow. But it was huge—a mansion bungalow. Mary heard her heels click on the stone path. She wore a linen mididress that hit just above the knee, a matching jacket, and low-heeled shoes with squared toes and daisy-shaped buckles. The shoes matched the leather of the snap-closed purse. She had put on a full face of base, lipstick, eyeliner and powder. Her hair was up and high, a hairdo. As she got ready, each detail of makeup and clothing had made her feel braver. She was putting on armor. It girded her, using the innocuous mascara wand and smelling the crisp linen. She felt hidden and quite capable. Clean and ladylike and dangerous.

Go ahead, underestimate me, she thought. When she arrived at the front step, she had a confident but blank smile.

A middle-aged woman opened the door. She also had a blank, unreadable smile.

"I'm Mrs. Malcolm, the housekeeper. I'll see that Mrs. Benton gets your letter." She barely looked at Mary as she took the envelope.

"I'm so sorry to have missed Mrs. Benton."

"I'll tell her you were here." Mrs. Malcolm began to close the door.

"May I use your washroom to freshen up?" Mary said. The housekeeper didn't hesitate.

"It's right over here," she said, and Mary followed her to a small bathroom under the main stairwell. Mary closed the door and gently placed her purse on the closed toilet lid. She looked in the mirror and took a deep breath. A wave of tightness moved through her stomach and chest. She grasped the sink and thought for a second she might faint. She ran the water and took several deep breaths. She put her face down to the faucet and drank directly from the running water. She thought of all the terrible, ugly things that had built this opulent, ugly house.

Under the sink was an oak cabinet with two hinged doors in the front. She opened it. In addition to the plumbing she could see a round toilet brush and a bottle of Mr. Clean. She lifted the purse from the toilet and kneeled in front of the cabinet. She placed the purse carefully inside, under the curve of plumbing. Holding the handle in her left hand, she opened the clasp with her right. A clock face, some wires and a mound of molded plastic no bigger than two fists.

She looked at her watch.

She put her hand in the purse and held the clock face steady.

She pulled the pin up until it clicked.

She listened for the faint ticking.

She inhaled.

She let go.

Jason's Journal

IT DIDN'T HAPPEN the way I imagined it would. No drama, no epiphanies. No breakpoint. Just a gradual and increasing distance. I feel so disloyal copping to this, kind of sad really. What I mean is, I never listen to the Beach Boys anymore. Not a note, not ever. The plastic-sleeve-encased vinyl sits untouched in a box in my room (in chronological order of release, of course). I still admire them, appreciate them, but it is almost purely intellectual now. I don't have the deep-felt desire to listen over and over. I honestly never thought the day would really come. And although it is sad, it is also kind of a relief, a liberation. As more time goes by, I discover other things to fill that now vacated space. Or perhaps I found the other things first and that's what pushed the Beach Boys slowly to the perimeter. All I know is I now have time to listen to my Kinks records, a band I have come to really admire. Although I somehow don't anticipate a connection quite as deep as the

Beach Boys. That was, perhaps, a one-off. And other interests and thoughts, some even unrelated to vintage music, have settled in, even flourished.

As I said, it wasn't dramatic or at all deliberate. I just started to turn to those records less and less. And when I did listen to them, my mind wandered more and more. I skipped songs. Or maybe it is as simple as I wore out the old material and I ran out of new material to listen to (it is—after all and despite all the bootlegs—ultimately a finite set of work).

Don't get me wrong. It is not as though I am about to put my half-speed-mastered 180-gram-vinyl *Summer Days (and Summer Nights!!)* up for auction on eBay anytime soon. Not the rare 1965 British-issue 45, mint and in original sleeve, of "God Only Knows" backed with "Wouldn't It Be Nice" (worth a considerable amount in the collectors' market). Not even my used, cheaply issued compact disc version of *The Beach Boys Love You* (featuring odd, synthetic-sounding keyboards and arguably the strangest album the Beach Boys ever made). No, I will keep all the LPs, all the CDs, all the singles and all the EPs for two important reasons:

First, at some point enough time will have gone by of not listening that I'll listen again and it might sound fresh and new. It could again totally engage me, maybe in even deeper ways because I'll be an older, and presumably deeper, person. I might find things in it I never was able to hear before in my younger life. I might become just as enchanted, just as joyously captivated. I could fall in love all over again. All of that could come to pass. It is possible, isn't it?

The second reason I feel compelled to keep these artifacts is because of something I am quite certain will transpire. I need these records because one day, years from now, I will listen to this music and I will remember exactly what it was like to be me now, or me a year ago, at fifteen, totally inhabited by this work, in this very specific place and time. My Beach Boys records sit there, an aural time capsule wired directly to my soul. Something in that music will recall not just what happened but all of what I felt, all of what I longed for, all of who I used to be. And that will be something, don't you think?

Acknowledgments

The following people answered many questions and gave their time to me: Beep Brown, Blake Hayes and Tim Horvath of Cherry Valley, New York. Kristi Kenny at Left Bank Books, Eric Laursen of AWIP, Carter Adamson of Skype, Dustan Sheppard of ICQ. Richard Frasca. David Meyer. George Andreou.

Thank you to Liza Johnson for letting me see her movie. And all the other people who helped me. I am indebted to Cecil B. Currey and his essay "Residual Dioxin in Vietnam."

Thanks for the practical help that makes writing time possible— Jessie and Ted Dawes, Terry Halbert and Bill Coleman. Special thanks to Willy Brown and Rebecca Wright for the Roseboom Housing Fellowship.

I am so fortunate to have Nan Graham as my editor. Thank you for all your time and attention. Thank you also to Alexis Gargagliano for her hard work. And to Melanie Jackson for her enthusiasm and encouragement.

Thank you, Don. Thank you, Gordon.

Finally, I would be remiss if I did not send a huge and never-ending shout out to Clement and Agnes for all their inspiration and patience.

About the Author

Dana Spiotta is the author of the novel *Lightning Field,* a *New York Times* Notable Book and a *Los Angeles Times* Best Book of the Year. She lives in Cherry Valley, New York, with her husband and daughter.